HARD HIT

J. B. TURNER
HARD HIT

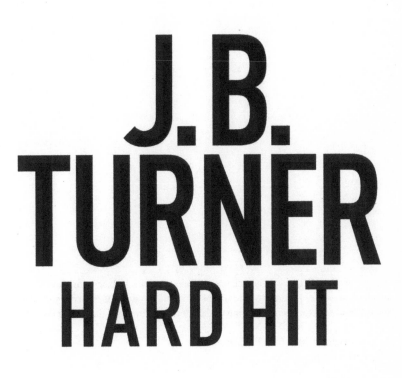

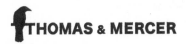

THOMAS & MERCER

Text copyright © 2019 by J. B. Turner
All rights reserved.

Published by Thomas & Mercer, Seattle

www.apub.com

Amazon, the Amazon logo, and Thomas & Mercer are trademarks of Amazon.com, Inc., or its affiliates.

ISBN-13: 9781542006651
ISBN-10: 1542006651

Cover design by @blacksheep-uk.com

Printed in the United States of America

For my late father

Prologue

Dawn on a bleak Bronx highway.

The driver of the black Bentley sniffed hard, weaving in and out of traffic, cocaine burning through his veins. He turned up the air-conditioning to the max. Cold air blasting his skin. Pulsating hip-hop bursting out of the speakers. Heart pumping. Mind racing. Slicing in and out of lanes. He tailgated a car for a few miles on the Cross Bronx Expressway. He felt euphoric. Then he got off at an exit and headed south through Washington Heights and Harlem.

The streets were empty.

He drove faster as the lights ahead changed.

Traffic picked up. His senses were being assaulted. The lights from oncoming cars were a blur.

He turned onto Park Avenue and accelerated hard. He ran a red light. Horns blared.

He glanced in the rearview mirror again, his heart hammering. The drugs were coursing through his blood.

His cell phone rang. "Sir, they want to know where you are."

The man felt his blood pressure spike. He sniffed hard. His nostrils felt numb from the residue of cocaine. He swallowed as the drug lingered in the back of his throat. "Tell them I'm en route."

"*En route? Very good, sir. What should I say has caused the delay?*"

"*That's none of their business.*"

"*Sir, you have three meetings lined up before the breakfast.*"

The man laughed. Up ahead he saw a green light. "*Can't someone else say a few words until I get there? It's just a business breakfast.*"

"*With respect, sir, it's being attended by the leading international entrepreneurs. And you have those meetings too . . .*"

The man drove on, the road ahead clear. "*Why so early? It's crazy.*"

"*Where have you been, sir? We've been worried.*"

The man laughed again. "*Having fun. Look, I'll be there soon. I promise.*" He ended the call as the green light changed to red.

Suddenly a female jogger wearing headphones stepped out in front of him. He plowed through her, sending her flying into the air.

A dull thud. Dull.

Numb.

That was all he felt as he accelerated away.

One

The heat was brutal. Ninety-five in the shade. And no break in sight.

Jon Reznick pulled down his baseball cap to shield his eyes from the blistering late-afternoon sun. He was standing on the edge of the crowd at the North Atlantic Blues Festival, a bottle of beer in his hand. Sweat stuck his T-shirt to his back. His throat was parched. The air was like glue. Guitar riffs hung on the stifling air.

But not a breath of wind.

That by itself was unusual for Rockland, Maine. A heat wave was blanketing the entire Eastern Seaboard of America. As it had been for the last week. Reznick couldn't remember another summer day this hot.

Reznick was about to head to the bar for another beer when his cell phone rang.

"Is this Jon Reznick?" a woman's voice asked on the other end of the line.

"Who's this?"

"Detective Isabella Acosta, NYPD, Nineteenth Precinct. Am I speaking to Jon Reznick?"

"Yes. What do you want?"

"Do you have a daughter named Lauren?"

An image flashed in his mind: Lauren's beaming smile when she'd returned home to Rockland for spring break. She was in New York

City now, working a summer internship. Reznick's gut tightened. "Yes, I have a daughter named Lauren. What happened?"

"Jon, she was in an accident. She's in the hospital."

"What's her condition?"

"I can't say. But you should get here as soon as you can."

Two

It was just after midnight when Reznick arrived at Weill Cornell Medical Center on the Upper East Side of Manhattan. A doctor and a nurse were standing by Lauren's bed. She was hooked up to an IV line. Reznick sat down beside her and stroked her hair; dried blood caked a wound on her head.

Lauren had tears in her eyes when she saw him. "Dad, you didn't have to come all this way."

His head was swimming as he struggled to take in how vulnerable and childlike she looked. "What happened?"

"I can't really remember." She winced and screwed up her eyes. "Goddamn migraine."

The doctor introduced himself. "We've done scans and they're clear. The headaches are coming and going, but we're keeping an eye on it."

"What exactly happened?"

"I believe it was a hit-and-run, not far from here. She was out jogging around five thirty. A car hit her in the crosswalk."

"That's more than eighteen hours ago. I only heard about it late afternoon."

"I have no idea why it took the police so long to get in touch with you. The good news is, we are pleased that your daughter, despite cuts, bruises, abrasions, and occasional migraines, does not appear to have suffered any lasting damage. But we will be keeping her here for a couple of days for observation."

"Thanks, Doctor. I appreciate your time and attention."

The doctor handed Jon his card. "If you need to speak to me, this has my cell phone. Now, if it's alright with you, I need to attend to a new patient who's just been admitted."

Reznick waited until the doctor and nurse were out of earshot before he kissed the back of his daughter's hand. "I love you."

Lauren smiled. "I'm so sorry, Dad."

"Don't worry. Dad's here. It's going to be OK."

Three

A pale morning light was flooding through the windows of the ICU room when Reznick awoke, his cell phone vibrating in his pocket. He sat up in the easy chair.

A nurse checking his daughter's vital signs smiled down at him. "Good morning," she said.

Reznick cleared his throat. "Yeah, good morning. How is she?"

"Dad, I'm fine," Lauren said.

"She's had a peaceful night. But we'll be doing more tests in the next hour or two."

He pulled his cell phone from his pocket. "Excuse me, I've got to take this call." Reznick got up and walked out into the corridor.

"Detective Acosta, NYPD, Nineteenth Precinct," she said when he answered.

"Morning."

"Mr. Reznick, I wanted to meet you face-to-face to give you an update on where we are with our investigation. Are you available in an hour?"

"Not a problem."

"You want to meet for coffee?"

"Where?"

"Ritz Diner isn't far from the hospital."

"See you then."

Reznick ended the call and spent a few more minutes with his daughter. He gazed down at her, relieved that she was alive. He went to a restroom and freshened up before going out.

The broiling heat hit him as soon as he stepped outside the hospital. He was starving and headed into the diner.

Reznick sat alone in a booth overlooking First Avenue.

"Hey, what can I get you, honey?"

He ordered a breakfast of pancakes and black coffee.

The waitress took his order and smiled. "Coming right up."

Reznick gazed out at the hustle and bustle of the New York streets. The taxis. The garbage trucks. FedEx. UPS. The movement. The people. Going about their business. His daughter should have been enjoying walking and jogging these same streets. But he was hopeful it wouldn't be long until she could get back to doing what she loved.

Reznick ate his breakfast, trying to enjoy the sustenance. A few minutes later, the waitress cleared the table. It was then that a woman in her late thirties, with dark-brown eyes and shoulder-length hair pulled back tight, walked in.

"Sorry for keeping you waiting," Detective Isabella Acosta began.

Reznick shook her hand as she sat down opposite him. She wore a navy suit, well cut, with a cream blouse, gun holstered to her belt.

"Morning meeting ran over."

Reznick smiled.

"Sorry also to meet under such circumstances."

Reznick nodded. "I'm just glad my daughter is alive, first and foremost."

The waitress refilled Reznick's cup, and Acosta ordered a latte.

Acosta waited until the waitress was out of earshot. "You OK?"

"I'm fine."

Acosta smiled.

"So, any progress on interviewing the driver?" Reznick asked.

"We've identified the vehicle. And we're going to be interviewing the owner of the vehicle very shortly. But so far we haven't managed to identify who was driving."

Reznick shrugged. "What seems to be the problem?"

"Surveillance footage is mostly centered on the moments after the accident. We are, however, trawling all the business and traffic cameras in the neighborhood, including our own CCTV cameras, to see what we can find."

"And it takes time, I'm guessing."

"We have techs working on that issue as we speak. A ton of footage, but none is of a high-enough quality to definitively show how the accident happened. We're also checking Lauren's cell phone, but we're running into problems with access. There's a four-digit passcode. She couldn't remember it last night, so I guess I'll try and talk to her again this afternoon. Hopefully she can help us with that."

"Sure."

Acosta gave a sympathetic smile. "What are you going to do in the meantime? I mean, while she's here in the hospital."

"Me? Watch over her. That's what parents do, right?"

The waitress returned with Acosta's latte. Acosta fingered the cup for a few moments before saying, "I have a son—well, it's my partner's son, but I still worry about him like no one's business."

"He in school now?"

"Summer vacation. He's at camp upstate. First time he's been away from home. And it's hard. We miss him like crazy."

Reznick nodded, not wanting to pry. His thoughts turned to Lauren. He couldn't believe how fast she'd grown up. She'd been a daddy's girl when she was younger. But over the years he'd watched her change. After her mother's death, yes, but especially since she had gone off to college. She'd gotten tougher. More resilient. Independent. Not afraid of hard work. Standing on her own two feet. Working in the city this summer. Jogging in New York City. He hoped that the accident wouldn't make her more cautious.

"Anyway, while you're hanging around town, I'm at the precinct seven days a week, or so it seems lately. And you have my number there, as well as my cell."

Reznick nodded. "Sure thing."

"There's something else I wanted to talk to you about."

Reznick gulped down the rest of his coffee. "What's that?"

"My boss said he'd been contacted by the FBI in New York. He was told that you do some work for them? But that you're not a special agent."

Reznick said nothing.

"Do you work for the FBI, Mr. Reznick?"

"Call me Jon. Yes, I work for them from time to time."

"You mind me asking what sort of work you do for them?"

"I consult on issues which concern the FBI. National security."

"Who do you report to?"

"Assistant Director Martha Meyerstein. You want to give her a call?"

Acosta took a pen out of her jacket pocket and scribbled the name on a napkin. "I'm assuming she's in DC?"

"Correct. So, you said your boss was contacted by the Feds. Were they giving him a heads-up about trying to keep me in check?"

"Not in so many words. He was told that you do valuable classified work with the FBI. And you usually operate on highly classified investigations. But it was mentioned that you are unorthodox and don't play by the rules."

Reznick couldn't help feeling a bit annoyed at how the Feds were dealing with this. He had put his life on the line for them on several occasions during top-secret and dangerous investigations. That included rescuing Meyerstein from the clutches of the Russian mob.

"I want to help, Jon. That's why I'm here. But you have to realize that you going off script, following your own agenda, it's not advisable."

"I got you."

"I don't want to have to arrest you for interfering with an investigation."

"There'll be no problem with me. I just want to make sure my daughter recovers fully. I want her well. I want her back with me. And I want the NYPD to arrest the person who did this."

"New York can be a brutal place, Jon."

"I know that, trust me."

"No one seems to have time to worry too much about other people. Life moves fast. It's tough. Relentless. A grind. Shit happens every day here. I've got a job to do. And I hope you understand that."

Reznick glanced out the diner window at the traffic on First Avenue. "You don't have to worry about me."

"Promise?"

"You have my word."

Four

It was dark when the Gulfstream carrying Aleksander Brutka touched down at Lebanon Municipal Airport in New Hampshire. A limousine whisked him and his bodyguard the short journey across the state line to the small town of Norwich, Vermont. Quiet, rural. Nestled just outside town was the colonial house where his grandfather lived.

Brutka and his bodyguard stepped out of the car. The air was sticky. He walked up the gravel path to the newly painted white door. He knocked four times, as he always did, and waited. A few moments later, an old man with rheumy eyes opened up.

Brutka stepped forward and hugged the man tight. "Grandfather, how are you this fine summer night?"

His grandfather dabbed his eyes. "Better for seeing you, Aleksander. Come in."

The bodyguard headed back to the car as Brutka shut the front door and followed his grandfather down a narrow corridor. Black-and-white pictures of rural Vermont scenes lined the walls. He was shown into the living room, where he pulled up an easy chair beside his grandfather.

His grandfather grimaced as he sat down, then smiled, wheezing slightly at the exertion. "I'm too old."

Brutka leaned forward and patted the back of his grandfather's hands, resting on the armchair. "Nonsense. You'll reach one hundred, mark my words."

"If only. But I fear Father Time catching up with me." The old man licked his parched lips.

Brutka stood and headed to the fridge in the kitchen, pulled out two bottles of spring water, and two glasses from a cupboard. He filled up his grandfather's glass and chopped up a lemon, which he knew the old man liked. He returned to the living room. "Here, drink this. You'll be dehydrated if you don't drink. It's very hot outside."

The old man drank the cool water, closed his eyes, and handed the glass to Brutka.

"Better?"

"Yes, Aleksander, such a good boy."

Brutka took a sip of his water and placed both glasses on the sideboard. "I'm sorry I couldn't make it last weekend," he said. "I've got a lot going on."

"You are the only one who visits me," the old man said. "Everyone else has forgotten about me. Everyone. Your father is too busy, I understand that, but thank God I have you."

"You'll always have me, Grandfather. I thank God I still have you."

The old man cleared his throat and beckoned Brutka closer. "I rely on you so much," he said as Brutka sat.

"It's my pleasure."

The old man let out a wheezy sigh and his watery eyes scrutinized Brutka's face. "Tell me, I know you're a very busy man, but how have you been? Are you enjoying your life? A man needs to relax. Take time to enjoy the good things."

Brutka smiled ruefully; high living was not something he skimped on. "I have a full social life," he said.

"And a girlfriend? You need to think about settling down."

"Absolutely correct. But I need to find the right girl."

"I was lucky . . . Your grandmother, a fine woman. An upstanding, good woman, who loved her husband, her children. She would have been so proud to see how well you have done."

The old man furrowed his brow slightly as though something was troubling him. "America is a great country, but I feel . . . I don't know what I feel."

"Tell me, Grandfather. Speak honestly to me. What is it? Is there something bothering you?"

"I feel . . . even after all these years, as if they might find me."

Brutka leaned in closer. "Grandfather, listen to me very carefully. Do you trust me?"

"I trust you with my life."

"That's good. As long as I draw breath, I will ensure no one finds you. I know many people. And rest assured, you are safe here. No one will find you here. I promise."

The old man remained quiet for a few moments before speaking. "I asked to speak to you face-to-face. And you came within hours."

"As soon as the plane's crew was ready, I headed up here. I said I would always be here for you, Grandfather. And I mean what I say."

The old man nodded, eyes downcast.

"Is there something wrong, Grandfather? You seem lost in thought."

"A friend of mine, he's retired, a veteran, and he helps his wife run a coffee shop on Main Street. He mentioned in passing a man who visited a few months back, very pleasant, working on his laptop."

Brutka shrugged. "I do it myself. You can write articles, memos, emails while enjoying a coffee."

"Yes. This man, he came in every day for a week or so, said he was on a road trip. But only a few days ago, the same man returns to the coffee shop. And he has his laptop."

Brutka nodded. "The same guy?"

"Yes. And you know what he asked?"

"What?"

"He asked if my friend knew a guy called Bud Smith."

Brutka stared at his grandfather. His blood ran like ice in his veins. "What did your friend say?"

"My friend asked who the guy was and why he wanted to know."

"Your friend didn't know the guy, right?"

"Complete stranger. The guy just shrugged, finished his coffee, and left."

"That's interesting."

"There was one thing my friend found out about the guy."

"What was that?"

"Said he saw his driver's license when he paid the bill. Tom Callaghan. New York."

Brutka made a mental note.

"Aleksander, I don't want anything to happen to me."

"Trust me, leave this to me. I will find out who this Callaghan is. And I'll deal with it." The old man nodded, a tremor in his hand. "You still have the gun I gave you?"

"Yes, I have it."

"Make sure it's close at all times. Just in case you need to use it."

The following morning, a tangerine dawn spread across the sky, its light catching the glass on the huge residential towers overlooking Manhattan's East River.

Aleksander Brutka was already racking up the laps in his rooftop pool. The sun warmed his back. It felt good. But his thoughts were still preoccupied after his trip to Vermont. The presence of the stranger asking about Bud Smith was troubling. He felt sick thinking his beloved grandfather was being disturbed and unsettled at his age. His grandfather had fled Eastern Europe with his young son, Brutka's father, along with countless other refugees, after the Second World War. And he had built up a successful hotel business, growing to love everything America had to offer. Brutka had already put in some calls to find out what was going on. But his instincts told him that Tom Callaghan, if that was indeed his real name, was not good news.

Brutka pushed those thoughts to one side while he swam and began to focus on the new day ahead. He had his own issues he needed to sort out. He was due to meet with his lawyer today to discuss the jogger he'd hit on the Upper East Side. And he wanted to feel as if he was on top of everything that seemed like it was piling up at the same time.

He swam on. Lap after lap. Slowly, he began to feel sharper as the endorphins kicked in, his mood becoming elevated. Today he was ready to face the world anew.

He loved swimming outdoors. The twenty-five-yard rooftop pool was where he went to gather his thoughts. Clear his mind. But also to keep fit. It was the reason he'd splashed out $70 million on the penthouse for his thirtieth birthday. The swimming was part of his morning ritual. He had started swimming when he was a student at Deerfield Academy, a boarding school in Massachusetts. He'd had excellent swimming coaches and had become a state champion when he was sixteen.

He took pride in his morning ritual.

When he'd started his job in New York five years earlier, he'd often stayed in a suite at the Four Seasons. And he'd often had to share his early-morning swim with other guests.

Having one's own rooftop pool, and being able to swim during a blistering heat wave, wasn't far from heaven in his mind.

His bodyguards stayed in the rooms below. An elevator from his floor gave him private access to the parking garage. It was discreet. If he was returning with a girl—or, as was more often the case, girls—no one knew.

Then in the morning they would be given the usual two thousand dollars for their time and escorted off the premises by his bodyguards. Brutka liked his life. His father liked it less. Aleksander knew he'd been indulged, not least with a world-class education. First at Deerfield. Then at a top liberal arts college, Williams, where he had studied economics. Then Harvard Law School.

Three years as a tax lawyer was all he had been able to endure. When an opening in New York became available, it was a perfect opportunity to enjoy the privileges, access, networking, and power brokering that accompanied the diplomatic position at the UN.

He jetted across the world but always returned to his perfect home, high in the sky. He loved New York.

Just over an hour later, after a healthy breakfast of oatmeal, freshly squeezed orange juice, and green tea, Brutka was sitting in the back of a limo, snared in Midtown traffic.

"How are we for time?" he said to his chauffeur.

"We're fine, sir."

Brutka's cell phone rang. He saw the caller ID and his heart sank. His father.

Shit.

"Father, how are you today?"

A long sigh. "Aleksander, I was just informed of the accident. Please explain yourself."

"It's all in hand."

"Do not lie to me, son. I don't abide liars. So what's the latest?"

"We believe that the car, the Bentley, may have been involved in the accident, and it was being used, unauthorized."

"So who was it?"

"We don't know, Father. I have my security people investigating to find out what the hell went on. It's crazy. I'm frankly appalled."

"Son, are you saying you weren't driving or in the vehicle?"

"Precisely."

"I've also just spoken to the State Department. They want this cleared up."

"I can assure you that whoever is responsible will be held to account."

His father sighed deeply. "What did your lawyer say?"

"I'm meeting him in fifteen minutes."

"Listen to what he says. Do you understand?"

"Yes, Father. There's something else, unrelated to this ghastly accident."

His father cleared his throat. "What?"

"I visited Grandfather. And he mentioned that a man by the name of Tom Callaghan was in Hanover a few months ago, asking about Bud Smith. Recently, this guy was back, sniffing around."

"Do we know who Callaghan is?"

"Not yet, but I will."

"I don't like the sound of that. Keep me informed. But for now, see your lawyer, and take his advice."

The offices of Morton and Charles were on the eighty-second floor of a building in Midtown. Brutka was greeted by Lionel Morton, a rotund, bespectacled man wearing a navy suit, crisp white shirt, and navy silk tie. Understated. Not flashy.

They followed Morton's secretary into the boardroom, where Brutka was shown to a comfortable leather chair. Sepia pictures of old New York lined the mahogany-paneled walls.

Morton pulled up a chair and sat down. He waited until his secretary had left the room before he started to scribble on a notepad. "So . . . we got a problem, right?" he said.

Brutka sighed. "A most unfortunate situation."

"As you know, our firm is on a retainer, so my services are available around the clock, and I'll be doing my utmost to maintain your diplomatic position here in New York. So, what exactly were you doing when this incident occurred?"

"Sleeping."

"So who was driving?"

"We don't know. But we'll find out."

Morton scribbled more notes. "Have the police been in touch?"

"Yes, they have."

"And?"

"They came by my apartment, but my aide said I wasn't in."

Morton pinched the bridge of his nose, as if slightly exasperated. "There must be surveillance footage from the embassy showing who took the vehicle."

"We're looking into that."

"So you're saying that an employee at the embassy took this vehicle, was involved in a hit-and-run accident, and no one knows who the hell it was?"

"It doesn't look good, I know. But we'll find the culprit."

Morton sighed. "I have to say, this is problematic."

"I agree. But we'll find who did this."

"Aleksander, it's important you do. And quick."

Five

The light was fading outside the diner. Reznick was finishing up a dinner of steak and fries when his cell phone rang. The caller ID showed Weill Cornell Medical Center.

"Mr. Reznick?"

"Yes, who's this?"

"Raj Patel, Surgical Intensive Care Unit. You need to return to the hospital, sir, right away."

"Intensive care? I don't understand. I was just speaking to my daughter a couple of hours ago."

"Your daughter is now in the ICU."

"Why? What's the matter?"

"Her condition has deteriorated. Badly."

"What exactly do you mean, Doctor?"

"You need to come now, sir."

Reznick's mind was racing as he ended the call. He left two twenty-dollar bills with the check and ran out onto First Avenue. Then he sprinted to the hospital.

He was breathing hard when he stepped out of the elevator and into the ICU. Lauren's eyes were closed, tubes coming out of her nose, the machine she was hooked up to beeping. He sat down beside her and stroked her hair.

The doctor introduced himself. "Your daughter had a major episode in the last hour. We needed to induce a coma."

Reznick heard the words but couldn't seem to process them. "Why?"

"Her condition changed suddenly. She began to complain of terrible pressure in her head. We did some more scans. And we could see that there was swelling. Intense pressure on her brain was rising fast. We had to do a procedure to relieve it."

"I thought she was going to get better."

"So did we. We brought her into the ICU. She's receiving the finest medical treatment. But I'm not disguising the fact that this is a severe setback."

Reznick felt a stabbing pain in his chest. "You need to be very honest with me. What are her chances?"

The doctor nodded. "Lauren is fighting for her life. I'm very sorry I don't have better news."

"What are her chances?"

"Honestly? We don't know yet."

"Take a guess, Doc."

"It's an uphill battle, that's all I can say."

With a sympathetic look, the doctor left, and Reznick leaned in close to his daughter's face. "Hey, honey, it's Dad." He felt his throat tighten. His flesh and blood was lying in a coma. "I want you to know that you're in a fantastic hospital, and the doctors are going to make you better. But you need to do me a favor, honey. I know you can hear me. You look like you're just sleeping. But I want you to listen to what I have to say: you're going to fight this. You're going to be strong. And you're going to dig deep. Your mother was a fighter. She never gave up. Ever. She was tough. And I'm going to ask you to be tough like you've never been before. When you're ready, you wake up."

Reznick felt tears in his eyes.

"Remember what I said to you when you were a little girl? You remember? I said, *I will never leave you. I will always be here for you.*

J. B. Turner

Whatever it takes. That was my promise. And I keep my promises. I'm going to be here for you when you need me. But now you just have a nice long sleep, and when you're ready to wake up, Daddy will be here."

Reznick stroked Lauren's silky hair and hummed a lullaby as the respirator beeped, the machine keeping her alive. He stayed by her bedside for an hour before he left to speak to the doctor again. "Can she pull through? I need to know."

The doctor sighed, his gaze wandering around the ICU.

"It's a simple question, Doc."

"It's not a simple question. We just don't know. But yes, she can pull through. She's young. She seems healthy and fit. But it's going to take all her strength and good luck to come out the other side of this. It's important you understand that."

The rest of the night, Reznick sat by his daughter's bedside. Listening to the machine breathing for her. The beeping. The drip. Time meant nothing. He was terrified of losing her. Since his wife, Elisabeth, died on 9/11, Lauren was all he had. She was just like her mother. With the same stubbornness. The same fierce intelligence. The way she talked about music. The way she argued her point. Even her posture when she read a book. The similarities were uncanny. But mostly, Reznick was reminded of his late wife in his daughter's smile and the way it lingered in his mind long after she'd gone.

He held Lauren's warm, clammy hand and prayed. Eventually, he felt himself drifting away into a sea of darkness and said a final silent prayer for God to watch over his daughter.

Six

When Reznick awoke at his daughter's bedside, his cell phone was vibrating in his pocket. He sat up in the easy chair.

A nurse checking his daughter's vital signs smiled down at him. "Good morning," she said.

Reznick cleared his throat. "Yeah, good morning. How is she?"

"No change yet."

Reznick took out his cell phone. "Excuse me, I've got to take this call." He got up and walked out into the corridor.

"Jon, it's Detective Acosta," she said when he answered.

"Morning."

"Mr. Reznick, I just heard about Lauren's condition. I'm so sorry."

"Appreciate that."

"I wanted to meet you to give you a brief update at the station on where we are with our investigation. Are you available in an hour?"

"Not a problem."

"We're a fifteen-minute walk away."

"See you then."

Reznick ended the call and spent a few more minutes with his daughter. He gazed down at her, in shock that he might very well lose her. And there was nothing he could do about it. The more he thought about it, the darker his mood grew. He went to a restroom and freshened up before heading out. He needed to do something.

Anything.

It was eight blocks to the Nineteenth Precinct on East Sixty-Seventh Street.

Reznick spoke to the guy at the desk, and he was told to take a seat. Twenty minutes later, Detective Acosta appeared.

"Sorry for keeping you waiting," she said when she came to collect him from the reception area. "Had to take a couple of urgent calls."

Reznick shook her hand and they headed up to the second floor. He followed her into a cramped office area, past a handcuffed young thug being brought in, down a corridor and past some officers drinking coffee, and into her windowless office. She shut the door behind her.

"Pull up a seat," she said.

Reznick sat down. The computer on her desk had a small soft toy on the top of the monitor. The screen showed what looked like incident logs. Pinned to the bulletin board above her desk were the telephone numbers of other Nineteenth Precinct detectives, a calendar, newspaper clippings of cases, a small American flag, and a couple photos of Acosta smiling proudly, her arms around a boy, presumably her son.

Acosta pulled up a seat and sat down. "You want coffee?"

Reznick shook his head. "What do you know?"

Acosta sighed.

Reznick leaned back in his seat. He sensed she was leading up to an important point but didn't quite want to say it.

"I can only imagine what you're going through. We're very sorry. But what I have to say is going to be, I'm afraid, of little consolation to you."

"Do you want to get to the point, Detective? Are we going to see an arrest? What exactly happened?"

"We believe—though the investigation is in its early stages—that the driver was under the influence. The car was being driven erratically. We don't know under the influence of what, that's still to be established."

"I don't understand. Why is he not in here right now, under arrest?"

"Ordinarily, that would be the case, Mr. Reznick. Believe me, the NYPD would love to put the driver of this vehicle away. But this is no ordinary case. Sadly."

"We seem to be going around in circles, Detective. Why is this no ordinary case?" Reznick leaned closer. "You mind explaining?"

Acosta sighed. "You need to trust me on this, Mr. Reznick. I want to help. And I hope I can. But I can't tell you any more right now."

Seven

Martha Meyerstein was at her desk on the seventh floor of the J. Edgar Hoover Building in Washington, DC, looking over briefing notes on an ongoing investigation when the phone rang. She sighed and picked up.

"Meyerstein."

"Martha, you got five minutes?" The voice belonged to FBI Director Bill O'Donoghue.

"Right now?"

"If you don't mind."

Meyerstein cleared her throat. "Not a problem."

She headed down the corridor and knocked on the Director's door.

"Come in!" he shouted.

Meyerstein opened the door and saw O'Donoghue behind his desk, looking over a file. "Sir?"

"Pull up a seat, Martha," he said without looking up.

Meyerstein shut the door behind her and sat down. O'Donoghue appeared more drawn and tired than she'd ever seen him. The fallout from recent events during which Jon Reznick had freed a former Delta buddy from a psychiatric hospital that, unbeknownst to the FBI, was part of a shadowy top-secret Langley black-ops program had strained relations between the FBI and the CIA to the breaking point in recent months. The antagonism between the agencies had spurred off-the-record quotes in the *Washington Post*, believed to have originated from within the CIA, suggesting that O'Donoghue was considering retirement. He had shrugged off the gossip, as he usually did, focusing on the job. He still worked grueling sixteen-hour days. And he was as demanding of his staff as ever. But Meyerstein knew from private conversations with him that he was increasingly concerned that the fractious relationship between the two agencies was a threat to national security.

O'Donoghue began, "Martha, I was looking over your memo about Reznick's daughter. I appreciate the heads-up. I had no idea."

"The New York field office is being kept abreast of any developments. They're liaising with the NYPD. I believe they're meeting later today."

"And they're keeping a lid on Reznick's connection to us? I mean, this is not something we want becoming common knowledge, that we have an interest in this man."

Meyerstein shifted in her seat. "Absolutely. I've been assured by Jacob Hartmann in the field office that he has personally taken charge of this, and only he is speaking with the precinct commander."

O'Donoghue nodded. "I know what Jon can bring to the table. He's helped us with some of our most challenging investigations. He's brilliant. He's brave. He's a warrior. I don't deny any of those things. But he's mercurial. And I've got to be honest, he worries me. He worries me immensely. We're under scrutiny right now like never before—in part because of his actions. We can't underestimate how one wrong move or comment could bring all manner of hell down upon us."

"Couldn't agree more."

O'Donoghue sighed. "These are dangerous times not only for America but also for the Bureau. The last thing we need is for this thing to blow up in the media and expose Reznick and his daughter to public attention. His role with us is somewhat . . . How can I put it?"

"Covert?"

"*Vague* might be better," O'Donoghue said wryly. "Some of the actions he's taken on American soil . . ." He shook his head. "The FBI is not above the law. And that includes Jon Reznick."

Meyerstein nodded. "I don't disagree with any of that, sir."

"Just so we're clear."

"I'm guessing that's not why you called me into your office."

"No." He flicked over some papers on his desk before he fixed his gaze on her. "I'm concerned that Reznick might try and interfere with the police investigation. Ruffle feathers, so to speak."

"His goddamn daughter is fighting for her life, sir, as we speak."

O'Donoghue stared at her, eyes heavy. "That's beside the point. Reznick is our responsibility. I need to know that he's not going to do something crazy."

"I understand that perfectly," Meyerstein said, tamping down her impatience, "but it doesn't sit well with me that our primary worry is whether he'll embarrass us when we should be concerned about who put his daughter in a goddamn coma."

O'Donoghue raised a brow at her tone. "It is what it is, Martha," he said mildly. "So . . . are you on board?"

"Do I have a choice?"

"We always have a choice."

Meyerstein sighed. "What are you proposing, sir?"

"Jon Reznick is our guy. He's worked for us for years. Sensitive operations. National security. Highly classified, as you know. It's important that we make sure things don't get out of control."

"What do you want me to do?"

"Get to New York. And be my eyes and ears."

"You want me to keep Reznick under surveillance?"

"I want you to do what it takes to ensure that Reznick doesn't go rogue."

Eight

Reznick looked through a window next to his daughter's bed to the broiling New York streets below. Cop cars speeding past the baking sidewalks. Shadows encroaching from the high-rise residential buildings all around. He was filled with a sense of foreboding for Lauren's future. No one down there cared about his daughter's predicament. Why should they? They had their own concerns. Worries. Fears. The day-to-day grind of living in this crowded, crazy city.

He wanted Lauren back to being the beautiful, smart young woman she was. The daughter who was doing great stuff at Bennington College in Vermont. The daughter who should have been living the New York dream while working a coveted summer internship. He was hurting. Deep down, he felt a chasm within him. An emptiness. And it was growing.

She was everything he had ever wanted in a daughter. His late wife had only known Lauren as a baby. Elisabeth never got to see the confident, outgoing young woman who was planning to work toward a PhD in English literature. Lauren should have had the world at her feet. And she would. Maybe not today. Maybe not tomorrow. But he had to believe that she'd recover.

Reznick turned around and saw a nurse monitoring her vital signs. The nurse looked up at him and smiled. "Hi, Mr. Reznick."

"Still the same?"

"She's stable."

Reznick nodded. "That's something."

The nurse smiled but didn't say anything.

Reznick needed to clear his head. He went out into the hallway and called Detective Acosta. Her cell phone rang five times before she answered.

"Acosta." The tough, no-nonsense voice of a cop.

"Detective, it's Jon Reznick."

"Hey, Jon, how's Lauren?"

"No change. Listen, I'm sorry to bother you. I was calling to ask about the perp."

"What do you mean?"

"Well, are you any further along with interviewing the driver?"

"I was just about to talk to him."

"Who is he? What can you tell me about him?"

"Jon . . . gimme a break. You know I can't divulge that." She hesitated, and Reznick thought she was about to take pity on him and tell him what he wanted to know. Instead, she said, "There's more to this case than meets the eye. I can't promise the outcome of our investigation is going to be satisfactory to you, but I can promise that I want to nail this guy just as much as you do."

"What exactly do you mean by that?"

Acosta sighed. "I've already said more than I should have. Let me do my job, Jon, and you go be Lauren's father. I'll call you when I can share more."

Nine

The interview room at the Nineteenth Precinct was stifling as they waited for their suspect. Acosta was drumming her fingernails on the wooden desk as her colleague, Detective Sergeant Kevin McGeough, flicked through his notes. She felt sweat sticking her shirt to her skin and dabbed her brow with a handkerchief. An electric fan in the corner was moving the warm, dead air around the room without any discernible effect. She was reminded of her cramped childhood apartment in an un-air-conditioned walk-up in the Bronx. Sweltering summer nights, the sound of police sirens cutting through the night air. Neighbors screaming at each other. But also the sound of her mother's crying because of their hand-to-mouth existence. The arguments. The struggle to make ends meet. The struggle to put food on the table. The grinding poverty. She felt a perpetual mixture of gratitude and astonishment that her current life was so comfortable. "When's the goddamn air-conditioning going to get fixed?"

McGeough shrugged. "Later today, I heard."

"This heat is killing me."

"Sure it's not the menopause?" McGeough said with a smirk.

"Fuck you." She looked at the clock. They had been waiting for twenty-five minutes, and still no sign of the diplomat or his lawyer. "The guy's running late."

"He's a busy guy," McGeough said, leaning back in his chair and stretching.

She sighed as she began to look again at the papers in front of her. The medical reports on Reznick's daughter. The useless, grainy images captured by dashcams in several vehicles in the vicinity of the accident, observers unable to identify who was driving the vehicle that had hit Lauren Reznick.

Eventually, half an hour later, just as she was getting ready to post-pone the interview, Brutka and his lawyer, Lionel Morton, strolled in.

Acosta looked up and nodded. "Please take a seat, gentlemen. Appreciate your time."

The pair sat down opposite Acosta and her colleague. Morton opened up his briefcase and pulled out a pad and a pen and began scribbling notes. Brutka's gaze wandered around the interview room as if his mind was elsewhere.

Acosta switched on the digital recorder. She stated the time and place and who was present in the interview room.

Morton cleared his throat. "I'd like to apologize for our tardiness. Aleksander was dealing with an urgent church matter. His friend and pastor at the Ukrainian Orthodox Cathedral at West Eighty-Second Street was looking for advice. An elderly widow who is facing eviction. The situation has, thankfully, been resolved. I'm sure you understand."

Acosta nodded. "Not a problem."

"We intend to fully cooperate."

"Thank you, Mr. Morton." Acosta looked long and hard at Brutka. "Sir, can you talk me through what happened with regard to your car, a black Bentley SUV, colliding with a young woman on East Sixty-Eighth Street three days ago?"

Brutka looked thoughtful. "Thanks for allowing me the opportu-nity to clarify this terrible situation. I was as distressed as everyone else when I heard the news."

"Forgive me, sir, but I'm sure you'll appreciate that I have to ask difficult questions."

"Indeed. Of course."

Acosta sighed. "Were you driving the vehicle when this incident happened, sir?"

"Most certainly not."

"So you were not behind the wheel when this accident happened?"

"Categorically not."

Acosta's instincts screamed that he wasn't telling her the whole truth. "Were you in the vehicle at the time, sir?"

"No, I was not. I'm shocked at what's happened. And I hope the young woman who was injured makes a full recovery."

Acosta cleared her throat. "Would you care to share with us who was driving your car?"

"We're investigating to figure that out."

"We have footage of someone driving your vehicle at the time in question. Do you mind if I play this, sir?"

Brutka shrugged. "Please do if you think it will help."

Acosta picked up the remote and played the clip on the big-screen TV hanging on the wall. She hit pause, freezing the video just before the accident. "We can see quite clearly that it's your vehicle, registered to your address in the city, at the intersection where the jogger was hit. A very expensive car, I've been told. So my question is, this is clearly a car that you use, correct? Would you accept that?"

"Yes, I would."

"Good. And the man behind the wheel?"

Brutka took a pair of glasses out of his jacket and peered at the screen. "It's a very fuzzy image. That's unfortunate. But I can assure you it was not me."

"Is it possible, sir, that someone else, who was unauthorized to use your vehicle at the time, was driving this vehicle?"

"It's possible, of course."

Acosta was mildly irritated by the man's unhelpful answers. "Perhaps a member of your staff?"

"Quite possible."

Morton leaned forward and smiled. "My client is quite willing to provide you with a written statement. He denies being the driver."

Acosta sensed there was something not quite right about Brutka. Something was off. "There would be one way we could determine if you were in the vehicle. If we had access to your cell phone, then we could determine your location."

Morton intervened. "Detective Acosta, Article 27 of the Vienna Convention, if my memory serves me well, says that the host country must permit and protect free communication between diplomats and their home country. So Mr. Brutka would be falling foul of that if he handed over his cell phone, wouldn't he?"

McGeough stared long and hard at Brutka. "Mr. Brutka, I understand and appreciate that you are a diplomat of some standing. The question remains, though: If it wasn't you, who was it? Did someone steal your car from the embassy grounds? If so, why wasn't it reported? Why was it returned? There must be footage showing the person who took it."

Brutka nodded. "That's a good point, and we are looking into that as we speak."

Acosta looked long and hard at Brutka before she smiled. "A young woman is now lying in a coma. She is fighting for her life."

Morton immediately sat straight up and pointed at Acosta. "I think my client has been up-front about this incident. Now . . . unless you have any further questions, this meeting is over."

Ten

The hours dragged as Reznick sat at Lauren's bedside, feeling helpless. His head was swimming. The person who'd nearly killed his daughter was still out there. He felt a simmering anger ready to boil over.

He needed to clear his head, get some air. He kissed Lauren on the check. "Won't be long, honey," he said. "I love you."

He headed out onto the stifling streets. After walking along East Sixty-Eighth Street for half a dozen blocks, he crossed Fifth Avenue and reached Central Park. Sweat caused his T-shirt to stick to his back. He put on his sunglasses and pulled on his baseball cap as the sun beat down on him.

He walked through the park and headed across to Gapstow Bridge. It was a place with poignant memories. He remembered standing there with Elisabeth all those years ago. Just a young man in his early twenties. Not a care in the world. Before his whole world collapsed.

He turned and faced The Plaza hotel, where they had gotten married. His wife's folks had wanted a big wedding. And all his Delta buddies had turned up. Rowdy, unruly, some crazed, all drunk off their asses by the end of the night. Former Delta operator Harry Leggett mimicking Michael Jackson's moonwalk before collapsing in a heap, provoking raucous laughter. It was August 14, 1999. It seemed like yesterday. But that was two decades ago. Elisabeth's family had been

J. B. Turner

horrified by Reznick's friends' behavior. But that only seemed to make the contrast between his friends and the rest of the guests even funnier in Reznick's eyes.

The thing he remembered more than anything else about that day was just how beautiful Elisabeth had looked. Their first dance. He couldn't even remember the song. Why was that?

He turned and saw couples walking hand in hand. He saw a pair of cops speaking to a young kid holding a skateboard. And he saw families taking selfies, laughing, joking. Tourists. Maybe from the Midwest. Maybe from Europe.

Reznick walked slowly across the bridge, taking one long, lingering look back at The Plaza, before he headed on through the park. The smell of cut grass and cigarette smoke hung in the air. He walked on, deeper into the park. Past young folks lying on the grass, headphones on, soaking up the rays. Tourists lounging on benches, watching the world go by. Sweating joggers. And those just ambling around.

What was he doing here?

Should he be by Lauren's bedside, hoping for the best? Something within him was calling for him to do something. Anything. The question was, what?

He knew he should stay out of it. That was the smart thing to do.

But Reznick wanted to know who the driver was. He needed to know. It was bugging him. He pulled out his cell phone. He pulled up the number of a guy in Miami. A reclusive hacker who had helped him in the past. A hacker who had previously worked for the NSA. Now the guy was off the grid, working for wealthy individuals and corporations who could pay him to access information.

The hacker answered immediately. "Yo, Mr. R., how goes it? Long time no hear. You OK, man?"

"I've been better."

"Every time we talk you have some problem."

Reznick shielded his eyes from the sun. "This is different."

"How?"

"First, I want to know if you can help me."

"In what way?"

"I need to get some information. Sensitive information."

A beat. "So we're talking illegal shit, right?"

"Technically, that's correct. But this is personal."

The hacker was silent for a few moments, as if wondering what this was all about. "What do you mean, personal?"

Reznick sighed and explained.

"Shit, man, I'm sorry. So, let me get this straight, your daughter's in a coma? Are you kidding me?"

"I wish I was. It's a big ask, I know. But I need some help."

"Sure I can help, Jon. And you're wondering why this guy hasn't been arrested?"

"Right."

The hacker sighed.

Reznick squinted, despite his sunglasses, as the blazing sun flickered between the leaves on the trees.

"That's bad what he did, man. But I don't want you finding this guy and killing him. I can't have that on my conscience."

Reznick said nothing.

"I take it from that silence that you're not ruling it out."

"Can you help me? Yes or no."

The hacker hesitated.

"You've helped me before," Reznick said. "And I'm very grateful. I hope we can trust each other."

Another sigh. "So the cops have a name?"

"I believe so."

"Ordinarily I might, depending on how long it took, charge ten thousand."

"That's not a problem. I'll wire it, like before."

Another sigh.

"Look, if it's too much trouble, forget it. No hard feelings."

"Wait!"

Reznick held the cell phone tight to his face. "What?"

"Know what I like about you, Jon?"

"What?"

"You put yourself on the line time after time. The last time it was an ex-Delta buddy up in that hospital in upstate New York, right?"

"I couldn't leave him there."

"Well, you know what? I admire that. A lot. Tell you what I'm going to do, Jon. This one's on me."

"What?"

"No charge. I'm not making any promises. But I'm going to try and find this guy."

"Just get me a name, that's all I want."

"Leave it to me."

Reznick headed back to the hospital and bought a bottle of cold water from a hot dog cart. He finished it before he reached the hospital. When he returned to the ICU, an ashen-faced doctor gave him an update. The news wasn't good. They might have to operate to relieve the pressure on Lauren's brain.

Reznick listened as if in a daze, struggling to take it in. He waited until the doctors had left before he sat down next to Lauren, holding her hand. He leaned in close, kissing the back of her hand. "I know you won't be able to hear me, darling, but I just wanted you to know, on the off chance that you can, I want you to know that Daddy's here. I want to help you. So do the doctors, darling. But you've got to fight this. You're a smart girl with great prospects, and we're not going to allow any accident to dictate how your life will turn out. Your mom was a fighter. You think she got to her position at such a young age without being tough and smart? You're damn right she had to be all those things, and more. Know what we're going to do? When you open your eyes again, we're going to spend some serious time together. Just me and you. I know you like New York. So we'll walk across this whole city."

The beeping of the machine keeping her alive was all the response he heard.

Reznick leaned forward and stroked his daughter's hair. "That's a promise. We'll spend time in Central Park. We'll eat hot dogs. We'll walk in the rain. And I swear, I promise, that we're going to get through this."

A nurse came in to check the machine that was beeping, marking down the readings. Then she quietly moved away.

Reznick waited for a few moments before he spoke again. "I was over in the park earlier. Saw The Plaza. Where your mom and I got married. Long time ago. I don't talk too much about her, I know, but you remind me of her. Very determined. Very focused. And if she were here, she'd be saying the same thing. She loves you. And she is not going to allow you to go down without a fight. So I want you to hear my words. I pray that you can. And know that I'm here with you, for you, and so is your mom, always."

He leaned in closer.

"This man might've hurt you. He might've hurt me. But I can take it. And so can you. You're going to heal. And you're going to get strong again. I know you can hear me. My voice might be echoing around your head. Maybe very faintly, I don't know. But I know you can hear me. Lauren . . . I love you, honey."

Reznick sat by Lauren's bedside for an hour, holding her hand. The sound of his cell phone ringing in his pocket finally snapped him out of his thoughts. He checked the caller ID but didn't recognize the number. He got up, kissed his daughter on the cheek, and went outside to the corridor to take the call. "Yeah?"

"Mr. R., OK to talk?" The hacker.

"Sure, go right ahead."

"Aleksander Brutka. Ukrainian national living in New York."

Relief to finally get an answer mixed with a strong temptation to hit something. "Are you sure it's him? I mean, are you really sure?"

"Just looking at the police report now. He was the one the police were interviewing. But there is no definite visual proof."

Reznick mulled over what other information he wanted. "Do we know where he lives?"

"I just pulled up his financial records. This dude lives in a brand-new residential tower, penthouse apartment. Rooftop pool overlooking the East River."

"His own rooftop pool?"

"Belongs to the penthouse."

"What's the address?"

"Three forty-six East Forty-Sixth Street."

Reznick made a mental note of the address as he contemplated his options. "I owe you one. Thank you."

"You owe me nothing, man. Just be careful."

Eleven

It was a run-down part of East Harlem. The *barrio*. Brutka was sitting in the back seat of the Bentley as the car cruised past dilapidated houses. He stared through the tinted windows as he watched a poor Hispanic man limp down the sidewalk, cell phone pressed to his ear.

His cell phone rang.

"Mr. Brutka?" The private investigator.

"Any progress on finding out who this Tom Callaghan is who was up in Vermont?"

"It's his real name, and I know who he is. He lives here in New York. Do you want the details?"

Brutka watched a teenage mother chewing gum, pushing a stroller along the sidewalk and past the graffitied steel shop shutters. "No. But this guy . . . he's based in New York?"

"We're building up a profile on him. We believe he lives in the Flatiron District."

"Stay on it. I want a dossier in forty-eight hours. I want to know everything about who he is, why he was up there, what he knows."

Brutka ended the call. His coke-addled mind was racing. He wasn't thinking clearly. He was trying to keep track of everything in his head. What he knew. What he needed to do. Who he had to see. The girl he'd knocked down. Meetings. Calls. Appointments. Lawyers. He was thinking of his grandfather. His father. And his personal responsibilities. He was thinking of girls. And he was wondering if he was being followed. Was he being followed right now? Did Tom Callaghan know about him too?

The thoughts increased his anxiety.

A few minutes later, Brutka's mind managed to focus back on the present as the car pulled up at a run-down apartment block, part of a notorious housing project.

The chauffeur turned around. "Do you want me to come in, boss? It's pretty sketchy around here."

Brutka shook his head. "Seen worse. Just wait for me. Keep your eyes peeled. I shouldn't be too long."

He got out of the car and was greeted by a super with a limp who had been given a five-thousand-dollar bribe, then shown to the elevator.

Brutka rode it alone to the nineteenth floor. The doors opened. The smell of piss and marijuana hung heavy in the air. He stepped out of the elevator and turned right, walking down the corridor to the last apartment, 1903. He knocked hard.

The door opened. Carmel, a glassy-eyed young white girl with peroxide blond hair, stood there smiling at him. "Hi," she said, pecking him on the cheek.

Brutka brushed past Carmel, and she shut the door behind him as he slumped down on the sofa. She put on some chill music, then fixed him a single malt scotch on the rocks. He inhaled the peaty, smoky aroma and smiled before knocking it back. His stomach burned with the liquor.

"Another one, baby?"

Brutka nodded and she handed him another. He nursed this one, watching the amber liquor mix with the ice.

Carmel leaned in close. "You got any blow?"

Brutka looked at the girl and smiled, stroking her hair. "What do you think?"

"You never let me down."

"We've got an arrangement. And I always keep my side of an arrangement. But it's not a one-way street."

Carmel nodded, eyes wide, eagerly waiting for her hit.

Brutka took a bag of cocaine and a bag of crack rocks out of the inside pocket of his jacket and handed them to her. Within a few seconds, she was eagerly chopping the coke into several thick white lines on a vanity mirror lying on the stained wooden coffee table.

He handed her a fifty-dollar bill, and she rolled it up. Then she hoovered up three lines of the best coke in New York.

Carmel's eyes rolled around in her head for a few moments as the euphoria washed over her. She fixed her glassy gaze on his as a smile crossed her face. Then she began to laugh uproariously. "Man, you look funny."

Brutka smiled.

"You're real serious today. You don't want to do a line, baby?"

Brutka grabbed her by the hair and pressed his face close to hers. "Listen, you fucking uneducated piece of shit, you'd be back in that freezing shithole apartment block in Kiev with your mother, four brothers, and two sisters if it wasn't for me, am I right?"

"Yes, baby."

"You fucking show me respect. Obedience."

"Yes, baby."

"Who got the visa for you and your sister?"

"You did, baby."

"I will look after you. But you need to know that you work for me. I control you. I fucking own you."

A look of fear flashed on the girl's face. "What's wrong, baby? You don't seem your usual self. Can I do something to make you feel better?"

"You must never cross me. If you do, you will end up back in Ukraine. Do you want to go back to that?"

Carmel shook her head, tears in her eyes. "I understand, baby."

"Fix me another scotch."

The girl did as she was told.

Brutka swallowed the tumbler of scotch in two gulps. It burned his insides again. Warming. He felt content. He took out a fresh fifty-dollar bill from his pocket. He rolled it up and leaned forward over the lines of cocaine. Then he snorted five lines in quick succession.

The drugs hit his system full-on. He felt wild. Crazy. He began to laugh. Carmel laughed with him.

Brutka got up and looked out the window at the grimy buildings frying in the summer heat. "Do you like it here?"

"It's OK."

"Better than fucking Kiev, right?"

Carmel pulled out a pipe, loaded it up with a lump of crack, fired up the lighter, and sucked up the vapors. Her eyes went bloodshot. "Boom!"

Brutka sat back down and took the pipe, and she popped a huge chunk of crack into the mesh base and lit a match as he inhaled deeply. He felt the drug hit his brain like a hurricane. Wiping him out. Revealing his true self. He began to scream and laugh.

He stood up and took off his belt. He wrapped the thick leather around his fingers and touched the silver buckle. He stared down at Carmel, who was looking up at him as if in a dream.

"You wanna start now, baby?"

Brutka smiled. "You bet."

Then he began to thrash the belt buckle down hard onto the girl's face, drawing blood. She tried to scream. Her eyes were wild, terrified. Then he grabbed her neck with his huge hands and began to choke her.

"How does that feel?" he snarled through gritted teeth.

Carmel's eyes were huge as her fear engulfed her.

Brutka crushed her windpipe until she stopped moving, unconscious. But he didn't stop. He exerted more pressure, choking and choking, liking the feel of power, of control. "I fucking own you!" he screamed.

Time passed in a blur until, eventually, he let go of her, and she collapsed onto the carpet.

Breathing hard, he leaned down and checked her pulse. Nothing.

He had choked the life out of her. Fuck. He'd gone too far. Way too far. And after he'd promised himself he wouldn't do this again.

Brutka stared down at the junkie girl's lifeless body, her dead eyes open and staring. He'd miss her. But at least he still had her sister. Leaving the drugs and the money behind, he left the apartment and got back in the SUV. He felt a little crazed, was still breathing rapidly.

"Everything alright, sir?"

"Everything's just fine."

Brutka pulled out his cell phone and made a call to a French guy who sorted out any "situations" for him. He rattled off the address.

"What's required, sir?" the Frenchman said.

"I think the apartment needs to be professionally cleaned. It's very untidy."

"I know just the people."

The line went dead.

Twelve

Reznick felt like he needed his own space instead of sleeping by his daughter's bedside every night. He checked into a room at the low-key Bentley Hotel on East Sixty-Second Street. He was going to be around for a few days at the very least, maybe weeks. He showered, shaved, and lay down on the bed and caught a few hours' sleep.

When he woke, he felt more refreshed than he had for a while. He put on some fresh clothes—a navy polo shirt, jeans, and a pair of sneakers—and headed down to the bar. He took a seat on the outdoor patio, shrouded in plants and topiary that shielded guests from prying passersby.

Reznick ordered a bottle of red wine and knocked back two glasses in double-quick time. He began to feel more relaxed. His thoughts turned to the man who had caused the accident. Slowly he began to strategize.

He had a name. And he also had an address, a penthouse apartment on the top of a luxury residential tower in midtown Manhattan.

Reznick wondered, not for the first time, what he was going to do with that information. He was tempted to head straight there and confront the guy. But what use would that be? The NYPD were on it, after all.

However, he knew deep down that he wanted more. He wanted Brutka to suffer as his daughter had. He believed this was the central motivating factor. He wanted revenge. An eye for an eye.

He wondered how he could leverage what he knew. The bottom line was that his daughter would still be in a coma no matter what he did. Whatever happened to Brutka, or whatever Reznick did, wouldn't change that. Not one iota.

So that was it, then? Revenge? Did he just want to teach the fucker a lesson?

His cell phone, sitting on the table, began to vibrate.

Reznick picked up. "Yeah."

"It's Acosta."

Reznick wondered what she wanted at this time of night. "Hey . . . Any news?"

"I'd like to talk to you, Jon."

"What now?"

"If possible."

"I'm not far. Just around the corner having a drink at the Bentley Hotel."

"See you in a little while."

Reznick asked for a second glass.

Fifteen minutes later, Acosta walked in looking harassed and stressed. She pulled up a chair beside him and glanced around. "Sorry, I just had to have a quick chat with my boss," she said.

"Tough day?"

"Every day is tough. Some tougher than others. But they all kinda merge into one another over time."

Reznick poured a glass of red and handed it to her. "This might take the edge off."

"I wouldn't bet on it." Acosta took a large gulp of wine. "That's nice." She looked around and into the bar. "They've redecorated. Nice place."

"Close to the hospital."

"Not far from the station house either. Anyway, just wanted to see how you were doing. I can only imagine what you're going through. It isn't easy. The days must seem like years."

"You have no idea."

Acosta gazed into her wine for a few moments, as if deep in contemplation. "I've been doing some checking up on you, Jon, discreetly."

"Why?"

"It's what cops do."

"Find anything interesting?"

She sighed as she shifted in her seat. "I reached out to a few people I know in the FBI, but also in Homeland Security."

"What did you find?"

Acosta lowered her voice. "I didn't realize you had been a Delta operator."

Reznick sipped some wine. "Yeah, I was in Delta. A few years ago. Actually, quite a few years ago. I don't talk about it much."

"My brother, he was in Afghanistan. Delta too."

"Might've known him. What was his name?"

"Diego Acosta."

Reznick shook his head. "Sorry, name doesn't ring a bell."

"He died two days after arriving in Afghanistan. Shot by a member of the Afghan police who were with him."

"Jesus Christ, I'm sorry. That's brutal."

Acosta sighed as she looked around the patio. "I so wanted my brother back. It's family. We were really close. I wanted him to be safe. I prayed he would be safe. Each and every night he was away. But . . . it wasn't meant to be. My prayers weren't answered."

Reznick nodded.

"I wish . . . I wish he would walk in right now and I'd see his face again." She shrugged. "But that's just never going to happen."

"You want to hold on to things that are dear to you. Family. Loved ones."

Acosta sighed. "Maybe I've overstepped by coming here."

"We're just having a drink."

"I just wanted to do everything I could to help, even if it's just trying to reassure you that we're doing everything we can."

"I appreciate that."

Acosta sipped her wine. "That's good."

"Should be at that price."

She smiled. "You must've known some Delta operators who didn't come home."

"Oh yeah. Too many. Never leaves you. Little fragments of conversation can put me right back there. Flashbacks. That kind of thing."

"My mother still doesn't sleep too well, all these years later. Sometimes when I stay over at her place, up in the Bronx, if I can't sleep I see her in the middle of the night standing at the window, looking out into the darkness, as if she's expecting Diego to come home any minute."

Reznick nodded.

"Anyway, I don't know why I told you all that. Just thought it was important."

"I understand."

Acosta put the glass to her mouth. "The people I've spoken to about your more recent work say you're a badass. Their words."

Reznick shrugged. "People exaggerate. Say things."

"They say you took down an Iranian crew almost single-handedly. I also hear you foiled a bioterror plot in DC."

Reznick pinched the bridge of his nose. He wasn't at liberty to share such sensitive pieces of intelligence as that, even if he was in the mood to brag, which he never was.

Acosta smiled. "Real buttoned up. My brother was the same. Wouldn't tell me a thing. Not a goddamn thing. Even when I pressed him, when he was home on leave, he told me nothing."

Reznick knocked back his glass of red and poured another, topping up Acosta's glass. "I'm guessing you didn't come over here to talk to me about your brother."

Acosta leaned forward, holding her glass. "Jon, I think it's important that I keep you abreast of where the investigation is. I'm under no obligation to do so. But I think, especially in this particular case, and with your background and clearance, you have a right to know."

"I'd welcome any insights."

Acosta sighed. "Yesterday you wanted to know when I would be interviewing the driver."

Reznick nodded. "And how did it go?"

"He said he wasn't driving. We have surveillance footage that shows his Bentley. But we can't be sure who was behind the wheel. So we're at sort of a dead end."

"You kidding me?"

Acosta shook her head. "The guy has impeccable credentials and no criminal record." She averted her gaze for a few moments. "Jon, there's something I've got to tell you. This is going to be tough to swallow, I know. First, even if we can prove he did this, we can't arrest this man."

Reznick took a few moments to process the information. "I'm sorry, what?"

Acosta sighed. "He's a diplomat posted here in New York. Which means he has diplomatic immunity."

Reznick sat straight up. "Are you saying there's nothing we can do? What about my daughter? What about the law?"

"He's protected by the law. International law. Vienna Convention. I'm so sorry."

"Son of a bitch! So why did he agree to an interview?"

"I don't know. Perhaps to show he's being helpful to the police."

"Fuck!"

"We *have* learned one thing. On the morning your daughter was struck, he would have been en route to an early-morning diplomatic breakfast. We checked. And double-checked. So, even if he was driving, he was carrying out his duties when the accident happened, which means—"

"Full diplomatic immunity. I know." Reznick swore under his breath. "Is the State Department aware of this? And if so, why haven't they made him persona non grata? That's what usually happens."

Acosta didn't reply.

"His home country, wherever the hell that is, could waive diplomatic immunity."

"From what I know, that isn't going to happen in this case."

Reznick took a few moments to process the information. "Why not?"

Acosta looked at him sadly. "The guy has friends in high places."

Thirteen

The following morning, as a pale-orange sun filtered through the blinds, Meyerstein was sitting in the twenty-third-floor office assigned to the FBI's fresh-faced Assistant Director Nick Peters, the man in charge of the New York office.

"So, Nick, I heard your guys had an unusual assignment last night?"

Peters smiled from behind his desk. Meyerstein had known him for the better part of a decade. A hardworking, dedicated Nebraska native who had risen to be one of the FBI's best men in the field. Whether it was terrorism, mob activities, or joint terrorism task forces, Peters had an exemplary record and was much admired by those who knew him. He also wasn't fazed by New York—its myriad challenges, the size of the city, or the unique problems a world city could throw at him. "You could say that, Martha."

"So what happened?"

"The Director wanted us to keep a close eye on Reznick."

Meyerstein nodded. "So what've you got?"

"I know Reznick reports directly to you. And I know what he brings to the table. But you can forget any thoughts you had of keeping Reznick from getting involved in this police investigation." Peters handed her several black-and-white photos. They showed Reznick meeting with an attractive woman in a bar, drinks in hand. "Detective

Isabella Acosta seems to be going out on a limb for Jon Reznick. I think we've got a problem."

Meyerstein stared at the pictures. She saw the way the detective smiled at Reznick. And the way he seemed at ease in her presence. "Interesting. And who contacted who?"

"She called him."

Meyerstein scrutinized the photos again, flipping through them. "She's pretty."

Peters nodded.

"Did we get audio?"

"Not this time," Peters said.

"It's important that Reznick doesn't get involved in any way with this diplomat who hit his daughter. This concerns me."

"Me too. We're getting a warrant signed this afternoon so we can get what Reznick and Acosta are both saying on their cells."

Meyerstein looked at the photos for a few moments. It made her feel awkward eavesdropping on Reznick, knowing him as well as she did. But the last thing they needed was for Jon to go after a protected diplomat. That was an international incident waiting to happen.

"She might've just been lending a sympathetic ear. Keeping him up to date with any developments," Peters said.

"Very personal service for a New York City detective. I'm not buying it. I imagine she has other cases to worry about."

Peters nodded. "You think she's feeding him information? Identity?"

"Maybe. It does concerns me that she might be divulging information, sensitive information."

Peters rubbed his face, frustrated. "As if we don't have enough on our fucking plate."

"Well, Reznick is technically still our responsibility. And we need to ensure that the United States does not break international law. We all know how well diplomats are protected."

"You really think Reznick is capable of getting that information and would be willing to act on it?"

Meyerstein sighed. "He's capable alright. Will he act on it? I don't know."

"You've worked with him for years, right?"

"One thing I've learned is that Jon Reznick is not afraid to take risks when the stakes are high. To put himself on the line. I'm concerned that with his daughter in the hospital, he might do something risky."

Peters flicked through a manila file on his desk and scanned a couple of pages. "So, he lost his wife on 9/11. So losing his daughter, or even *potentially* losing her, could spark something in him."

"We can't rule that out. He can be highly disciplined. But there is an unpredictable and, frankly, combustible side to his nature."

Peters leaned back in his seat, biting on the end of a pen. "I've spoken to Commissioner Jacobsen, and he says that he's already spoken with Acosta's boss. The precinct is dealing with it, but I agree: there needs to be sensitivity around this. The State Department has called me three times in the last forty-eight hours."

"Interesting. And Detective Acosta is based on the Upper East Side?"

"Nineteenth Precinct."

Meyerstein gazed at the photos again. "I'm concerned."

Peters steepled his fingers and shrugged. "It's not illegal what she's doing."

"I've heard about going above and beyond the call of duty, but this looks like she's blurring boundaries."

"By all reports she's a very good cop. Fine detective. Grew up in the Bronx with a big family. Mother worked three jobs to help them survive."

"That's tough."

"What're you thinking, Martha?"

Meyerstein got up from her seat and walked over to the windows overlooking the lower Manhattan skyline. "You ever met him?"

"Reznick? No. What's he like?"

"Doesn't take crap. From anyone. Tough. Uncompromising. And he doesn't do boundaries. Rules. Laws."

Peters leaned back in his seat and sighed. "Fuck. So he's not going to like the fact that the man responsible for his daughter's hit-and-run is going to walk free."

"Jon will know that already. If Acosta hasn't told him, I'm sure he's found out."

"What then?"

"That's what worries me."

Meyerstein wanted to speak to Reznick face-to-face, but also to see how Lauren was. She was escorted to the ICU by a nurse and met the doctor in charge of Lauren's case. She showed her FBI ID and he escorted her to Lauren's room. She stopped outside the door and looked through the glass.

Reznick was sitting at his daughter's bedside, holding her hand. He seemed to be speaking quietly. Meyerstein's instincts were to leave them alone, not disturb the moment. But she had a job to do, regardless of her personal feelings.

She gently pushed open the door and approached the bed. Reznick turned to face her.

"I hope you don't mind me being here," Meyerstein said.

He didn't say anything, just turned back toward his daughter.

"If you want, I'll leave. Just say the word."

Reznick leaned forward and kissed Lauren on the forehead, then got to his feet. "Nice to see you. Let's grab a cup of coffee."

Fourteen

Reznick felt good to be with Martha. He admired her work ethic, intelligence, and tenacity. He had known and worked with her for years. But there was still an underlying tension between them. It seemed to linger. He always attributed it to the serious work she did and the sensitive nature of the jobs he got involved in.

They took the elevator to the ground floor of the hospital and made small talk as they walked to a nearby coffee shop on East Sixty-Sixth Street, covering everything from the heat to the President's latest outburst.

It wasn't often that they encountered each other anywhere other than across a desk. He couldn't help noticing her light, citrusy perfume. It smelled nice.

Reznick went up to the counter and ordered an espresso for himself and a frothy latte for Meyerstein. She chose a quiet corner table and sat down. He picked up the two coffees and joined her.

"I hope you don't think I'm intruding," she said.

"You're doing your job. I get it."

Meyerstein smiled. She looked tired, worn down by the job. "I just want to help. I want you to know we're here for you."

Reznick sipped the strong espresso, feeling the caffeine buzz hit his system almost immediately. "I understand what you're doing. And it's not a problem. Seriously."

"What do you mean?"

"I know why you're here. Why you're *really* here."

"You do?"

Reznick leaned in close. "You've got a diplomat who's out of control, unaccountable to anyone, who nearly killed my daughter. And you have me, an FBI . . . adviser, and the Feds think I need close watching. Am I right?"

"I can't confirm what you've just said."

"You don't have to."

"How did you find out so much?"

"It doesn't matter. We all have our ways, right?"

Meyerstein sighed and seemed to force a smile. "This is killing me, Jon. I've never met Lauren until today. I'm sorry it's under such circumstances. But I have a job to do."

"You're going to lay down some rules?"

"I would call it advice. Guidance."

Reznick shrugged. "Go on."

"And I make no apology for that."

"Fair enough. Wouldn't expect anything less."

"I say this as a friend and colleague who admires you very much: you need to back off. I know how you'll be working this. You'll be figuring out what happened, who did it, and what you can do about it. It's natural. Now I don't want to get into a big argument about this. But you need to accept that some events are outside our control."

Reznick stared long and hard at her.

"Now, I want to help, but you have responsibilities when you work for the FBI. We have rules. And protocols."

"I get that."

"So I want you to think really carefully about what I know you'll be considering."

"And what's that?"

"Don't think you can go around New York trying to hunt down the person who did this in order to avenge your daughter. That's not going to happen. You need to accept that."

"Someone important did it. Someone with diplomatic immunity who is going to get off scot-free. Someone important enough to get you to fly up from DC to warn me to back off."

Meyerstein's gaze wandered around the rest of the coffee shop, fixing on a younger woman with a laptop and some papers on the table.

"I already know the guy's a diplomat."

"This won't end well, Jon."

Reznick shrugged.

"Who told you?"

"You know I can't say."

Meyerstein stared at him. "Do you know how much I care about you, Jon?"

Reznick was taken aback. He shifted in his seat and averted his gaze for a few moments. He felt uncomfortable with this line of conversation. But something about her gentle tone of voice caught him short. He looked at her and shrugged. "No, I guess I didn't. But thanks for telling me."

"I mean . . . I don't want you getting into trouble. There have been some close scrapes. But . . . you need to just back off on this."

Reznick smiled. "I hear what you're saying."

"This won't end well for anyone, Jon, if you head down that path."

"I know who he is. Just so you know."

Meyerstein shook her head. "Not good, Jon. Not good at all."

"Martha, when people get involved with my family, they get involved with me. This guy almost killed my daughter. She's still fighting for her life."

"You need to let the law takes its course."

"Are you telling me I should turn the other cheek?"

"That's exactly what I'm telling you to do."

"My daughter can't turn the other cheek. She's in a goddamn coma. My beautiful daughter. Unable to move. Unable to breathe without a machine."

Meyerstein looked around the coffee shop again. "There are rules, Jon. There are laws. You do believe in the rule of law, don't you?"

"I believe in right and wrong. This guy is in the wrong. He also broke the law."

"But international law deems that diplomats are protected. America's diplomats are protected too, because in many countries the laws differ from the ones we're used to. It has to be that way for everyone for international relationships to work. Don't you understand? As hard as it is to hear, the protocols at work here are bigger and more important than Lauren. Than you."

"I understand that. But that doesn't concern me. This guy is walking around, and no one seems to be able to get him the hell out of this country. That's what I don't understand."

Meyerstein met his gaze. "Let me make one thing clear. Take my advice and head back to the hospital and be with your daughter. But if you go down the path I believe you're about to go down, the Feds will come down on you hard."

When Reznick returned to Lauren's hospital room, a bouquet of white lilies was sitting in a vase of water at her bedside, accompanied by a small envelope.

Reznick looked at the nurse. "Who's that from?"

The nurse smiled. "Aren't they lovely? They just arrived." She handed him the embossed envelope from a New York flower shop. "Probably her college friends. A couple have called asking how she is."

Reznick looked at the envelope. "Do you mind if I open it?"

"Not at all."

Reznick opened the envelope. Inside was a note. It read: *Dearest Lauren, So sorry to hear about your accident. Praying you have a full recovery. Thinking of you and your family, AB.*

"Who's it from?" the nurse asked.

Reznick stared at the note, rereading it. He felt as if his skin were burning. He'd considered acceding to Meyerstein's request, staying out of the investigation no matter how likely he was to disagree with its outcome. Focusing on Lauren and her health. But he recognized the initials on the note. *Aleksander Brutka.* The bastard wasn't content to just get away with his crimes. He was playing a sick little game at Reznick's expense. Enough was enough.

Fifteen

Reznick threw the flowers in the trash as questions began to rage inside his head. He paced Lauren's hospital room like a caged animal. How had the guy gotten her name? He didn't think the cops would have released that. So that left only the possibility that the diplomat had managed to acquire that information illegally. Perhaps through similar channels to the ones Reznick had used to secure the name of the diplomat.

He wondered what sort of person would mow down an innocent girl in a crosswalk, not stop at the scene of the accident, and then send flowers with his initials on the card. He assumed that the guy was playing mind games. Fucking with them. The diplomat didn't know that Reznick had his name and could match the initials. But the tone of the note was as if it had come from a friend. A person who cared.

Then again, perhaps it was something more sinister.

Was this an attempt by a degenerate diplomat to worm his way into her life? Was he a drunk? Did he use drugs? Perhaps the diplomat wanted to ensure his victim's silence.

Reznick picked up the card again and read the words. He had to respond. This was a direct provocation. The actions of a manipulative and dangerous man.

The more he thought about it, the more enraged he felt.

Reznick thought back to his meeting with Meyerstein. She had warned him not to get involved. He assumed she had been instructed by the Director of the FBI to head to New York to keep him in check.

Reznick felt conflicted. He didn't want to go against Meyerstein or jeopardize his relationship with her and the FBI. But he wasn't the sort of guy who could just walk away from this. It wasn't in his nature. Besides, this asshole needed to know who he was dealing with.

The guy had crossed the line. Doing nothing was not an option.

Reznick had the guy's name. And he had an address. He just needed a plan.

Was he going to turn up at the guy's apartment, get in, and somehow try to lay him out cold? As a form of retaliation?

It was an appealing thought. But he knew the chances of getting into an upscale apartment building were pretty low. Sure, there were ways. Maintenance guy fixing some air-conditioning ducts. Delivery guy. Mailman.

Reznick figured that a guy like Brutka would have a layer or two of security in-house. Close protection. Outer layer. And electronic surveillance cameras.

The longer Reznick considered it, the more convinced he became that it was a futile thing to attempt. What was he going to do? Kill the guy in cold blood? It might avenge his daughter, teach the guy a lesson. But what would come of it?

He would go to jail for years. His daughter, meanwhile, would be without the only family she had.

Lauren needed her father.

Reznick tried to push his raw anger aside as he weighed the consequences. He quickly rationalized that it was intolerable not to confront this guy, no matter the price he might have to pay later.

He began to refocus on where Brutka lived. He needed to get an idea of what the building looked like. Access areas. Entry point. Any luxurious apartment building like that would be heavily guarded. And have a 24/7 front desk.

It was then that the germ of an idea began to form.

Reznick felt his senses switch on. He headed out onto the broiling New York streets and across to Barneys on Madison, where he bought a nice suit, shirt, tie, and new shoes. Then he went back to his hotel room, showered, shaved, and got changed.

Reznick put his 9mm Beretta in his waistband and called up the hacker.

"Hey, Mr. R. Any update on your daughter's condition?"

"No change."

"I'm sorry, man. That's terrible."

"She's in the best hands. So that's something."

"What can I do for you?"

"Got a slightly unusual request."

"On this, whatever you want, I'll get it."

Reznick smiled. "We need to meet up for a drink sometime."

"I'll think about it. You worry me, Reznick."

"I need another favor."

"Name it."

"I want you to call the real estate brokers who are in charge of selling and renting out apartments at the residential tower where Aleksander Brutka lives."

"Shit. You really are going to kill him, aren't you?"

"Highly unlikely."

"So what's the purpose of you going there?"

"I don't know . . . I want to send him a message."

"You want to shake the tree?"

"That's exactly what I want to do."

"When do you want to do this?"

"Soon. Get me an appointment as soon as you can, ideally within the next few hours. Say your client, a high-net-worth individual, wants to be shown the best apartments they have available."

The hacker started to laugh. "You really are a crazy motherfucker."

Sixteen

The thirtysomething female Realtor was standing outside the apartment building to greet Reznick when he arrived. "Mr. Reznick?"

"The very one."

"So nice to meet you, sir." The young woman was shielding her eyes from the blazing sun. "Welcome to One East River. Are you in town on business?"

"I'm bored with staying at The Carlyle. Need something permanent. I also do a lot of business with the United Nations, so I'd like to be a helluva lot closer to see my clients."

"Which company do you work for?"

"Offshore banking, mostly . . . Tax advice, that kind of thing. Can't say too much more at this stage."

"Not a problem. Let's head inside."

The young Realtor got a security badge for Reznick, and she whisked him to the thirty-second floor and swiped her card to access a stupendous apartment. Light flooded through the floor-to-ceiling windows, which gave sprawling views over the East River. She showed him around the spacious rooms. Then out onto the wraparound terrace. "Isn't this something?"

"How much?"

"It's listed at twenty-five million dollars. But if you deal directly with me, we could be talking twenty-two. Sound good?"

Reznick stared out over the water and looked up at the penthouse terrace at the top. "Great place."

"It's very discreet."

"Friend of mine lives in the penthouse," he lied. "He recommended I check it out."

The woman smiled. "You know Mr. Brutka?"

"Aleksander? Sure, very well indeed. We've done business together for years. Very smart man."

The woman laughed. "I actually brokered the sale of Mr. Brutka's penthouse."

"Is that right? That's terrific. That makes perfect sense. Well, I've got to say I can see why he's so enamored of this place."

"So . . . do you have a date when you'd like to move in?"

"I was hoping within the next six weeks."

"That's perfect. By the time we get the paperwork taken care of, it'll all be ready for you. We can provide the services of a top New York interior designer if that's required too."

"Absolutely." Reznick went back into the apartment. "Any suggestions for what would work in this space?"

"For me personally? Minimalism. White. A less-is-more kind of thing."

Reznick checked his watch. "I've got an appointment uptown in an hour."

The Realtor tucked some hair behind her ear. "So is this apartment to your liking?"

"It's more than to my liking. I'll be in touch very soon."

The Realtor blushed. "That's wonderful. Our firm is based in the building, seven days a week."

Reznick said, "You got a restroom I can use before I head to my meeting?"

"Of course. Follow me."

The Realtor headed out into the hallway and pointed to a double door and sign at the end of the corridor. "The restroom is right there, Mr. Reznick." She handed him a card. "My office is two floors down—can't miss it—if you want to pick up a brochure on your way out."

"You got it. See you in five minutes."

Reznick waited until she pressed her thumb against the elevator and the doors had closed. He went into the restroom. Saw a smoke detector. He pulled out paper towels and stuffed them into a trash can. He pulled out a lighter and lit the paper. The flames took hold. Black smoke drifted up toward the ceiling.

The piercing sound of the smoke alarm ripped through the air.

Reznick headed out to the corridor, smashed a glass fire alarm, and pressed the button. The sound of the wailing alarm was deafening, echoing through the corridors. He headed into the stairwell and bounded up three flights of stairs two steps at a time.

He came to a secure door with a video intercom.

Fuck.

He buzzed repeatedly.

A few seconds later, a huge thickset white guy, vaguely Slavic, stared through the video panel.

"This is a private area, sir," the guy said.

"Emergency. Fire. You need to open up."

"Sir, I cannot leave my post."

"Listen to me. Open up. This is an evacuation. I need to speak to your boss."

"Who are you?"

"I'm the executive manager of the building."

The guy buzzed opened the door, and Reznick pressed the Beretta to his forehead. "On your knees."

The guy tried to grab the gun, but Reznick smashed him in the side of the neck first. The man went down in a heap. Reznick hauled the guy out onto the carpeted landing, his foot keeping the door open. He rifled through the guy's pockets and pulled out a cell phone and a swipe card.

Reznick left the guy immobilized and headed down a marble corridor to where a desk and chair sat outside the penthouse apartment. He wondered if that was where the security guy he had taken out was usually positioned. It made sense. He swiped the card and pushed open the door.

He took a few moments to look around the extraordinary duplex penthouse. Whitewashed walls, floor-to-ceiling windows, huge photographs of iconic New York architecture on the wall.

Reznick spotted the surveillance cameras discreetly positioned. He padded across the huge space and pounded up the stairs to the next level. Through more floor-to-ceiling glass he saw the turquoise waters of the penthouse pool with the killer views.

He looked around at the walls. These were adorned with black-and-white portraits of Aleksander Brutka in and around New York. Photos of him in fast luxury cars. With models. At parties. The Met Gala. Black-tie events.

In the corner of his eye, a huge man, as big as a mountain, appeared with a knife.

The guy was grinning like a madman, ready for a confrontation. He lunged forward. Reznick feinted and grabbed the guy's arm, pulling his fingers back until he dropped the knife. But the guy immediately wrapped his arms around Reznick in a bear hug. He felt the life being crushed out of him. Slowly. He leaned forward and then smashed his head back into the guy's face. And again. And again. The crunch of the man's nose breaking was accompanied by a groan.

Reznick elbowed the guy in the throat, bringing him to his knees. Then he stepped forward and kicked the guy square in the head, breaking his jaw and leaving the guy out cold.

He checked the rest of the penthouse. Through the windows at the far end of the outdoor deck, adjacent to the pool, a man in his early thirties, wearing shades, was drying himself beside the pool.

Reznick slid back the glass doors, walked up to the man, and pointed the gun at his head. "Aleksander Brutka?"

The guy nodded slowly. "What is going on?"

Reznick pressed the gun tight to his head. "On your knees."

Brutka sighed as he bent down. "Sir, what in God's name is going on here?"

Reznick shook his head. "Do you know who I am?"

Brutka shook his head. "I've no idea who you are. You've just barged into my apartment with a gun! I've never met you in my life."

"My name is Jon Reznick. You ran down my daughter. And left her in a coma. You understand now?"

Brutka's eyes were hooded. "What—?"

"Shut the fuck up. I'm doing the talking. Where I come from, if you commit a crime, you pay a price."

Brutka shook his head. "I understand now. You think I was driving the car. I can assure you that's not the case. I've spoken to the police."

"Then you send my daughter flowers with a little note. Who does that?"

"I just wanted to express my heartfelt sorrow. I own the vehicle, and it was taken without permission. I didn't realize that would offend you, sir. I hope you can accept my sincere apologies."

"No, I fucking don't! I think you're lying! Here's what's going to happen. Do not ever, ever contact my daughter, myself, or the hospital ever again, do you understand?"

Brutka nodded. "Yes, I do."

"You only get one warning. You will leave this city. You stay away from my daughter. Am I making myself clear?"

"I understand how you must feel. And for what it's worth, I'm truly sorry."

"Trust me, don't make me come looking for you."

Reznick knew he had to get out of there. He turned on his heel and strode out of the apartment. He took a different stairwell and went down three floors to where he'd been shown the apartment. Then he took the elevator to the lobby.

He sensed the cameras on him, scanning his every move.

Then Reznick headed out the front door onto the boiling New York streets.

Seventeen

A few minutes later, Aleksander Brutka was drinking a double scotch in his penthouse to settle his nerves. He sat and seethed as his head of security, Maurice Blantone, began reviewing the surveillance footage. He had been tempted to fire his whole security detail. But he had put that on the back burner until this matter was resolved.

Blantone pressed the remote and the video began to play on the huge screen. A sharply dressed white guy wearing sunglasses strolled through the lobby with the real estate agent. The man in the footage turned and looked up at the cameras. Then Blantone froze the image. "This is our guy?"

Brutka stared at the man who had breached his security. "That's him. Jon Reznick. So this is the girl's father?"

"That's the name he gave. He obviously wants us to know that. But this is no ordinary, run-of-the-mill tough guy. And he's not an opportunist."

Brutka shook his head. He felt his heart beginning to race.

"We need to be careful how we react. That may be what he's counting on—you reacting."

"So many questions. How did he know I was the one who ran into his daughter? Was my name leaked by the cops?"

"Aleksander, don't go there. Don't start making assumptions. I also don't think it was a good idea to send the flowers. It doesn't look good."

"Don't tell me what I should or shouldn't do. I get enough of that talk from my father. So I want to know how this happened. The guy just strolls into my apartment complex with the Realtor. Then somehow gets past two of my security detail? How is that possible?"

"We need to really work out some options. We don't want to over-react. Or make the wrong call. I've got a bad feeling about this guy. About this whole incident."

"Let me make one thing clear: I call the shots. I will decide."

Blantone sat down beside Brutka. "How long have I known you, Aleksander?"

"A long time."

"Since you were a boy. I worked for your father. And he has entrusted your security and well-being to me."

"My father can't know about this. He'll ask me to hire that French security firm who were protecting my cousin in Kiev."

"We have this covered."

"Do you? He just strolled in here! What the hell am I supposed to think?"

"I don't know much about this guy yet, but I do know that it takes a certain type of man to do what this Reznick guy just did."

"He told me to leave town. *He* told *me*! Aleksander Brutka! The son of the Ukrainian President!"

"I want to offer a suggestion. First, we need to learn exactly what this guy is all about."

Brutka looked at the screen. "I want to know everything about him. What does he do? Where does he live? What makes him tick? I want to know if he drinks. Does he do drugs? Does he chase women? I want to know everything there is to know about this bastard."

Blantone nodded. "I've already got things underway."

Brutka finished his scotch and threw the glass against a wall; the shards smashed to the floor. "You fucking better. No one fucks with me. Sort this out. And then I'm going to kill Jon Reznick."

Eighteen

Reznick caught a cab five blocks from Brutka's luxury apartment and headed uptown. He knew he had crossed a line and the cops would have every right to haul him in and charge him. But at that moment he didn't really care.

The cab dropped him off outside the hospital, and he headed inside. He met with the doctors. But there were still no signs that Lauren was ready to be weaned off the drugs, the first step in slowly waking her from the induced coma.

He was starting to fear the worst. Was she slipping away? Or was she healing and just needed more time?

Reznick spent a couple of hours at his daughter's bedside. Talking to her softly. Telling her how much he loved her. He felt drained and closed his eyes while he held her hand.

He could have killed that fucker Brutka in cold blood. That was what he'd wanted to do. But then he would have lost. His daughter would have lost. But still there was the lingering feeling that he wanted Brutka dead.

Reznick went out into the hallway and made another call to the hacker.

"I need one final favor," he said.

"Shoot."

"I want you to remotely activate Brutka's lawyer's cell."

"You want to listen in?"

"Set it up so that whenever he calls or receives a call from Brutka, I get a message."

"An audio link?"

"Exactly. It might provide some useful intel."

"That's way out on a limb, Jon."

"Don't do it if it compromises you."

A beat. "You're nuts, you know that."

"Tell me about it."

"Leave it to me, man."

Reznick went back to his daughter's bedside, dozing off to the sound of bleeping from the machine.

The following morning, Acosta turned up at the door to the room. He knew why she was there.

Acosta cocked her head, signaling she wanted to talk somewhere else. They headed to a nearby diner. He ordered coffee and brunch for them. After they'd finished, the straight talk began.

Acosta leaned across the table. "Dumb move, Jon," she said. "You don't strike me as a stupid man. What were you thinking?"

Reznick shrugged.

"The diplomat's lawyers have been in touch. And they are not happy."

"Are you referring to Aleksander Brutka, member of the Permanent Mission of Ukraine to the United Nations?"

"How the hell did you get that name? I certainly never gave it to you."

Reznick sighed. "You wanna keep your voice down?"

"How did you get the name?"

"I don't know what you mean."

"Don't jerk me around, Jon! I thought we were operating on trust."

"So did I."

"I never gave you the name."

"I never said you did. You withheld that."

Acosta looked around the diner for a few moments, clearly exasperated. "What has gotten into you?"

"Nothing's happening, that's what."

"This is a police matter, Jon. We have to deal with our suspect in a lawful manner. I'm sickened by what happened to your daughter. We all are. But you have to let us do our jobs."

"But you're not. Nothing is happening. Hour by hour, day by day, nothing. He's still free."

"You're not the law, Jon."

Reznick shook his head. "The NYPD are beholden to some archaic Vienna Convention bullshit. This is America, not Austria. Who the hell calls the shots?"

"It's complicated. This is politics. And that's when things get fucked up."

"Damn right it's politics. Dirty politics. And that guy is not being held accountable."

Acosta rubbed her eyes. "Know how I first heard about your visit to his apartment?"

Reznick shrugged.

"Brutka's lawyer."

"He called you? Why you?"

"They think I leaked Brutka's identity. And now he's out for blood. He's talking about suing me. Suing the NYPD. My boss is not happy. And he's being pressured by both Brutka's lawyers and the State Department. It was a dumb stunt you pulled, and now I'm getting the blame. They know I've been talking to you. So now you've got a problem with me *and* the NYPD."

"I have no problem with you. And I certainly have no problem with the NYPD. My problem is with Brutka."

"Says you. But things have spilled over a bit, don't you think?"

"It's just the opening skirmishes. Things will get meaner."

She looked at him open-mouthed. "Are you trying to start a war with this guy? This is a respected diplomat."

"Did you know he sent my daughter flowers in the hospital? After nearly killing her and refusing to admit it."

"What?"

"Flowers. And a note." He pulled the card out of his back pocket and handed it to her. "Signed *AB*."

"Maybe he just wanted to say he was sorry."

"I'm not buying it."

Acosta shook her head. "I still can't believe you did that. They said you had him at gunpoint. Set off a fire alarm and assaulted a security guard."

"Why don't you arrest me?"

"The State Department has already contacted my boss saying not to drag you into this."

"That's right. They don't want this going to trial. They know how it would look."

"Jon, you're not thinking clearly."

"I've got his attention. And I'm prepared to do whatever it takes to protect my daughter. This guy is dangerous."

"I know your background. And I understand how you must feel. But this can't go on. It was reckless. This diplomat is well respected. And under international law, if that had been cops storming into his private apartment, we would have been in deep shit. This guy has full diplomatic status, and you need to back the fuck up."

"Things have only gotten started."

"Brutka's lawyers will come for you. You do realize that, don't you?"

"I'm counting on it."

"And he'll have the full weight of the law behind him too."

"Well, that's fine with me."

"Jon, I think you want to provoke him. Is that what you're doing?"

"I'm letting the guy know that I want him the fuck away from my daughter. I want him out of New York."

"That's not your call. We have no proof he was driving. So he's innocent."

"I'm not buying that crock of shit."

"And also, my colleagues might very well come looking for you."

Reznick shrugged.

"You want to bring him out into the open, get him to make a move, don't you? Is that what this is?"

"I've said enough. Let's leave it at that."

"Jon, you're not listening. You could be hauled in and charged. Brutka himself could bring charges against you."

"Do you think he wants this incident to be splashed all over the papers?"

"Is that what you're banking on?"

"I'm counting on him not wanting a scandal, but being forced to make a move, one way or the other."

"And what if he sends people out looking for you?"

"Then I'll be waiting for them."

Nineteen

Acosta felt stressed and angry after the meeting with Reznick. She headed back to the precinct and was handed a cup of coffee by Detective Sergeant McGeough.

"You look like shit," he said.

"Thanks for that confidence booster. What're we going to do with Reznick?"

"The boss is furious, as you can imagine. We should really bring him in."

"I just spoke to him."

"You did? Where?"

"Diner a couple blocks away."

McGeough arched his eyebrows. "What's he got to say for himself?"

"He's defiant. Almost like he wants a war."

"I think the boss is hoping that since the diplomat doesn't want to get involved, and since Reznick's daughter is still in a coma, it's going to blow over."

Acosta sighed and sipped the lukewarm coffee. "I don't think that's what Reznick has in mind."

"He's a whackjob. He held a diplomat at gunpoint. That's nuts."

"We have no evidence that happened. Just Brutka's word against Reznick's."

McGeough shook his head. "Whose side are you on?"

"Oh, fuck you!"

"Isabella, we know Reznick was there. We've seen the footage."

Acosta nodded. "The guy is former Delta. So was my brother. I know what they're like. And what they're capable of."

"And you were chatting with him?"

Acosta shrugged. "What can I tell you? He's a straight shooter. I like him."

"You need to be careful, Isabella. I'm serious."

Acosta slumped in her seat and skimmed through a pile of Post-its.

McGeough shrugged at her. "Catch you later," he said as he turned to head out of the office.

"Yeah, whatever." She stared at the bits of papers. One of the phone numbers stuck out. A number she knew. She dialed quickly.

"Detective Acosta?" The voice sounded frightened.

"Yeah, what's happening, Daniela?" A junkie girl she had tried to help when she worked in East Harlem.

"I'm scared. I don't know who to talk to. I don't trust the other cops. I spoke to a guy at the Twenty-Eighth Precinct. He had an attitude when I called and then hung up."

"Slow down, Daniela. You know me. I'm listening. What's bothering you?"

"I think I'm being followed."

Acosta scribbled a note on a fresh pad. "Who's following you?"

"I'm scared. I think they're watching me."

"Who?"

"Friends of a guy who controls me. The guy who beats me up. They're out there. Watching me."

"I need a name."

"I recognize the cars. I'm really scared."

"You got a license plate?"

"My vision isn't so good since he attacked me the last time. Migraines. I think I might have a detached retina."

"You need medical attention."

"You know how it works, Isabella. If I turn up at the hospital, he'll know about it. I don't have insurance. I don't have papers. I ain't got nothing."

"And you don't know who this guy is?"

"No. But I took a picture of him when he passed out last night."

"That's something. Let's talk. Face-to-face. I'll get you some medical attention."

"He's crazy. He has friends. They scare me. They turn up any time day or night. Looking for favors."

Acosta closed her eyes for a moment. It was an all-too-familiar situation. A girl with a drug habit too scared to give a name. But the guy is still free to continue with his criminality. Brutality. Violence. Psychological torture. Intimidation. And far worse.

"They treat me worse than an animal! I have no one to help me."

"We need to get you out of there, Daniela. Your silence only helps him. You need to speak out, about whoever is responsible. At the very least we can move you and protect you."

The girl began to sob. "I'm scared."

"I'll send a car from the Twenty-Eighth to pick you up. I know a guy there. Get a bag packed. How does that sound?"

"Don't be too late."

Acosta put in a call to a colleague, Gabriel Montero, at the Twenty-Eighth Precinct in East Harlem. She explained the situation. "I really need this."

Montero listened in silence. "I've got some stuff to sort out. I can get there in two hours."

Acosta groaned. "Gabriel, I want her out of there now."

"If it's critical, she needs to call 911. Otherwise, I'll get to her when I can."

"And two hours is the best you can do? The absolute best?"

"Take it or leave it, Isabella. I've got two shootings to deal with in the meantime."

Acosta sighed. "Fine. Just get her to safety. It's a priority for me. Let me know when it's done."

The rest of the afternoon saw Acosta tied up with interviews of suspects in robberies of Upper East Side liquor stores and an attempted homicide outside a bar.

When she was finally finished, she called Gabriel to make sure he'd had Daniela picked up.

Gabriel picked up on the sixth ring. "Yeah?"

"Just checking in to make sure Daniela's safe."

Gabriel let out a long sigh. "I sent a couple of my guys up to her apartment."

"And?"

"No answer."

Acosta groaned. "Are you kidding me?"

"They were there for ten minutes, banging on her door, ringing the bell. They went back half an hour later. Nothing. She's not home."

"Or maybe she's not answering."

"My guys identified themselves as NYPD. But nothing."

"What about the super in her building?"

"He said she hung around with a bad crowd. But we knew that already."

"Shit."

Acosta ended the call, got in a squad car, and sped uptown to the apartment at the East River Houses. It was a public housing project that still had drug and gang problems despite the efforts of police from the Twenty-Eighth Precinct. She pressed the buzzer and identified herself, and the super let her in.

Acosta followed him into the elevator, and they rode it to the ninth floor.

"She's a junkie, you know that?" he said.

"Yes, I do. Does she get visitors?"

The super shrugged. "I can't keep an eye on everything. People come and go. They bring people in that don't live here. It's not good."

The elevator door opened, and she followed the super down the corridor. It smelled of piss, and stale smoke hung heavy in the air.

The super said, "I try my best, but kids these days, you know what they're like."

Acosta knocked hard on the door and repeatedly rang the bell for a couple of minutes. "She's not answering. Fuck," she said. "Open it up."

The super did as he was told, pushing open the door. Acosta went in first and looked around the unfurnished apartment. It was bare. Not even a mattress. No sofa. Nothing. "Where's her stuff?"

The super shrugged.

Acosta saw a shelf full of drug pipes, a lump of hash, a small rock of crack. She went into the bathroom.

Lying sprawled on the linoleum floor, eyes wide open, vomit and blood dried on her dirty T-shirt and jeans, was Daniela.

◦

Twenty

The Uber's air-conditioning was on full. It was a sweltering 100 degrees outside. Reznick drank a bottle of water while he caught a ride from the Upper East Side back to midtown Manhattan, a couple of blocks from the UN, a backpack at his feet. He wanted to know if Aleksander Brutka had left town or if he was still hanging around.

He stepped out of the cool taxi and into the dirty steam-bath air, slinging the backpack over his shoulder. The smell of rotten trash from a nearby dumpster assaulted him in the breeze.

Reznick donned his sunglasses and walked half a block to the corner of East Forty-Sixth Street and First Avenue. Thirty-five stories above him was the luxury tower where Brutka lived.

Reznick turned around. The building was diagonally across from the UN headquarters, farther down the street. He took a pair of powerful binoculars out of his backpack and trained them on the highest floor of Brutka's building. He scanned the glass tower exterior, the sun sparkling like a million reflective mirrors, until he spotted the penthouse's wraparound terrace. He pulled it into focus.

He was too close to get a good look, so he walked farther up the street until he saw a vehicle entrance, which led, no doubt, to underground parking.

Twenty yards farther down the street, the Venezuelan flag flew over their UN mission.

Reznick crossed over First Avenue and stood beside a UN gatehouse. Using the binoculars, he scanned the terrace again. Suddenly, he saw a man standing there. Smiling. Wearing a white polo shirt, cell phone pressed to his ear, laughing, as if he didn't give a damn. He was positive it was Brutka.

The bastard. Still there. Not a care in the world.

But he needed to be sure.

He put the binoculars in the backpack and pulled out a camera with a telephoto lens. He trained it on the terrace. Then he took several dozen photos, hooked up a high-speed USB cable to his cell phone, and downloaded the pictures. He emailed the photos to his hacker's email address with a message: *Identify this guy.*

Reznick deleted the email and "bleached" his Sent folder so no one could follow the trail. He knew the hacker would be using cutting-edge encryption so no one could track him. But he didn't want to take any risks.

He stowed the gear in his backpack, slung it over his shoulder, and pulled out a bottle of water from a side pouch. He gulped down the water in a few swallows. He ditched the empty plastic bottle in a trash can. A minute later, his phone rang.

"Mr. R., just checking that you sent me this."

"I did. I hope that's OK. I don't want to be too presumptuous."

"Hey, I like what you do."

"So, this pose you any problems?"

"I'm assuming you think this might be your diplomat."

"Got it. I'd like to know for sure."

"I've checked online images of him. Sure looks like him."

"I need to be 100 percent."

"I'll run some pretty cool face-recognition software."

"How long until we know for sure?"

"Gimme an hour."

The flashing lights from some vehicles headed down First Avenue caught Reznick's attention. He watched as they slowed to a stop across the street from where he stood. There was an NYPD vehicle in the lead, an SUV behind it, and a sedan behind that. All lights flashing. Out of the SUV emerged two officers wearing black clothing and sunglasses and sporting semiautomatic rifles. They crossed the street and walked right up to Reznick.

The smaller of the two got in his face. "Good afternoon, sir. You mind explaining what you're doing here?"

"And who are you guys?"

"We're from the NYPD Hercules counterterrorism team. Show me some ID."

Reznick pulled out his wallet and handed over his driver's license.

"Rockland, Maine. Can I ask what you're doing here, sir? We spotted you using binoculars and photographing one of the buildings at UN Plaza."

Reznick shielded his eyes from the sun. "Is that illegal, Officer?"

"No, it's not. But we need to know why you were photographing potentially sensitive areas of New York City. Thousands of diplomats live and work in this part of town. I'm assuming you know that."

"Is that right?"

A man emerged from the rear car across the street, cell phone pressed to his ear. As he approached Reznick, he ended the call.

The man stood in front of Reznick, the armed officers flanking him. "We need you to come downtown, sir."

"Why?"

"We need to ask you some questions."

Thirty minutes later, Reznick was in an interview room at a downtown precinct with two counterterrorism officers from the NYPD, a burly middle-aged man wearing a tight short-sleeved shirt and a younger woman. After a few minutes of introductions and setting up the video and tape recording, the burly guy kicked off the interview.

"What were you photographing so close to the United Nations, Mr. Reznick?" he asked.

Reznick leaned back in his seat, arms folded. "I haven't done anything illegal."

"You need to answer the question."

Reznick sighed. "Am I supposed to be helping you with your investigation or what?"

"Just answer the question, if you don't mind. Why were you watching that building, One East River, and taking photographs?"

"What do you know about me?"

The female detective said, "We know you work off the books for the FBI. Classified."

Reznick said nothing.

"Are you working on a particular job for the FBI? It's important we know this."

"No. I'm not working for the FBI on this matter."

The woman scribbled some notes. "I appreciate your candor. Is what you're doing related to what happened to your daughter?"

Reznick stayed quiet.

The guy showed still images of Reznick arriving at the apartment complex with the Realtor, taken by a camera from the Venezuelan UN mission nearby. "You've also taken a look around inside this building, haven't you? And a complaint has been lodged by a resident's attorney."

Reznick just stared at him.

The woman smiled at Reznick. "Jon, we know your background. We know what you're capable of. And I, for one, am very sympathetic to what you're facing."

"My daughter's in a coma. Do you know that?"

"I understand," she said. "But you need to realize, the law matters. We do things by the book."

"I keep on hearing that. The law. The law. No one is above the law. Except when they are, apparently. I'm talking diplomatic immunity."

The guy cleared his throat, looking increasingly agitated. "Mr. Reznick, what you're doing is surveillance, I get that. But you can't go around spying on people. Diplomats. Whoever you think was involved in this terrible accident."

Reznick said nothing, feeling a seething anger building inside him.

The woman said, "Jon, can I ask, what did you hope to achieve?"

Reznick shrugged.

"I would suggest," she said, "that what you're doing is deliberately letting him know, or us know, that you are monitoring him, right? You want him to know that you're there."

Reznick was impressed. She knew what he was doing. And why. "Good analysis."

"I'm ex-military myself. I know about these things. And would I be right in suggesting that you want this man to know that you are not going away? That you know his identity? You want to unnerve this guy. Get him to react, to make a mistake?"

"Can't disagree with any of what you said."

The burly cop said, "Let's talk about this guy you believe lives in this building. What can you tell me about him?"

"What do you want to know?"

"I want you to be upfront with us."

Reznick stared at the cop. "OK. I have reason to believe that Aleksander Brutka, UN diplomat for the Ukrainian delegation, was responsible for nearly killing my daughter while he was driving to a function. Official business. And that means that he is protected."

The cop averted his gaze, glancing at some notes on the desk. "Let's suppose what you're saying is correct. That such a person is living at that address. How did you find out his identity? This absolutely has not been shared with you. I know. I've checked."

Reznick stared at the man. "I've got nothing to say about that."

The woman said, "Jon, it's important we know how you got that information. This is national security we're talking about."

"Are you saying American national security is at risk because of me?"

"I'm saying, with respect, that spying on UN diplomats, who are allowed under the Vienna Convention to operate here, is illegal. We, as the host country, must protect and permit free communication between diplomats. We must also protect their mission from intrusion or damage. This extends to their private residences."

Reznick leaned forward. "You're very fond of quoting the articles of the Vienna Convention. Article 9 says the host nation at any time and for any reason can declare a particular member of the diplomatic corps persona non grata. Which, roughly translated, means we can get rid of those diplomats who have committed crimes in the host country."

"Are you finished, Mr. Reznick?"

"So the question is, why the hell hasn't this guy been made persona non grata?"

The female cop said, "I think we're getting off base now, Jon."

"I don't think we are. Am I supposed to just sit back and take it, knowing that the guy is still free to walk around New York, attend meetings, live his life, after leaving a young American girl in a coma? My daughter. Are you fucking kidding me?"

The guy pointed at Reznick. "Enough!"

"Don't point your finger at me."

"This isn't going to end well, Reznick."

"My daughter is in a goddamn coma, and you're saying it's not going to end well? For me, things can't get any worse. And I'm not going to rest until I get some answers."

The burly cop shifted in his seat. "You're out of line, Reznick. Who the hell do you think you're talking to?"

"Shut up and either arrest me, charge me, or whatever it is you guys are supposed to do, or get out of my face."

The woman rubbed her eyes, clearly at the end of her patience. "You need to know that we will not tolerate the harassment of a UN diplomat here in New York City. We will not tolerate any further incidents."

"You finished?"

The woman nodded.

"Good. Well, I will not tolerate this criminal in our midst. Are we done?"

The guy nodded.

"Then I want to go and see my daughter. That alright with you guys?"

"Stay out of trouble, Jon," the woman said. "Next time you're going to jail."

Twenty-One

A burnt-orange sun washed over the Manhattan skyline as Brutka sat beside his pool enjoying a glass of champagne after a late-afternoon swim. His cell phone vibrated with a message.

He picked it up and checked the caller ID. It was the private investigator.

"Just wanted to let you know that the dossier on Tom Callaghan is taking a little longer than we expected to pull together," he said.

"Why?"

"It's complicated. He's got his hands on some sensitive historical documents. We're trying to verify what he knows."

"So tell me: What's this guy's job?"

"He's a journalist."

"The guy asking around in Vermont?"

"He's the guy. We have connections to various journalists in New York, and we're working these sources."

"When will I get the dossier?"

"As soon as I have the full picture, you'll have it."

"Get to work."

Brutka ended the call. His mind began to race again. He thought of his grandfather. He thought of Callaghan. A journalist. What did he know? Was he onto them? He tormented himself as the questions piled up again.

Fifteen minutes later, Brutka received a text message from his head of security. Blantone wanted to speak with him in person on "urgent" business. Brutka replied that he would meet him in the secure conference room of the Permanent Mission of Ukraine to the United Nations on East Fifty-First Street.

Half an hour later, after showering and changing into a suit, Brutka sat down at the head of the conference table as Blantone leafed through his notes. "You said you wanted to talk to me face-to-face about this?"

Blantone put his finger over his mouth, got up, and whispered in Brutka's ear. "Give me your cell phone. Right now. Do not speak."

Brutka wondered what was going on. He took the phone out of his jacket pocket and handed it to Blantone. The security expert, who was also a senior political attaché to the embassy, calmly walked out of the room for a few moments before returning.

"What was all that about? Is something wrong?"

Blantone sat down in front of his papers. "I called in a cybersecurity expert to scan your premises and devices. The only thing compromised? Your lawyer's phone."

"What?"

"Someone—we don't know who—has activated the microphone on your lawyer's device, turning it into what the Feds like to call a roving bug, so everything you said while there and your position would be known to the individual or group who accessed it."

"And they can tell that?"

"It's done remotely."

Brutka contemplated the situation. "Is Reznick a computer expert?"

"No. But we can assume he knows someone who is."

"Fuck. So he could've been listening in since when?"

"We're doing some more tests on the lawyer's cell phone, but it looks like it's been at least twelve hours."

"Could it be the FBI?"

Blantone shook his head. "Possible, but not likely in this case."

"So, in effect I am being spied on through my lawyer. Confidential communications relating to the business of our country have been compromised. That is clearly a major breach of the Vienna Convention."

"Among other things."

"Unless . . . Tell me, what else do we know about this Mr. Reznick?"

"You're going to like this."

"I'm assuming you're being sarcastic."

Blantone nodded and smiled. "Former Special Forces, Delta, and occasionally, in the last few years, employed by the FBI."

Brutka rubbed his hands across his face. "That changes things. So either Reznick is working alone and using a specialist he knows to help him, or the FBI is using his daughter's accident as a convenient cover. Implicating Reznick while they carry out surveillance work for the American government."

"It's very serious."

"We need to let our lawyers know."

"I've already briefed Morton."

Brutka nodded. "Very good. What did he say?"

"He said we have a major problem."

"We'll see. I have friends in high places."

"You don't seem too concerned."

Brutka got up from his chair and kicked it over. "I don't seem concerned? I'm furious, you idiot. And I'm very angry at this Reznick character. I mean . . . what the hell is he doing?"

Blantone sighed. "It's personal, clearly."

"Is it possible this guy will just go away?"

Blantone shrugged. "Doesn't seem likely."

"Someone gave him my name."

"We're still looking into that."

"My money says it's the cops. That bitch detective Acosta."

Blantone said, "There's something else."

"What?"

"Reznick has been busy again."

"I keep hearing the name Reznick. What is it with this guy?"

"He's rattling a few cages, boss."

"I know that."

"You don't know the latest."

Brutka stared at Blantone. "What?"

"Seems he's not content with just taking a tour with the Realtor. I have it on good authority that he was picked up by the NYPD a few hours ago, sniffing around the block again. Taking pictures of your residence, apparently. Photographed you using a telephoto lens."

"So my lawyer's cell phone has been bugged, Reznick has violated my private residence, and he's harassing me, stalking me. Am I missing something?"

Blantone sighed. "Aleksander, we need to not react. You shouldn't have sent flowers and a note expressing your sorrow. You just riled him up."

"I was trying to be nice."

"You were trying to be provocative. We need to take stock. Morton is drafting a letter. He's demanding a meeting with the FBI."

"What else?"

"He's going to be demanding answers. And he's going to be demanding that Jon Reznick be arrested and charged with multiple offenses. But that will be risky. If any of this comes out in the press, they'll be all over the hit-and-run. Enough public outcry and your father might insist you head back to the Ukraine for a spell."

Brutka turned and looked out over the Midtown skyline. "Tell Morton to hold off for the moment." He tapped a finger against his lips, thinking. "This guy Reznick is only hanging around New York because his daughter is in the hospital here, right?"

"Correct."

"Perhaps that's something we need to look into."

Blantone scribbled some notes. "Just to clarify . . . you want me to look into moving his daughter to a different hospital? That's what you're saying?"

"Why not? We could use it as leverage. We'll drop any legal action if she's moved out of New York."

A smile crossed Blantone's lips. "Man, that's cold."

"It's business. I'm a diplomat, conducting the business of my country. Recognized and protected under international law."

"Very true."

"One final thing."

"Sure."

"Reznick seems to be bringing this imagined antagonism between us to my front door. Literally."

"True."

"I think it's time he got a taste of his own medicine."

Blantone looked a little uncomfortable. The security chief grimaced as if suffering from bad indigestion. "I'm not sure you're thinking rationally. And I'm begging you not to go down that route, Aleksander."

"I disagree."

"My honest opinion, sir?"

Brutka shrugged. "By all means."

"I think it would be prudent to let it go. Let the law take care of Reznick."

"I'm rather fed up hearing that guy's name."

"Sir, it's imperative that we have a proportional response. A measured response. What if this is the sort of overreaction he's hoping for?"

"I don't give a damn what he's hoping for. He's making a fool of me. And I don't like it. He needs to be taught a lesson."

Blantone nodded. "Very well. When do you envision issuing our response?"

"When the opportunity arises. Sooner rather than later. Let him know that this won't be allowed to continue. Enough is enough."

"What if he doesn't get the message?"

Brutka leaned back in his seat and stared at his underling. "Your job, Blantone, is to make sure that Mr. Reznick definitely gets the message."

Twenty-Two

Reznick was starting to think that Lauren might never emerge from the induced coma. He felt that every hour she was unconscious made it less likely that she would make a full recovery. Reznick gazed at his daughter, his heart breaking. He asked question after question of a series of doctors. They each listened, and they all explained it was simply a matter of watching and waiting. They talked about brain scans. They showed him Lauren's results. Pictures of her swollen brain. He listened as if in a dream. He felt as if he was going out of his mind.

Reznick stroked his daughter's hand. It felt surprisingly warm. He pressed her hand against his cheek. He wanted to be reassured that she was alive. Still with him. The machine was keeping her breathing. The beeping relentless, like a metronome.

He wanted her to wake up, but he worried too. Would her brilliant mind still be able to think the way it had before? The doctors hadn't mentioned anything about that. Were they holding something back?

A nurse appeared, smiling. "Hi, Mr. Reznick," she said. "We're going to give your daughter a sponge bath."

"Sure, sorry, of course." Reznick got up and looked at the nurse. "The doctors showed me a bunch of images of her brain. And it's still watch and wait. Is she going to be OK?"

The nurse sighed. "It's really difficult, Mr. Reznick. From what I know, and from her notes, they're soliciting opinions from several specialists in this area."

"And they all agree on the prognosis?"

"They all agree. Look, you must be tired. Maybe get away from here for a little while, get some shut-eye. Maybe come back later and see how she is."

Reznick smiled. "Yeah, you're right. I'm dead on my feet."

"Are you afraid she's not going to wake up?"

"That and her being brain damaged."

"It is a potentially life-changing incident. But what the doctors have done is the best course of action. What her body needs is time to heal."

"Amen to that. Thank you."

"You're welcome."

Reznick felt marginally better after talking things over with the nurse. He left the hospital and headed back to his room at the Bentley. He put in a call to Acosta, but there was no answer. He wondered if he should call Meyerstein. She would be sympathetic. Of that he had no doubt. But he didn't really feel comfortable reaching out to her.

He stared out the window and was tempted to head down to the bar and get drunk.

The more he considered it, the more he realized that he had to curtail his urge to drink himself into oblivion. A few beers or glasses of wine were one thing. But in the twelve months that followed Elisabeth's death all those years ago, he had plunged into excessive drinking. It was like he would never emerge from the darkness.

It reminded him of his father's demons. He had used alcohol to numb the pain of his nightmares and bad memories of Vietnam. Mangled bodies screaming in his head. He had wanted to quiet them. Nothing more. Reznick's own mind was itself awash with bad stuff. Death. Destruction. He had mostly managed to compartmentalize it through the years. Pushing that stuff to the darkest recesses of his mind.

But occasionally the bad memories emerged like ghosts, encroaching on his world. As if to remind him of what he had done. What he had seen.

Reznick switched on the radio at a low volume. It was tuned to a classic rock station. They were playing Bob Seger's "Against the Wind," a song he remembered from his childhood. His father had played it often. It seemed to offer solace. Plaintive lyrics. The grind. The road ahead.

He lay back on the bed and stared at the ceiling.

He thought back to Rockland in the early eighties. He was a boy lying on his bed at night, listening to his father downstairs sobbing hard after his mother's funeral. He hadn't felt like intruding on his father's personal grief. So he had just lain there and stared at the freshly painted ceiling until he fell asleep. Eventually, he woke up in the middle of the night and went downstairs.

His father was staring into the fire, a half-empty tumbler in his hand, tears streaming down his face. He remembered his father turned around and stared at him glassy eyed, then pulled him close and tight. As if afraid to lose him.

Reznick had sat with his father the rest of the night. And they had talked. They had talked about life. Death. Vietnam. About America. But most of all he had talked about his wife, Reznick's mother. A woman who had worked. Who had sacrificed. And put up with his father's mood swings.

A woman who had wrapped her arms around her husband. She had held him close as he had sat hunched in silence in his chair beside the back window. Beer in hand, a black mood engulfing him. She had always seemed to know when to listen. When to chide him for being morose. Or to rouse him for work. Most of all from that night, Reznick remembered his father talking about family.

Blood is thicker than water, Jon.

That was what he said that night. His father talked in a low, gruff voice. He wasn't a big talker. He looked at Reznick and said the words that never left him:

When I'm gone, you only have yourself and your own flesh and blood to rely on.

As the years passed, the words had lingered with Reznick. He took them to mean that he needed to be self-reliant, look after himself and look after his family.

His father had the frontiersman spirit. He didn't want handouts. He didn't want charity. He had believed that an able-bodied man shouldn't rely on anyone. It was a matter of honor. A matter of pride. But most of all, it was about what it means to be an American.

The family had lost its beating heart when Reznick's mother died.

His father didn't know how to cook. How to keep the house nice. His mother had done all that. But over the days, weeks, and months, his father had begun to learn. He learned to do all those things. There was little money left over. But his father had taught him things that money couldn't buy. He had taught him how to hunt. To trap. And to fight.

When dawn broke on that winter morning after the funeral, his father, still reeking of drink, had gone upstairs, showered, shaved, and dressed for his shift at the sardine packing plant in Rockland. Reznick still remembered the terrible hurt and sadness in his eyes. His father hadn't wanted to face the world. But there he was, the day after the funeral, doing what had to be done.

Reznick's father had hugged him tight before he headed out the door. Reznick had watched his father walk down the dirt road that led into town as if it were just another day.

The sound of the fire trucks, sirens, traffic and never-ending noise in the background snapped Reznick back to reality for a few moments.

The song was still playing. The sound was like a cocoon. *Against the wind.*

He felt his eyes closing.

Reznick's thoughts returned again to his childhood. The early eighties. His father sitting in the corner as a blizzard tore through Rockland, beer in hand. Fire lit, logs crackling, his dad staring at the flames, tears in his eyes. This song was playing. It seemed to stir something in his father like nothing else.

He loved this song. His father seemed to find solace within it. A beauty. A cry from the heart mourning a lost youth. A lost life. A lost love.

Reznick's father always kept his hair short. Marine cut. He had always wondered what his father thought when he looked at the long-haired Seger on the album cover. But it didn't bother Reznick's father. He loved the sentiments. Raw. From the heart. Painful. Grieving. But above all else, truthful.

He wished his father was with him now. He would know what to do. Reznick wondered if he shouldn't just grab a gun and head on over to Brutka's. Kill the fucker. That was what his father would have done. But he wasn't his father.

Reznick knew that sometimes the simplest solution wasn't the best. Killing the man might assuage the terrible anger within him. But he knew that then he would have lost. And his daughter would have lost.

It would be a Pyrrhic victory.

He finally felt himself drifting to sleep, saying a silent prayer for his daughter.

When he awoke, he went into the bathroom, splashed some water on his face, and popped a couple of Dexedrine, an amphetamine he had found useful in the past. Reznick had first started taking the drug in Delta Force during an extended combat operation. It had kept him and his fellow operators alert and focused throughout a mission. He washed them down with a bottle of water from his minibar. He called the ICU to see if there had been any change in Lauren's status. But nothing.

He felt frustrated.

Reznick did what he usually did. He needed to move. It helped him think. He needed to get rid of his aggression. The simmering anger. The endorphins would kick it. He got changed into a marled gray T-shirt, running shorts, and his Nike running shoes. He put on his headphones, cell phone playing an essential Radiohead playlist his daughter had recommended to him. He'd bought them tickets for the band's Madison Square Garden show coming up in the fall. But that wasn't important anymore.

He strapped his phone to his arm and headed out onto the bustling sidewalk. The heat of the New York summer night hit him after leaving the cool of his air-conditioned hotel. The traffic was snarled all around. Cops at an intersection pulling over a vehicle.

Reznick jogged down the sidewalk, avoiding the pedestrians, and crossed Fifth Avenue. He headed into Central Park and began to pound the trail. The music was loud. The blood was flowing.

He got himself onto East Drive. Then headed north, ready to do the 6.1-mile counterclockwise loop of Central Park. He'd done it many times before when he was in the city. It was a route that was long enough to get the heart pumping, short enough not to waste too much time.

He overtook some slower joggers and power walkers enjoying the warm night. He felt sweat beading his face, sticking his T-shirt to his back.

Slowly Reznick began to feel the endorphins kicking in. He felt sharper. Better. Stronger. His sluggishness was gone. He was also alert.

He ran hard, hundreds of yards ahead of the joggers he passed. Three miles in and heading down West Drive.

The guitar riffs and sonic noise from his headphones were all he could hear. Until the sound of high revs from a powerful motorcycle cut through the music for a split second.

Reznick instinctively glanced back. Two guys on a bike accelerating fast toward him. He jumped out of the way, took off his headphones. The bike came to a stop about fifty yards ahead of him, and the two guys, both wearing full-face helmets, got off.

The guys flipped up their visors and walked slowly toward Reznick, grinning wildly.

The passenger held a baseball bat in one hand while the driver brandished a huge hunting knife.

Reznick knew what this was all about. He took a step forward, adjusted his stride and went for the guy with the knife first. He kicked the guy in the groin. Then punched the knife out of his hand a split second later. He smashed his fist hard into the side of the guy's neck. The guy went down cold.

The guy with the baseball bat edged forward, more tentative now.

Reznick could see in the guy's eyes that he didn't like his odds. "Come on, son, what've you got?" Reznick took three steps forward and lunged at the guy.

The guy pulled back the bat. But Reznick was already in close and turned sharply, holding the guy's wrists. He twisted his grip and snapped the bat out of the guy's hands.

The guy moaned.

Reznick kicked the bat away, grabbed the guy by the helmet, and kicked the fucker hard in the balls. The guy yelped like a pig, face scrunched up inside his helmet, hands covering his groin, without even thinking.

Reznick ripped off the helmet and brought it down, smashing it into the guy's jawline. A crack, a sickening groan, and the guy collapsed in the heat. Reznick bent over and punched the guy repeatedly in the broken jaw until he passed out.

A passing cyclist shouted, "Hey, what the fuck, man?"

Reznick watched as the kid cycled on, pulling out his cell phone, no doubt calling the cops. He rifled through his attacker's pants pockets. Nothing. No ID. No cell phone. He went over to the other unconscious goon. But it was the same again. Nothing. No ID. No cell phone.

He took his own cell phone out of the Velcro strap on his arm and photographed both men.

He put the cell phone back in his arm strap, put his headphones back on, Radiohead blaring in his ears, and continued on his route, leaving the two guys lying unconscious on the Central Park jogging trail.

Twenty-Three

Meyerstein glanced at the clock. She began drumming her fingers, flicking through notes in the meeting room at FBI HQ on the twenty-sixth floor of the building in lower Manhattan. She sighed, still waiting for Aleksander Brutka and his lawyer, Lionel Morton, to show up. Eventually, thirty minutes later than the scheduled meeting there was a knock at the door.

The two men were ushered in.

Morton stepped forward and smiled. "I must apologize for our tardiness. Mr. Brutka had an emergency situation to attend to."

Meyerstein got up and shook his hand before she greeted Brutka. He wore an impeccably tailored dark suit, starched white shirt, light-gray tie, and a chunky gold watch. "I hope everything is OK, Mr. Brutka."

Brutka took a few moments to appraise the room, as if wanting Meyerstein to know he wasn't overawed or cowed by the impressive surroundings.

She sat down behind the large table as Brutka stared down at her.

"Yes, thank you." He brushed some imaginary dust or a thread off his suit before he sat down. Then he crossed his legs, examining his manicured fingernails.

Meyerstein smiled through gritted teeth. She was already annoyed. "So . . . let's get started, shall we?"

Morton opened a pad, scribbled a few notes. "I was assured this was just an informal chat, face-to-face."

Meyerstein fixed her gaze on Brutka, who was avoiding eye contact. "Are you OK, Mr. Brutka? You seem quite distracted."

Brutka looked up and stared at her. "I'm just a little distressed after the incident at my residence, as you can imagine."

"Well, I thank you for coming here with Mr. Morton. And I'd like to thank you both for being able to see me on such short notice."

Morton scribbled again.

"I'd like to record this meeting, if that's OK with you."

Morton turned and looked at Brutka. "Aleksander?"

"What?" Brutka snapped.

"How would you feel about this chat being recorded?"

Brutka leaned back in his seat and sighed. "No."

Meyerstein glanced across the table at Brutka. "Not a problem. No need to be formal."

Brutka nodded sullenly.

"So, I'd like to say that I'm speaking with the full authority of the Director of the FBI, Bill O'Donoghue."

Morton wrote that down. "Did he ask you to speak to us, or was this your idea?"

"This was my idea. I think it's important that everyone is clear where they stand."

Brutka began scrolling through messages on his cell phone.

"Mr. Brutka," Meyerstein said, "can I have your full attention, please?"

Brutka looked at Meyerstein with disdain. He made a show of putting his cell phone in his jacket pocket. "Sorry. Was just checking an email from one of my staff."

"Thank you."

Morton said, "Can you tell us what exactly you want to talk to us about, Assistant Director?"

Meyerstein leaned forward, hands clasped. She looked straight at Brutka. "Mr. Brutka, after much deliberation and inquiry into recent events, the FBI considers it best for you to voluntarily leave this country. We believe that any reasonable person would conclude that you have overstayed your welcome."

Morton leaned over and whispered briefly in his client's ear.

Brutka nodded.

"Assistant Director, we're rather taken aback," Morton said. "What are you talking about? We came here after a flagrant violation of the Vienna Convention when a man we believe to be named Jon Reznick broke into my client's private residence and held him at gunpoint! We were fully expecting an apology."

Meyerstein sighed. "You need to stop playing games, both of you. Does either of you want to talk about what happened last night in the park?"

Silence. Brutka stared blankly at her as Morton scribbled notes.

"Would Mr. Brutka like to explain why two security personnel from your embassy, both on the diplomatic list, were found unconscious last night in Central Park?"

Brutka leaned back in his seat. "I was very distressed to hear about that, as you can imagine. Attacks on diplomatic staff are outrageous. We have already lodged a complaint with the American government."

Meyerstein smiled. "NYPD cops in Central Park found these two gentlemen." She pulled out two color photographs showing the blood-soaked faces of the victims lying unconscious. "They had a rented motorcycle and, we believe, tried to attack a man in the park. Two against one. Unfortunately, they got the worse end of it. A lot worse. Which is not so great from their point of view. But the reality is, they are accredited members of the embassy. And, we believe, they pulled a knife and a baseball bat on a man. An unarmed man."

Brutka stroked his chin, looking at Meyerstein with a lingering and menacing stare.

"We have a description of the victim thanks to a statement from a cyclist. Was this a revenge attack on Jon Reznick as a warning, by chance? Revenge for him allegedly intruding into your private residence?"

Morton sighed. "This is an outrageous allegation. Is this deflection?"

"Not at all. Are you going to answer my question?"

"This incident has, I believe, no connection with Mr. Brutka. I'm appalled that you're even making that suggestion. These men were the victims of a quite disgusting, unprovoked attack."

"We don't believe that to be the case."

Morton was about to speak, but Brutka held up his hand to silence him. "Assistant Director, I am obviously as anxious as anyone to find out what exactly happened. But I'm wondering if the FBI are best placed to deal with this matter."

Meyerstein didn't drop her gaze. "What do you mean?"

"I mean, this Mr. Reznick is clearly an FBI operative. I'm talking conflict of interest. So I'm wondering if I shouldn't be asking for this matter to be investigated by those outside the confines of the FBI."

"That can be arranged. But be under no illusion. If we do that, you need to prepare yourself for the diplomatic fallout."

Brutka sat in silence, as did Morton.

"Go now, and you can leave the country of your own free will. Frankly, your criminal behavior is reprehensible."

Brutka gave a patronizing smile. "That is a scandalous suggestion, Assistant Director."

"Is it?"

"I am at a loss to understand how this investigation has led to this grotesque situation where I am being accused of criminal behavior. I'm aghast. And I'm wondering what's next. Are you planning to leak details to the press if I don't comply? Is that it?"

"Mr. Brutka, any other right-thinking country would have hauled their diplomat home by now. Running down a college girl who was out jogging, not stopping after the accident."

"I know I'm repeating myself, but I wasn't in the vehicle. We are conducting an internal investigation to establish who was driving."

"With respect, Mr. Brutka, we don't accept that explanation. And, last night, sending two goons to rough up the father of the college girl so soon after he confronted you. Is that just an unfortunate coincidence?"

"This is all very bizarre and unsettling. But as I continue to insist, I have no idea what exactly this is about."

"From where I'm standing, it doesn't look good. And let me tell you I'm not impressed. I think we both know that you're being protected by your father. Otherwise, you would have been off with the diplomatic bags on the first flight out of JFK."

Brutka shook his head.

"Your explanations are less than satisfactory. And entirely unconvincing."

"I don't accept that, Mrs. Meyerstein."

"That's Assistant Director Meyerstein. And the FBI, just for the record, believes you have overstayed your welcome."

Brutka shrugged. "I think we'll have to agree to disagree on that particular point. I represent the interests of the people of Ukraine at the highest diplomatic levels. Only the State Department can make the call."

"How can you be so sure that the State Department won't listen to what the FBI has to say?"

Brutka smiled. "One can never entirely be sure, Assistant Director, but we are always keen to reach out and continue dialogue and conversations. It's what diplomacy is all about, after all, is it not? About maintaining relationships. Strengthening ties. And believe me, we have very strong ties in the United States."

Meyerstein smiled. "I'm sure you do."

"Don't hesitate to contact me or Mr. Morton again if you have further questions." A cold smile crossed his face. "My door is always open."

Twenty-Four

Reznick woke from a fitful sleep at his daughter's bedside, cell phone ringing. He took a few moments to get his bearings. His mind flashed to the night before in Central Park. He had to assume that was why someone was calling him now. He kissed Lauren on the forehead. "I'll be right back, honey."

Reznick went out into the corridor and stood in an alcove for privacy. He didn't recognize the caller ID. He pressed the phone to his ear. "Yeah?"

"Is this Lauren's father?" It was the voice of Aleksander Brutka.

Reznick wondered how Brutka had gotten his number.

"I take it from your silence that this is Mr. Reznick. Nice to speak with you again."

"You still in town?"

Brutka laughed. "I do like you, Mr. Reznick. I like how direct you are. I admire that."

"You want to get to the point?"

"You know who I also admire, Jon?"

Reznick felt a chill down his spine.

"I admire your daughter. I've seen pictures of her. The pictures are in front of me just now. Facebook. What a marvelous invention. I can look at all her photographs. Are you on Facebook, Jon?"

Reznick felt his blood pressure rise as he began to pace the corridor. "So, the mask has slipped. Didn't take long."

"I particularly like the ones of her on vacation in her bikini. Lovely figure."

"You know the interesting thing about people like you?"

"No, tell me."

"Nothing. That's what's interesting about you. You see, for all your wealth, your millions, your connections in Washington, everyone who knows you privately loathes you. But I guess you know that already, right?"

"Deflection? How intriguing. I know a lot more about you now, Jon."

"I take it from this chat that you have no intention of leaving town."

"Very perceptive, Mr. Reznick. I'm staying put. And I'm beginning to be rather intrigued with you. Former Delta operator, American assassin, occasional consultant to the FBI on classified investigations. That's some résumé."

Reznick knew the guy was fucking with him.

Brutka laughed. "But getting back to your daughter. She's a high-quality girl, no question about that. She's also got an Instagram account. I like the picture of her in the coffee shop, laughing. So natural. Very photogenic. Quite beautiful. Wholesome. I like that look. A lot. You know, in Ukraine I could help her make a lot of money with that face."

"Stay the fuck away from my daughter, do you hear me?"

"To be frank, she's the kind of girl I'd like to get to know better, if you know what I mean."

"You get your kicks fantasizing about things like that?"

"I seem to have hit a raw nerve, Mr. Reznick."

Reznick closed his eyes. "Stay away from my family, do you hear me?"

"Or what?"

"You need to know one thing, you piece of shit: I eat fuckers like you for breakfast. And any tough guys you want to send my way to do your dirty work. Now I'm going to say this one more time: stay away from my daughter, you sick fuck."

"But Jon . . . that's rather hypocritical of you. Why should I stay away from her if you won't stay away from me? Bugging my lawyer's cell phone? Tsk, tsk."

"I will do whatever it takes to protect my family. My daughter's all I've got. And what you did, running her down without stopping, is breaking a bunch of laws. US laws. You're in America now, you piece of shit, or didn't you know that?"

"I feel like I'm repeating myself. I wasn't in the vehicle. At least that's what I told the FBI."

"You know, it's interesting. You sound an awful lot like a guy in the Marines I once knew."

"How intriguing. Tell me more."

"Like you, he never admitted when he was wrong. He made up excuses for his bad behavior. He exploited people who were weaker than him. He never took responsibility for his actions. And he had no remorse."

"How fascinating."

"He was eventually diagnosed with narcissistic personality disorder. And I'm guessing that's why you sent my daughter the flowers."

"I didn't know you were a trained psychologist as well, Mr. Reznick. You are full of surprises."

"Well, someone clearly needs to sort you out, you nutjob!"

"All this aggression. The FBI must be very annoyed with you, Jon. You do still work for the FBI, don't you? I just had a meeting with a woman you know. Assistant Director Meyerstein. Very fine woman. Lovely mouth. Nice ass too."

"You disgust me."

"Know what she wanted me to do? She wanted me to leave the country. Said the FBI didn't want me. They don't like me. Now, answer me this: Why would I do that?"

Reznick was pleasantly surprised and rather proud that Meyerstein had taken such a stance. "If you had an ounce of decency, you would be mortified by what happened. But I guess you get off on this kind of thing. Is that your thing, Aleksander? You don't mind me calling you Aleksander, do you?"

"Call me whatever you like, Jon. I'm thoroughly enjoying this exchange. Your daughter has a lovely cheekbone structure. Good breeding."

"Why don't you come over here and we'll iron this out man-to-man?"

Brutka laughed long and hard. "You see, Jon, I admire your bravado, but it's all bluster, isn't it? There are limits to how far even you'll go. Anyway, I hope you don't mind me taking up your time. I know you're a busy man. And one final thing before I go. You need to be careful."

"Wrong. You're the one that needs to be careful, you dumb fuck. If you know what's good for you, you'll disappear."

Brutka sighed. "No. I don't think I will."

Twenty-Five

The conversation had ignited a rage within Reznick that was close to boiling over. It was clear he wasn't dealing with a rational human being. This guy was a psychopath. No remorse. Quite the opposite. Disdain. And now veiled threats to his daughter.

Reznick had heard enough. The fucker hadn't gotten the message. He pulled out his cell phone and called the hacker.

"Need a favor," he said.

"What's going on, Mr. R.?"

Reznick explained the tone and nature of the call with the diplomat and the encounter with the two goons in Central Park.

"Shit. Are you OK?"

"I'm fine. They got the worst of it, trust me."

"Man, that ain't good."

"This Brutka is fucking with me. And he's enjoying it. But let's see if he enjoys fucking with me on my terms."

The hacker sighed. "Stay on the line. I'm going to do some analysis of your cell phone."

Reznick waited for a couple of minutes before the hacker came on again.

"So the guy was calling from a new cell phone, new encryption, the works. It might not even be his."

"Figures. He'd caught on that you were monitoring his lawyer's phone."

"But I've gone a step further. I've just activated the microphone on the diplomat's new phone, and it's picking up his voice clear as day—he's boasting to someone about his call with you. So they clearly think by changing phones you wouldn't be able to locate him."

"How did you do that?"

"Long story."

"Where is he? GPS location. Where is he right now? I want him face-to-face."

"He's having a drink in the bar at the United Nations."

"Shit."

"Not to worry. You want to get him face-to-face?"

"Absolutely."

The hacker went quiet for a few moments. "Give me a second."

"Can you get me in there?"

"I can."

"How?"

"Let me think . . . Well, I could construct a perfect UN identification."

"How would that work?"

"I can update the UN servers with new details which will comprise your ID. So you can pick up your blue UN pass as a returning delegate."

"Are you kidding me?"

"Dead serious."

Reznick was long past caring about the consequences of his actions. He knew he could be falling into a trap. But he didn't care. "And it'll work?"

"All you have to do is wear a nice suit since we're going to pass you off as a UN delegate."

"Where do I pick up the badge?"

The hacker hummed a tune for a few seconds. "Hang on . . . Let me see . . . Yeah, it's called the Pass and Identification Unit."

"I want to go one-on-one with this guy. Now."

Twenty-Six

Just over an hour later, the fake UN ID was delivered to Reznick's hotel by a friend of the hacker who lived in New York.

"Best of luck, man," the kid said.

Reznick tipped the guy a hundred bucks.

"Whoa, I didn't expect payment."

"Get yourself a beer for your trouble."

The kid grinned. "Take care, man."

Reznick suited up, put on his sunglasses, and called a cab. He had the driver drop him off two blocks from the UN building. He walked down the shaded sidewalk and approached the security screening area. He was asked to take off his sunglasses as his badge was activated. Security guards ran a wand over his body to check for weapons. Then his photograph was checked against the computer details.

He was escorted to the Pass and Identification Unit and handed his blue pass with his fake name, Roger McGurk. An Irish diplomat.

A woman behind the desk smiled. "We're good now, Mr. McGurk. Have a nice day."

Reznick smiled back and put his sunglasses back on. "Thank you."

He checked the signs and headed to the delegates bar overlooking the East River. His blue pass was scanned as he entered. The sun was streaming through the windows, making his sunglasses fit right in.

He walked up to the bar and ordered a club soda. He scanned the room. Small groups of diplomats and their aides chatting over drinks.

The bartender handed him his drink.

Reznick paid the bill. A short while later his cell phone rang.

"I'm monitoring the cell phone," the hacker said. "He's switched to a different one. The one he called you on is used by an aide. Look, I don't want to tell you how you to do your thing, but is it possible this guy is setting a trap for you?"

"We'll see soon enough. Where is he now?"

"He's still in the building. A side meeting with some Libyan diplomats in the fourth-floor dining room. Hang on . . . Stand by, man . . . OK, he's on the move."

"Where to?"

"You might be in luck. He's heading back down in the elevator. He's taking the Libyan delegation to the North Delegates' Lounge."

"That's where I am, right?"

"Yeah, he just got off on the second floor. He'll be with you . . . One minute, he'll be coming right your way. Good luck."

"Appreciate the heads-up, man."

"Take care."

Reznick put his cell phone back in his pocket and sipped his soda water. He listened to a couple of interns bitching about their Moldovan boss. Rents in Manhattan. Broken air-conditioning in the subway. And one was moaning about seeing a huge rat on the sidewalk.

A couple minutes later, Reznick got a visual on Brutka. He stole a glance at the big crowd of people, including security, who ushered him into the bar. His arm was wrapped around another diplomat as if they were old friends. They were surrounded by other assorted hangers-on and aides.

The group was shown to the far corner of the room, where there was a reserved table. Champagne was delivered, and Brutka led them all in a toast as they overlooked Manhattan's East River.

Reznick couldn't help but notice a burly security guy approach Brutka and whisper in the diplomat's ear.

Brutka listened intently and patted the security guy on the back before resuming his chat with the others.

Reznick walked up to the bar, facing away from Brutka and his group. "Club soda," he said.

The bartender served up his drink, and Reznick stood and sipped it. He began checking messages on his phones. Nothing.

Reznick glanced in the mirror and noticed Brutka moving away from the group. The diplomat had a cell phone pressed to his ear. Brutka stood only a few yards from him now, complaining loudly about "schedules clashing" and "intemperate language." He really was a loudmouth. Brutka began to bemoan the work of his housekeeper.

Then Brutka raised his voice. "I'm dealing with it, Father," he said.

Reznick kept his back to the diplomat but watched as Brutka drifted out of the lounge with two aides by his side. He waited a few moments. A minute or so later the two aides returned, one on his cell phone. Reznick called the hacker. "Where's our guy at this moment?"

A beat. "He's . . . Bathroom. Second floor. Opposite end of the bar from where you are now."

Reznick ended the call and strolled down a corridor and into the bathroom. He walked in and saw Brutka taking a piss, his back to the door. Reznick removed his sunglasses, set them on the counter, and began to wash his hands.

The diplomat turned around, zipping up his pants.

Reznick shoved Brutka's shoulder back with the palm of his right hand and, with his left arm, he put the diplomat in a choke hold. He squeezed the guy's neck tightly, and he buckled to the floor. Eyes rolling around his head as if he was ready to pass out. "You get a kick out of saying those terrible things about my daughter? You get off on that?"

Brutka moaned, eyes screwed up in pain.

"Think you can play games with me? You picked the wrong guy."

"Are you out of your mind? . . . I was just passing on a compliment! I admire your daughter and wish her a speedy recovery!"

"No, you don't. You were having a bit of fun at her expense, weren't you? You need to learn to show some respect, you spineless fuck."

"You're out of your mind. Stop!"

"You're not even sorry. You criminal piece of shit."

Brutka's teeth were clenched. "You misunderstand my intentions."

Reznick pressed his mouth to Brutka's right ear. "You need to get the fuck out of town before it's too late."

"I was not responsible for what happened—"

"Wrong answer." Reznick exerted more pressure on the guy's windpipe. "How does that feel? You feel out of control?"

Brutka rasped, "You're making a terrible mistake!"

Reznick hauled the man to his feet and grabbed him by the throat. He pressed hard into his carotid artery with his thumb. "You like that, tough guy?"

Brutka's eyes were wide.

Reznick dragged Brutka into one of the stalls by his hair. He rammed the diplomat's head into the toilet bowl, flushing the water onto his head. Time after time. The diplomat thrashed as he swallowed the water and disinfectant. Seconds passed. Reznick flushed the toilet again. And again. Until Brutka went limp.

Reznick yanked him up by the hair one more time. "Final warning," he said. He smashed Brutka's face down hard against the porcelain bowl. An anguished groan as blood and teeth splattered onto the tiled floor of the stall.

He dropped the diplomat onto the floor. Brutka lay motionless, blood oozing from his mouth.

Reznick stepped out of the stall. He checked himself in the mirror. He straightened his tie and picked up his sunglasses. Then he bent down and wiped the specks of blood off his shoes with a paper towel.

He threw the paper towel in the trash, then walked out of the bathroom and made his way through the lounge, down in the elevator to the ground-floor lobby, past security, and once again into the stifling New York air.

Twenty-Seven

Three minutes later, as Reznick strode north on Second Avenue toward Fifty-Second Street, a cop car pulled him over.

A cop pulled his gun on Reznick. "Freeze, fucker!"

Reznick stared at the cop.

"Slowly, hands on your head."

Reznick complied. A second cop handcuffed him and frog-marched him into their vehicle before taking him the short journey to the Seventeenth Precinct on Fifty-First Street. He was arrested, booked, photographed, and then strip-searched. Then he was taken to a windowless interview room. He was kept waiting for more than an hour.

Eventually, a detective entered the room with a cup of coffee and sat down opposite Reznick, flicking through a pile of papers. "I've been speaking to a few people about you. That's what took me so long. Seems like you've been having quite a few days in New York, Mr. Reznick."

Reznick stared at him. "My daughter's in a coma."

"Shit, I'm sorry . . . I didn't mean it like that."

Reznick nodded. "Sure."

"Jon . . . Can I call you Jon?"

Reznick shrugged.

"Jon, here's where I'm at. My boss wants to charge you with numerous offenses. Hard to know where to start. I mean, entering the secure area of the United Nations, are you crazy?"

"It's not me that's crazy. It's the guy who nearly killed my daughter."

The detective leaned back in his seat and showed his palms. "I understand. I'm the father of two girls. Trust me, I get where you're coming from. But come on, let's face it, this is off-the-scale nuts. And it's not a one-off. I'm reading that apparently you beat two guys unconscious in Central Park. Political and security personnel from the Ukrainian embassy. And now we've got a United Nations diplomat, Aleksander Brutka, who was attacked and left unconscious. Hell of a face you left on him."

"Will he live?"

The cop shrugged.

"He'll live," Reznick said. "I was only toying with the fucker. If I really wanted to put him to sleep, that wouldn't have been a problem."

"Here's the thing. The diplomat—once he recovers, if he recovers—is going to want to press charges. You're in deep shit."

"Trust me, I've been in worse."

The detective flicked through the files again and sighed. "I don't understand. It says in this file that it is *believed* that you work occasionally for the FBI. Some of the information seems to be redacted by the FBI and Homeland Security. You mind expanding on what that means?"

"I can't comment."

"I'm assuming the Feds don't know about this?"

"They will soon enough."

"How do you feel about that?"

Reznick shrugged. "Do you know anything about Aleksander Brutka?"

"You're the one that has to answer for your actions."

"He ran down my daughter, and still he's allowed to be accredited as a diplomat. How is that even possible?"

"You might want to take that up with the State Department."

Reznick folded his arms. "Might just do that."

"In the meantime, what are we going to do with you? You're turning into quite a nuisance."

Reznick sighed. "Listen, I've got no problem with the police. I'm just trying to get this fucker out of my daughter's life. No one seems to be able to do anything about him. He swans around as if he owns this city."

"He's not swanning around now, Jon. He's in the hospital."

"Good."

"That attitude isn't helping your case."

"You know what's going to happen?"

"What?"

"Brutka won't press charges. You know why not? Because it would mean he would get embroiled in a court case, and the hit-and-run story would all come out. He doesn't want that."

The cop shook his head. "You're killing me, man. This is crazy. You're a smart guy. But you can't be going around kicking the shit out of diplomats, no matter how appalling they are. What do you say? I don't hear any contrition."

"It is what it is."

The cop sighed. "Jon, you leave me with no alternative. You're going to be charged for this. You've gotten lucky so far. But your time's up."

Twenty-Eight

Brutka was lying in a Bellevue hospital bed, waves of pain erupting on the right side of his head as he was being examined.

The doctor shone a penlight in his eyes.

"Do you mind?" Brutka said, wincing at the light.

"OK, relax." The doctor switched off the light and conferred with his colleague. He checked the charts. Eventually, he looked down at Brutka. "Four missing teeth, loss of blood, but miraculously, no damage to the brain. Throat tender, not surprising. The CAT scans and MRI show no internal bleeding or other injuries. We were concerned about your jaw, but it's just severe bruising."

Brutka closed his eyes as the pain intensified. "When can I leave?"

"You need to stay overnight for observation."

"Tomorrow morning I'm free to go?"

"All things being stable, yes."

Brutka thanked the doctor. He was given some more pain relief, which took the edge off things. A few minutes later, the cops came and took a statement.

"We know who attacked you, Mr. Brutka," a police officer said, "and we're confident that we have the right man. It's just a matter of getting your statement about what happened, and then we can go about filing charges."

Brutka shook his head. "Officer, the NYPD have better things to do than chase down thugs like this. I don't want you to waste your time."

The cop looked at his colleague and then at Brutka. "Sir . . . I don't think you understand. This was a serious assault. He choked you."

Brutka swallowed hard as a nurse passed him a glass of water. He took a sip. It felt good. His throat was still sore and raw.

"The doctor said your vocal cords could have been permanently damaged."

Brutka sighed. "They weren't."

The cop shook his head. "Sir, I would strongly recommend you press charges. You were attacked."

"Officer, I'm a devout Orthodox Christian. And part of being a good Christian is forgiveness. I've already forgiven this man. I assume he has mental health issues, and for that we should offer prayers."

The cop glanced at his partner again, then cleared his throat. "And that's your final word?"

Brutka nodded, already beginning to plot his revenge against Reznick. A few minutes later, his cell phone vibrated on the bedside table. He picked up. It was a message from the private investigator. He had forgotten all about Tom Callaghan and the journalist's interest in his grandfather up in Vermont.

Dossier complete. TC knows everything.

Twenty-Nine

The following morning, Reznick was roused from sleep in a Manhattan police cell by a cop pointing a nightstick at him.

"Jon, you got company. Shake a leg."

Reznick got up and followed the policeman to an interview room. Inside, waiting for him was Meyerstein. He waited until the cop had shut the door behind them before he spoke. "What are you doing here?"

"You're in luck," she said.

"How so?"

Meyerstein cocked her head. "You're free to go."

"On whose orders?"

"I pulled a few strings with the NYPD."

Reznick had to sign some papers before he walked out of the precinct with Meyerstein and was shown into an SUV. He got in the back next to her and they were driven to the FBI's office downtown. Once they were inside a corner office, she shut the door and pointed to the seat opposite her desk.

"This your place these days? Very minimalistic."

"I'm working out of this office until further notice."

Reznick slumped in the seat. "Damn."

Meyerstein sat down behind her desk. "Not good, Jon, not good at all."

"I appreciate the help."

Meyerstein sighed. "Seriously, what the hell were you thinking? I've had the State Department screaming at me, my boss wondering if you should be put in a psychiatric unit, and all the while you're acting as if you've gone rogue. It's unacceptable. The only plus side is that Brutka isn't pressing charges."

"Why am I not surprised?"

"The guy isn't stupid. He doesn't want this to go to court. And then have to divulge the hit-and-run that started all this."

"Did you know that bastard called me? And that he sent my daughter, who he put in a coma, flowers?"

"It's not illegal, Jon. Christ, this needs to stop. I did warn you where this would lead. You've already been hauled in by the NYPD. Twice. It needs to end!"

"This ends when he's on a plane out of New York."

Meyerstein began to pace the room before she stopped and faced him, hands on hips. "We're at a crisis point, Jon, and I'm coming very close to just turning my back on you. I don't want to. But you're boxing me in. I want to help, but you're just defying my every request to stay out of this."

"It's not in my nature to let this go. I can't."

"What does that mean?"

"It means this is not over. My daughter is still hanging by a thread, and that fucker is walking around this city. And we don't seem to be able to do anything about it."

Meyerstein massaged her temples with her fingers. "I think we're going around in circles, Jon."

"I'm not going around in circles, Martha. It's the American government that refuses to kick that fucker out of our country. They choose to do nothing. Why is that?"

Meyerstein sighed, head bowed. "I'm trying to help you, Jon. But you're pushing me away. I can't get close to you. You don't seem to want to listen. It's like you're closed off. And it's worrying me. I'm concerned. For you. For your daughter. About how this will all end."

Reznick folded his arms and stared at the floor.

"You don't have anything else to say?"

"I look out for my family. You know that. My daughter is my only family. Brutka left her in a coma. And no one seems to give a damn."

"Not true."

"It's all protocol, diplomatic immunity, and some such other bullshit."

"The FBI recommended that Brutka leave the country."

Reznick rubbed his face as a wave of tiredness washed over him. "I'm very pleased to hear that. But why not the State Department? Are they protecting this fucker?"

"I've heard enough. You've crossed the line. I'm sorry, Jon, but you cannot continue to be part of the FBI after this."

"So be it."

"This didn't have to happen, Jon."

"If he had left the country, I would have been able to move on. But I can't with him lurking in the background. I'm telling you, he is a risk. A serious risk."

"Knocking his teeth out and choking him is not a rational response. It's an emotional response, Jon."

"Damn right it was."

"You should look after your daughter."

"I will. But you need to get a message to that bastard. He needs to watch his back."

Thirty

Just over an hour later, Meyerstein joined a high-level video conference with the FBI Director, Bill O'Donoghue, and the undersecretary of state for political affairs, Pat Sheen. She was alone in the New York conference room looking up at the big screens. She sensed that the meeting, arranged on short notice by Sheen, the highest-ranking member of the Foreign Service, was not going to go well.

She had run into Sheen at a security conference at Quantico a couple of years back. At the time, he was the manager of overall regional and bilateral policy issues, as well as overseeing bureaus around the world. He was hugely intelligent, unsurprisingly, and was known as an adherent of the realism school of international relations. Which was a fancy way of saying neoconservative. Basically, he believed in realpolitik whereby a nation is motivated by what is in its interests. It was a pragmatic approach to diplomacy and international relations. An approach where the personal infidelities of individual diplomats or politicians were not the be-all and end-all. Diplomacy was simply about what was in a nation's best interests. And Meyerstein knew that Sheen's viewpoint was that countries from the old Soviet Union, especially Ukraine, were in effect America's watchdog in Russia's backyard. Vital for American national security, both economically and politically.

Meyerstein took a deep breath before she switched on her microphone. "Good afternoon, gentlemen. Just wanted to give you an update on the situation in New York."

Sheen put up his hand. "Hi, Martha, glad we can hook up on this issue. It's causing me sleepless nights, let me tell you. I'm getting a lot of grief on this. From the White House and from the Ukrainians."

O'Donoghue said, "Martha, do you want to kick things off? It'll have to be quick."

"Sure thing," Meyerstein said, glancing at her notes. "Jon Reznick is, as you are both aware, the father of Lauren Reznick, and she is in a medically induced coma. Her condition is still cause for concern. But that aside, I've been quite clear with Jon that his actions are absolutely unacceptable, illegal, and have no place in our work. Accordingly, I have relieved him of any FBI duties with immediate effect."

Sheen said, "Martha, his behavior is quite disgraceful. And I think we should be considering having him prosecuted."

Meyerstein sighed. "I don't disagree with your assessment, but I think it's clear that Reznick's actions were a deliberate ploy on his part to provoke a response from Brutka. Unfortunately, it's gotten out of hand. Way out of hand."

Sheen said, "Aleksander Brutka is a respected and much-admired United Nations diplomat, a close friend of the United States. I've known him and his father for nearly a decade. I'm truly at a loss as to how this got 'out of hand.' We need to look at the big picture instead of getting fixated on what Brutka is alleged to have done in New York City."

O'Donoghue said, "Pat, what we're concerned about, and I've already raised this with a couple of your guys, is that Aleksander Brutka has not been deemed persona non grata by the State Department. I haven't received a satisfactory explanation of this decision. I believe if he is removed from the country, the whole dynamic changes. I'm referring to the hit-and-run on Reznick's daughter."

Sheen said, "They're allegations. We have no proof he was driving. Ordinarily, we would have thrown the book at him. But that's not possible in this case at this time."

Meyerstein said, "Why not?"

Sheen sighed and shook his head. "It's complicated. There are multiple factors we have to consider; you know how it works."

Meyerstein said, "Like his father being the President of Ukraine?"

O'Donoghue intervened sharply. "That's quite enough, Martha."

Sheen said, "No, it's fine, Bill. It's good to be up-front. And I've known both of you guys for a long time. A frank exchange of views is very important in my line of work. So here's where I'm at. I agree, Yegor Brutka has a blind spot with regard to his son. But you guys know that there are national interests at stake that we don't want to jeopardize. Ukraine is a valued and important partner in a very sensitive part of the world."

Meyerstein had figured as much. "I'm assuming you mean bilateral military exercises, intelligence sharing on Russian oil contracts, military deals, that kind of thing."

"I'm not at liberty to reveal specifics. But this is where we've got to see the big picture, Martha. I'm going to be honest with you. The government of Ukraine wants to become energy independent in the next few years. And they are working with several American corporations to advise them. But not only that, they want to diversify their energy supply. Not be dependent on Russia. We estimate that Ukraine has around nine hundred billion cubic meters of proven reserves of natural gas. And we are doing everything in our power to ensure Ukraine not only stays independent but thrives in the twenty-first century. It is absolutely in American interests to support them."

Meyerstein sighed. "While I understand the rationale, it's not a good look allowing this guy to get away with serious criminal behavior."

"Martha, I make no apology for putting these strategic aims ahead of what is clearly reckless and criminal behavior."

Meyerstein shifted in her seat, getting more and more irate. "So let me get this straight. We're prepared to turn a blind eye to what this guy did—leaving a young girl in a coma—because American national interests are at stake? So if he goes out, gets in his car, and kills an innocent bystander tonight or tomorrow or the day after, that's just the way it is? Really?"

"I understand your anger."

"The thing is, Pat, if it was a country with little economic clout or one where we had no national interests to protect, we would have thrown him out already."

Sheen smiled down from the screen. "Quite possibly. It's a very good assessment. It's a tough call, I accept that. Jon Reznick is a fine man. But I am responsible for doing what's right for this country, which takes precedence over one man's bad behavior. So, you're right. We are willing to turn a blind eye to this one serious offence which Mr. Brutka is alleged to have committed."

"For how long?"

O'Donoghue interjected, "That's a good question, Pat. The State Department must have a time frame for how long this could be tolerated."

"For how long, Pat?" Meyerstein snapped.

"For as long as it takes. It's not ideal. Far from it. But American geopolitical interests come first, last, and always."

Thirty-One

The SUV was crawling along Fifth Avenue. Reznick had been aware of it for a couple of blocks. He wondered if it was more of Brutka's goons, spoiling for a fight. He walked on, trying to figure out his next move. He didn't know who these guys were. But they clearly knew him.

His cell phone rang.

Reznick answered. "Yeah?"

"Jon . . . don't be alarmed. We don't mean you any harm. But we need to speak to you."

"Who's this?"

"We're in the big Jeep on your tail."

Reznick stopped and looked across Fifth Avenue. The vehicle had stopped in the traffic outside a townhouse being renovated, workmen toiling in the blazing heat. A cabdriver was screaming out his window at the SUV. Reznick crossed the busy street, jogging past the cab, which screeched to a halt.

"Hey, buddy," the taxi driver said, "tell your friend to get a fucking move on."

Reznick ignored the guy and knocked on the front passenger window of the SUV. Slowly it wound down. A guy wearing sunglasses and sporting a navy suit sat inside. He flashed a government ID.

"Steve Kelinski, State Department."

"You want a date or something, Steve?"

Kelinski grinned. "Smart-ass, huh? You wanna hop in?"

"Not really."

"Two minutes of your time."

Reznick looked around. "What's it about?"

"Got an ultimatum for you."

"Sounds ominous."

"You wanna jump in?"

Reznick opened the back door and slid in, slamming the door shut behind him.

The SUV pulled away slowly.

Kelinski took off his shades and turned around. "Jon, sorry we have to meet under these circumstances."

"You want to get to the point?"

"This can't go on. We've kept our distance until now. But that's over."

"If you say so."

"Listen. Brutka is an important man, Jon, and you pulling that stunt at the UN, that's not cool. What the fuck was that all about?"

"It's about defending my family."

"There are rules, Jon. And you are not above them. I don't care who you work for."

"Fuck your rules. And the same rules that apply to your diplomat friend."

"He's not my friend."

"Isn't he?"

Kelinski sighed and pointed his finger close to Reznick's face. "We have global responsibilities."

"Good for you."

"He's an important man. His country is vital to our national interests."

"Bullshit."

"I'm trying to be nice here, Jon."

"Am I supposed to be impressed with this bullshit? My daughter is in a fucking coma, and I'm supposed to care about the virtues of this shitbag diplomat?"

"Let me spell it out. Really nice and easy. The diplomat's country is vital to our interests. And we can't allow your behavior to spoil our relationship with his country."

"I don't give a shit about that. My only interest is my daughter and her well-being."

Kelinski shook his head. "Reznick, this little game of yours is up. We can't tolerate this any longer. And I'm going to lay it on the line so you can understand. You need to leave New York."

"And why would I do that?"

"You need to understand that you don't have the power in this situation, Jon. You might think you do, but you don't. We don't want you to get hurt."

"Is that a threat?"

"No. Just some guidance."

"Listen to me, pal. The only people hurt, apart from my daughter, are the diplomat, who's missing some teeth, and a couple of his goons, who attacked me. They're the ones who got hurt."

"This is not going to end well. So we're telling you nice and clear it's time to get out of the city."

"Really? So let me get this straight. Is the State Department now subcontracted to the Ukraine? Is that what you're telling me? Is that who's pulling the strings?"

Kelinski cleared his throat.

"You like running errands, Kelinski?"

"Are you trying to provoke me, Reznick?"

"Get a life, Kelinski."

"You're leaving New York!"

"Not possible. My daughter is in the hospital here."

"She has to go too."

Reznick grabbed the man by the throat. "What did you say?"

"You heard me!"

"Now you listen to me, my daughter can't be moved. She's in a goddamn coma."

Kelinski closed his eyes as Reznick loosened his grip. "Don't ever do that again."

"She's in a goddamn coma. So my answer is no, I won't be leaving New York."

"That's where you're wrong, Jon. The decision has been made."

"Bullshit."

"She will be moved to a new hospital. And you will leave New York. The security and national interests of the United States are in play."

Reznick shook his head. "Motherfucker. Are you kidding me?"

"Deadly serious. You've got forty-eight hours to get out of town."

Thirty-Two

A few hours later, Acosta had finished her paperwork for the day. She stifled a yawn; she hadn't slept much the past few nights. She was worried about the escalating scenario between Reznick and Brutka. But she was also wondering what all the political infighting between the Feds, the NYPD, and the State Department would come to.

The only one who seemed to gain from this mess was Brutka himself.

Acosta sympathized with Reznick's position. All the cops at the Nineteenth Precinct did. She felt sorry for him, alone in New York, his daughter fighting for her life. She knew he was going about it in a reckless manner. But she also knew that Reznick's actions had exposed a terrible rift between the NYPD and the FBI on one side and the State Department on the other.

Acosta sensed that matters were coming to a head. And it was all down to Jon Reznick, seemingly on a one-man mission to bring Brutka down, no matter the personal cost.

She secretly admired his direct, no-nonsense, take-no-prisoners approach. It would most likely be how her own brother, Diego, would have dealt with things if she had been the victim of a hit-and-run. These men were definitely cut from the same cloth.

Acosta had been toying with putting Reznick in contact with someone who knew far more about Brutka than she did. A guy she trusted.

She had been hesitating since she had first met Reznick. But she had heard about the ultimatum from the State Department, telling Reznick to leave town. It was the final straw.

She took a deep breath, wondering if she should do it. This wasn't how an NYPD detective should be acting. But Acosta reasoned that while she didn't condone lawbreaking, she was also human and wanted to help Reznick in any way possible in his pursuit of Brutka.

An email pinged in her inbox. Acosta had been waiting for the email for hours. She maneuvered the mouse and clicked to open the attachment from the NYPD Computer Crimes Squad. It was the last photo taken on Daniela's cell phone, found hidden inside a bag of frozen peas in her apartment. It took a few moments for her brain to process the image. It was a bloated Brutka, sleeping, white powder on his nose.

"What the hell?"

Acosta stared at the image in shock. Dumbfounded shock. It was the real Aleksander Brutka. Not the carefully cultivated persona of the smooth-talking elite diplomat. But a man who clearly lived a shadow life. A life of secrets. Dark secrets. A man with something to hide. The hit-and-run and leaving Lauren Reznick in a coma were just the tip of the iceberg. Aleksander Brutka was using drugs. And now here he was, on the cell phone of a dead hooker. Why? Did she want her abuser or dealer to be known if something happened to her? That made sense.

Her mind began to race. She thought of Daniela dying alone in her apartment, only hours after she had called, saying people were following her. She said there had been a car outside. Was this who'd killed her? Was this who'd ordered her murder?

The more Acosta thought about it, the more convinced she was that Aleksander Brutka was far more dangerous than she had first thought. She wondered why she hadn't figured it out earlier. It wasn't just the callous way Brutka had run down and left Lauren Reznick for dead. That was bad enough. But she was beginning to see how Brutka might also be to blame for Daniela's death, either directly or indirectly. The guy was appalling. He was a monster. The bastard had to be stopped. But how? As it stood, she was powerless. The thought of that arrogant prick going free depressed her as much as the thought that she hadn't been able to get Daniela to safety in time. A wretched end to her young life, in a shitty room in East Harlem, either overdosing or being made to look like she'd overdosed.

Acosta began to make the connections. Brutka wasn't just a drug user. He was almost certainly a drug dealer. And perhaps even a pimp. Was this guy, this fucking privileged diplomat, responsible for far more than just getting high and drunk driving? Was he the violent bastard who'd beaten Daniela, abused her, and drugged her? And did it really end with just Daniela? Or were there other victims?

She waited as she contemplated whether to speak to Reznick or not. She realized that what she was about to do might get her suspended or even fired. But despite everything, she found herself dialing his number.

"Yeah?" His voice was low.

"Jon, can you meet up for a drink?"

"Now?"

"Sure, why not?"

"That's fine. Where?"

"Baker Street Pub, an Irish sports bar, on First Avenue."

"See you there."

Reznick hung up.

When she arrived, Reznick handed her a beer as he nursed his own. She pulled up a stool beside him at the near-empty bar, a Yankee game being rerun on the TVs.

Acosta wondered if she was doing the right thing. She felt tense knowing she was acting completely out of character. She had two things she wanted to tell Reznick. She took a sip of the cool beer and looked at

Reznick. He looked tired, haggard. "You look like shit," she said. "You need to get some sleep."

Reznick took a couple of gulps of beer. "Lot on my mind."

Acosta edged closer, voice low. "I know. You really are a stubborn bastard, Reznick. Anyone else would've just moved on."

"Not the way I work. I didn't realize how many friends in high places this guy has."

Acosta said, "I heard you had a run-in with Brutka."

"And two of his goons the previous night."

Acosta shook her head. "Seems like you're on the radar of the State Department."

Reznick nodded.

"I heard you've been asked to leave the city."

Reznick shrugged.

"I'm not condoning what you did to Brutka, let's be clear, and I can only imagine what it must be like. But I'm telling you, your instincts on Brutka are correct."

"Look, I'm sorry for giving you so much grief on this. But I just can't let this go."

"Like I said, I'm not condoning what you've done."

"I want him off the streets. But somehow I'm the one being told to leave New York. I mean, what the fuck?"

"We all want him off the streets."

Reznick glanced up at the game on the TV.

"I heard the FBI wants him gone."

Reznick nodded. "It's the State Department. That's where the problem lies. Had a little chat with one of their guys this afternoon outside the park. Not far from here. In an SUV on Fifth Avenue."

Acosta sipped her drink. "Fuck."

"I'm assuming that the State Department guys don't normally go cruising around New York City."

"It's really disappointing that this is their position. In fairness, in the past, if it was diplomats charged with drunk driving, theft, or sexual assault, they were always hauled off home."

"That would make sense."

"Brutka is clearly being protected by the State Department."

"Which makes me wonder if that's why he acted with impunity."

"Here's the thing: Brutka wasn't on the radar of law enforcement or the Feds, although his habits might have been known to the State Department. I thought you might be interested to know that Brutka is, apparently, on the radar of a prominent journalist. This guy keeps his cards close to his chest. I trust him. I don't know what he knows about Brutka. But from what I'm hearing, he hasn't been able to lay a hand on him. Yet."

Reznick smiled. "Why do you think that is?"

Acosta sighed and leaned in close. "Why do you think? Money, influence, powerful friends."

Reznick was quiet for a few moments. "I'm assuming you didn't just want to meet to shoot the breeze, pleasant though it is."

"Not exactly. I wanted to talk to you about a couple of things."

Reznick shrugged.

"A little while ago I got confirmation about the overdose death of a girl up in East Harlem. Claimed she had been threatened, abused, beaten, treated like a sex slave, but didn't press charges. She was scared out of her mind. I spoke to her yesterday, and she said there were people outside her apartment. I put in a call, some cops went by a couple of hours later, but there was no answer. Eventually, I turn up at her apartment, super lets me in. Dead. Within hours of speaking to me."

"Fuck."

"She told me shortly before she died that she had taken a picture of the guy who beat her up after he'd passed out in her apartment. Guess who?"

Reznick fixed his steely gaze on her. "You're kidding me."

Acosta shook her head.

"Brutka?"

Acosta nodded. "It was him alright. So now there are more questions."

"But with the same answer."

"No doubt."

"There's a lot more to this guy than just a hit-and-run."

Acosta took a gulp of her beer. "I think you can assume Brutka's job as a diplomat is simply a cover for him staying in New York and doing whatever the hell he wants, no matter the cost. I would wager that this guy is involved in pimping, drug dealing, violence. Who knows? Maybe even murder."

"But what the hell can anyone do about it?"

Acosta leaned in closer. "That leads me to the second point. The guy I was telling you about. The journalist. He might be interested in your story."

Reznick sipped his beer. "I'm not that enamored of journalists, I have to tell you."

"He's a good guy. Very diligent. Very thorough. But also very discreet. He's got sources across the city. I know him. I know him well. And I trust him."

"Have you told him what happened to Lauren?"

"I mentioned it, yes."

Reznick nodded.

"This journalist, when I told him about Brutka and the hit-and-run, he began to open up a bit. Said he had been on the receiving end of Brutka's reach. Lawsuits against the *New York Post* like you wouldn't believe. The paper came under intense pressure to pull a story the journalist was working on. And guess what? Despite a major investigation into Brutka, which lasted for eighteen months, all that hard work amounted to nothing."

"They scrapped the investigation?"

Acosta shook her head. "Put it on hold. About a year ago the journalist said that a freelance reporter contacted the *National Enquirer* with another story about Brutka, and they had it all lined up. They bought the rights to it. Half a million dollars changed hands."

"So what the hell happened to the story?"

"I heard someone at the magazine got a call from someone to kill the story. They were paid another fat sum to spike the damn thing."

"Kill the story?"

"And that was the end of that."

Reznick sighed. "What about the journalist? How did that work out?"

"Here's the thing. I've been in touch with him. He says that the new editor wants to pursue this. But he wants more meat on the bone, so to speak. A few of his sources were problematic, since the victims were illegal aliens in this country. Ironically, from Brutka's own country. Ukraine. Prostitutes, mostly."

Reznick drank the rest of his beer and ordered up another round for them. He hunched over his drink. "So this guy has been investigating Brutka . . . He just needs more information?"

"The guy has a dossier on this scumbag. He's got the story. He wants to bring him down. So that's something you have in common."

"True."

"He knows everything about Brutka. But if you could let him know what transpired, in your words, it would give the story about your daughter's hit-and-run, the guys attacking you in the park, all that stuff, a way in. It would mean an overwhelmingly convincing firsthand account."

"You want me to speak to him?"

"That's up to you. But yeah, you could help him. His aim is to get even better evidence to nail the bastard. But he can also help you learn far, far more about the big picture. I think we're only scratching the surface. But the journalist, Tom Callaghan, knows the full story."

Reznick pondered what Acosta was saying. "I'm not going on the record."

"You don't have to. He just wants someone to tell him, not via NYPD sources, what really happened."

"The fun guy from the State Department I bumped into said I've got to be out of town in forty-eight hours. I think they're deadly serious."

Acosta sipped her beer. "You've got a window of opportunity. Your call, Jon."

Thirty-Three

The following morning, just before lunch Reznick met up with Tom Callaghan at the Old Town Bar in the Flatiron District. Inside, it was all dark wood and low lighting. A few barflies looked up from their beers.

A big, stocky guy signaled him from across the room. It had to be Callaghan. He wore a short-sleeved white linen shirt with a couple of pens in the top pocket, jeans, sneakers. "Nice to see you."

Reznick shook his hand.

Callaghan ordered a couple of Heinekens. He handed one to Reznick. "Wanna sit down?"

Reznick nodded and followed the journalist to a quiet booth at the far end of the bar. He sat down opposite the journalist. He felt as if he was being scrutinized. He looked around to get his bearings. "My kind of place."

"Favorite haunt of mine. Spend way too much time in here, my wife says."

Reznick sipped the froth off the top of the beer. His gaze wandered around the bar before he looked across the table at Callaghan. "Here are the ground rules: no photographs of me or my daughter."

"Not a problem."

"Also, you can't identify either of us, do you understand?"

"I just want to say that I have a daughter myself. And I can only imagine what you're going through. It's a terrible situation."

Reznick nodded. "Appreciate that."

"What's the latest on your daughter?"

"Still in an induced coma."

"Really sorry, Jon. Listen, can I say where you're from?"

"You can say I'm from Maine. And that my daughter was visiting New York. She's a college student, that's all I can say. That is accurate but doesn't reveal our identities."

Callaghan leaned across the table. "Fine," he said, lowering his voice. "Is it OK if I record this conversation on my cell phone so my editor has a verbatim account of our conversation?"

"Do not identify me. Am I clear?"

"Totally. That's fine. I want you to be comfortable. And I want to assure you that I protect my sources. This is important to me. Underpins what I'm all about."

Reznick sighed. "What do you want to know?"

Callaghan took out his cell phone and started recording. "Tell me what happened, in your own words."

"What do you mean?"

"How did you get involved with Aleksander Brutka?"

Reznick took a gulp of beer before he began a broad-brush overview of events, beginning from the moment he was told by cops that his daughter had been in an accident. He talked for nearly an hour, trying to fill in as much as he could. The surveillance of Brutka's building, gaining access through the Realtor, and telling Brutka to leave town at gunpoint. And he also mentioned what Acosta had revealed about the cell phone photo of Brutka lying passed out, discovered at the dead girl's apartment in East Harlem.

Callaghan was taking shorthand notes, flicking through page after page. "That's wild."

Reznick then went on to talk about how he got pulled over by the NYPD Hercules counterterrorism team when he put Brutka's apartment under surveillance. Then about attacking Brutka inside the UN.

Callaghan took a few moments to reply, as if assessing exactly what he'd been told. "Are you kidding me? Inside the UN? How on earth did you get in?"

"I know a guy. Hacker friend. Managed to get into their identification department."

Callaghan whistled. "And you . . . approached Brutka in the bathroom? Are you kidding me?"

"I had been keeping an eye on him inside for fifteen minutes or so. Then I got a chance to get him one-on-one. He didn't like that."

Callaghan was quiet for a few moments. "Was there something that made you want to confront him again?"

"He sent my daughter flowers. With a note. And he called my cell phone to say he was checking her out on Facebook. He said some vile stuff."

Callaghan nodded.

"In my eyes, he had crossed a line again."

"Couldn't agree more. Listen, what you're telling me matches the same arrogant, narcissistic, violent behavior I know he's capable of. Brutka is very dangerous."

Reznick sipped some more beer. "I'm not an expert, Tom, but he seems to get off on the thrill of it all. Knowing he can't be touched. I mean, who would send flowers to the girl he left in a coma?"

Callaghan shook his head and scribbled more notes. "I really appreciate you sharing all of this."

"I want to do anything to bring this fucker down."

"I don't want to underplay it, but your daughter, as you may know, is only the latest casualty."

Reznick said nothing.

"I know of at least eight young women who have been abused and assaulted by him."

"Eight? Are you sure?"

Callaghan nodded. "Nine if you include what Acosta said about the girl in East Harlem."

"Are you serious?"

"Deadly."

"How is this allowed to go on?"

"You wouldn't believe half of it."

"So are these New York girls?"

"They live here. But no. From abroad. Ukraine. He abuses them, I mean rapes. He also supplies drugs to them. They end up addicts. Terrible state of affairs."

Reznick was struggling to get his head around the magnitude of Brutka's crimes. "Detective Acosta mentioned just this one girl. Maybe some drug possession."

"That's only the girl she knows. I'm talking different areas of the city. Some out in New Jersey. Some in the East Village. Harlem. A couple in the Bronx. And not just drugs. This goes way beyond drugs."

Reznick sighed. "My main concern is my daughter. Acosta said your investigation was back on track at the highest levels within your paper."

"Absolutely. I've had guarantees, but the more case studies of this guy's criminality and abuse of power, the better. The public needs to know about this guy."

Reznick leaned in close. "The FBI wants him out of the country. So does the NYPD."

"It's the State Department protecting him."

"Have you ever heard of a case like this?"

"Never."

"Why do you think that is?"

Callaghan gulped the rest of his beer. "Geopolitics. Ukraine is, as you know, part of the former Soviet Union. And what happened there in 2014, the Euromaidan Revolution, was the overthrow of a Russia-friendly democracy. A coup. And guess who was pulling the strings."

"I can take a guess."

Callaghan nodded. "Ukraine has a lot of natural resources, and the CIA wants them to be less reliant on Russia, but there's also the possibility of opening up US military bases, effectively right on the Russian border. It's the Cold War take two."

"I'm guessing the fact that Aleksander's father is the president changes things quite a bit."

"There's kickbacks among contractors. Hundreds of millions in kickbacks throughout the government. Think tanks in DC. Lobbyists. PR companies. Greasing the wheels. He has threatened to withdraw everything if his son is punished."

Reznick nodded. "And you've got proof of that?"

Callaghan nodded. "Most certainly." He lowered his voice. "Jon, I've been told you're a former Delta operator."

"Don't identify me as such."

"How will I describe you?"

"Security consultant. Nice and generic."

"I hear you consult for the Feds, among others."

"I can't comment on that. And don't insinuate anything."

"Not a problem. What you know is only scraping the surface, Jon. Only the surface."

"What else have you found out?"

"A lot. It's not just abuse and drug use. He's involved in human smuggling. Drug trafficking. I have been told by three separate sources about cocaine and heroin shipments flown in from South America by a private jet he owns, and that the drugs were all labeled as diplomatic luggage. Couldn't be touched. Customs and the DEA reported that their sources told them that Aleksander personally oversaw this."

Reznick rubbed his hands over his face. "Jesus Christ. The scale of this is mind-blowing. What a fucking mess."

"Your little run-in with the State Department tells you that this relationship—economic, political, and diplomatic—takes precedence."

"When did you first become aware of this guy?"

"About five years back. Within six months of him taking up his post."

Reznick was starting to see the big picture. "So, they have mineral wealth and military leverage, right?"

"Ukraine is strategic to US interests. America wants them admitted to NATO. Russia doesn't want a Western alliance on its doorstep. With the rise of China, the reemergence of Russia, and also Iran, America is looking to consolidate its influence. They've got military bases across Europe. And this, in turn, is part of their geopolitical games with Russia."

"And Brutka just happens to be a Ukrainian diplomat with a penchant for sadism and drugs?"

"Tip of the iceberg. There are other girls being abused in the most terrible, systematic way. Brutka's role allows him to issue ten-year US visas for those girls he has handpicked."

Reznick closed his eyes and sighed as the scale of the criminality became even more apparent. "Let me make sure I understand. If we hadn't been turning a blind eye to Brutka . . ."

Callaghan leaned in closer. "He would've been sent home years ago."

"So he should have been back in Ukraine already?"

"Correct. Your coming forward gives me an opportunity to reveal this ongoing criminal behavior. And I'm very grateful for it."

"If it gets Brutka out of the country, then I'll be happy."

Callaghan sighed. "You've been very forthcoming. And I want you to know that I give you my word that this story will come out. Because it is far, far bigger than just Brutka."

"What do you mean?"

"There's something we have been working on. It's powerful stuff. A separate investigation. A parallel investigation, so to speak."

"Can you give me a hint?"

"I can't really."

Reznick leaned closer. "Tom, I'm sharing information with you. I hope you can reveal what you know."

"Jon, I'm a journalist, and when we're working on a story we don't want anyone else to catch wind of it. We want to get in first. Exclusive."

"Whatever you tell me is not going to be shared with other newspapers or TV channels, trust me. That's your story, fine. But at least share a bit of what you know. Quid pro quo."

Callaghan showed his hands. "OK, but seriously, this is just for you. I'm trusting you."

Reznick nodded.

"This is more than Brutka, the diplomat." Callaghan's voice was now a whisper. "Here's the thing. His father, Yegor Brutka, the President, hates Russia with a passion. Pathological. And I've been digging into his past. No official documents available. But about a year ago I managed to find out something interesting. All journalists have contacts they build up over time. Some very good contacts. And what I've found out shocked me and sickened me."

Reznick nodded.

"This is all going to come out when we publish. Brutka's father, who was a boy at the time, and the grandfather were smuggled out of Ukraine at the end of the Second World War."

"Refugees?"

Callaghan shook his head. "Try again."

"Not a clue."

"Brutka's grandfather, it turns out, headed up a Ukrainian paramilitary unit in 1941. He was believed to have been part of a group, along with the Waffen-SS, who carried out a massacre in Lviv, which was then in Poland, of thousands of Jews. Beat them in the street. Killed people with sticks, clubs, bare hands. Women stripped naked and paraded through the town."

Reznick felt sick in the pit of his stomach. "How do you know this?"

"Scores of eyewitness accounts and also American records. The Simon Wiesenthal Center unearthed corroborative evidence. Witness statements identifying the grandfather."

"So how the hell did they get into America?"

"Turns out we helped him disappear after the Second World War to the US."

Reznick shook his head. "And Brutka's grandfather was part of that intake?"

"That was only part of the story. Not only Nazi scientists who had experimented on Jews but also hundreds, maybe thousands, of Waffen-SS, Ukrainian, and Lithuanian collaborators immigrated here. No one knows the true numbers. People with blood on their hands. People that had carried out pogroms. Like John Demjanjuk."

"I remember that name."

"Demjanjuk was an autoworker, Cleveland. He had become a naturalized citizen. He was stripped of his citizenship and deported to Israel. It was said he was the guard known as Ivan the Terrible. Subsequently found guilty of genocide. Then cleared on appeal. Regained his US citizenship, then more allegations surfaced. This time in Germany. He stood trial a second time in Germany. His family said he was a Ukrainian prisoner of war in Germany. SS identity card."

"Tell me the rest." He pointed to his head. "This is just for me. I'm not recording this."

"Fair." Callaghan sipped his beer. "Brutka's grandfather, Ilad Brutka, used the name Bud Smith as his cover in the States. He was smuggled here in 1945 by the OSS, the predecessor of the CIA. Wound up running a small hotel in fucking Vermont. Cold War spy for America among the Ukrainian community in the States. Made money, bought more hotels. Became wealthy. His son, Brutka's father, returned to Ukraine. Became a lawyer."

"And we allowed that?"

"There's more. A lot more."

"Like what?"

"Tons of stuff. The father, currently the President of Ukraine, is backed by the far-right radical group Right Sector."

Reznick nodded. "They were the guys behind the coup in 2014?"

"Right. Anti-Semites, fascist to the core, part of the tradition that can be traced back to the Second World War. Very active in the eastern part of Ukraine, an area which wants to break away and be part of Russia."

"Let me get this straight. So the grandfather was a Nazi collaborator?"

Callaghan nodded. "He was there."

"How can you be so sure?"

Callaghan reached into his jacket pocket and handed over a grainy black-and-white photo. It showed a crowd, with a grinning twenty-something man in the foreground, pointing a rifle at a naked, terrified woman in the street. "Ilad Brutka, July first, 1941."

Reznick held the photo and stared at the woman's eyes, which seemed to be pleading for mercy. She was alone. At the mercy of a baying mob. He handed the photo back to Callaghan, who put it back in his pocket. "And you've verified that it's him?"

"We've had three forensic experts confirm that it's the same guy. The grandfather. Old passport photos, military ID photographs. That's him. He's a fucking animal. As is his father. And his grandson."

Reznick cleared his throat. "How has this not come out?"

"It will. You have my word. Very soon. The reason it hasn't come out yet is that the CIA, Justice Department, and the State Department have all been covering up the presence of Nazis and Nazi collaborators in our midst since the Second World War. And the paper came under immense pressure about my investigation. But the new editor isn't taking any prisoners. This story will run. And your testimony about what happened to your daughter and what actions you've taken has helped that. So thank you."

Reznick's head was swimming with the revelations. "You have to promise me. You have to get this published, whatever it takes. This is far bigger than just a hit-and-run."

"I know. The paper is behind me on this. But they want this story watertight."

Reznick gulped some of his late-morning beer. "I don't know if what I've told you will be of any use."

Callaghan shook his head. "Jon, this could be the straw that breaks the camel's back. I want to see this bastard hung up to dry. Your daughter, a young American student, in a coma because of this guy? This will cause an uproar. But the story of the grandfather overshadows even that."

"How long till you publish?"

"A week max."

Thirty-Four

Meyerstein was enjoying a sandwich at her desk when her phone rang. She had been expecting the call from Steve Kelinski, of the State Department.

"Assistant Director, apologies for the delay," he said. "I want to give you a heads-up on Jon Reznick."

Meyerstein put down the sandwich. "What about him?"

"We've issued him an ultimatum. He's crossed a line. And harassing UN diplomats is totally unacceptable. He also grabbed me by the throat, just so you know. Not a smart move."

Meyerstein closed her eyes, wondering what Reznick thought he was going to achieve with such tactics.

"We've tried to be understanding, but Reznick's actions have ruled that out."

"Steven, do you want to get to the point?"

"The point is, we've had enough. And we wanted to let you know that his daughter is being moved to a hospital in Maine, closer to Reznick's home."

Meyerstein took a few seconds to process the information. "His daughter? Are you serious? She's in a goddamn coma."

"I'm sorry."

"Who signed off on this?"

"Pat Sheen. It's from the top."

"I should have guessed. Is the State Department planning to ignore the concerns of the NYPD and the FBI, Steve? Seriously, is that what you're saying?"

"That's not our problem. Lauren Reznick is being moved. This is not up for discussion. But we thought it was common courtesy to let you know."

"Well that's damn decent of you."

Meyerstein got up from her seat, walked to the window, and stared out over lower Manhattan. "In all my years at the FBI I've never heard of such a thing. Not only to allow the criminal act of this diplomat to go unchecked, but to then move the victim simply to comply with the outrageous demands of that dirtbag Brutka and his father."

"Those are unsubstantiated assertions and you know it."

"Oh come off it, Steve. Do you really expect me to believe this bullshit isn't because of who Brutka is and who he knows and how important geopolitically his country is to us?"

"We're going over old ground. I'm not going to get locked into a discussion about this. It's happening. She is being moved."

Meyerstein stood and stared at the skyline, the Freedom Tower glistening in the sun. "When will she be moved?"

"It's happening now. As we speak."

Thirty-Five

When Reznick got back from the late-morning meeting with Callaghan and arrived at the hospital, his daughter was in a bed being carefully pushed down a corridor to an elevator. She was still connected to tubes and the machine.

"What the hell's going on?"

The doctor in charge shook Reznick's hand. He took him aside into his office and explained the situation. "I just want to let you know that I did not authorize this. No way."

"Who? Was this the State Department? I need to know."

"I can't say. I just know that the medical director sent me an email. The decision was made for him. When I tried to contact him, he just told me to get it done. I didn't have a choice."

Reznick felt pangs of guilt. He had left her bedside. "Maybe if I had been here I could've stopped it."

"Mr. Reznick, don't beat yourself up over this. Nothing could've stopped this happening. This is high level. The wheels are in motion."

"Where is she being taken?"

"I believe they're taking her to Maine."

Reznick was struggling to process what was happening. "I can't believe they're actually going ahead with this. This has got to be unethical."

"We didn't recommend this. All I know is that the State Department signed a medical waiver, and she's in their care until she gets to the hospital in Maine."

"I need to be with her."

"There's still time. The ambulance will be leaving soon, though."

Reznick thanked the doctor for all his efforts and his honesty. He took the elevator down to the ground floor and saw his daughter lying on the bed—accompanied by two nurses, two doctors, and an anesthetist—being lifted into the back of an ambulance with the ventilator. He showed his ID and hopped in with her.

The ambulance was headed out of Manhattan to East Farmingdale, Long Island. Small airfield.

Then they were transferred to a fresh crew on an air ambulance.

The whole time Reznick sat beside his daughter, still being artificially kept alive. He kissed her forehead before takeoff. "I'm sorry, darling."

The doctor sitting beside her, monitoring her condition, turned to Reznick and smiled. "Sir, I promise, while this situation is not ideal, she's going to another great hospital. She's in good hands."

Reznick patted the doctor on the back. "Appreciate that, thank you."

The flight to Bangor took just under two hours.

When the plane landed, Reznick helped the nurses and doctors lift the gurney and load it on to another waiting ambulance. Lauren was transferred to the ICU at Eastern Maine Medical Center. A short handover from the mobile team of medics, then the Bangor team of specialists got to work and started fresh tests.

Reznick sat down at her bedside and began talking softly to his comatose daughter.

A nurse joined him. "We'll look after her, Mr. Reznick."

Reznick nodded. He knew Lauren was getting the best treatment possible. But he also felt hollow inside, believing he had let his daughter down. "I know you will."

Thirty-Six

The days that followed were a blur for Reznick. He felt empty. He lost track of time as he sat at his daughter's bedside. Every waking hour he now watched over her like a hawk. He wondered if she would ever get better. When a doctor entered her room, Reznick looked for signs in the doctor's eyes. He was looking for a glimmer of hope. And he also prayed. Not outwardly. Silent prayers. Sitting by her bed, eyes closed, feeling as if his heart was being ripped out, beseeching a greater power—God, anyone—to save her. To help. To pull her through.

On the fourth day, the lead doctor on the case asked to speak to Reznick in private.

The doctor led him to a small sitting room. Reznick felt his stomach tighten, wondering what he was going to say.

"Take a seat," the doctor said.

Reznick sat down, privately steeling himself for a bad prognosis.

"I have some news."

Reznick stared at the doctor, part of him not wanting to hear what he was about to say.

"We believe she's ready," the doctor said. "We want to wean Lauren off these drugs over the next day or so," he said. "There are signs that she's ready to be woken up."

Reznick was at a loss for words for a few moments.

"This is positive, Mr. Reznick."

Reznick felt a wave of mixed emotions wash over him. Part of him was glad they were going to try to wake her up. But part of him was fearful that she would be damaged. "Doctor, that's the best news I've had for a while. For a long, long while."

"I'm not promising anything. But it's important that we take this step and start the process."

Reznick ran his hands through his hair; he was exhausted from lack of sleep and stress. "How long will this take?"

"We should be in a better position to establish how she's coming along in the next forty-eight hours. Familiar voices are very helpful. A familiar, soothing voice."

Reznick nodded. "Do you want me to speak to her?"

"The drug dosage is being dropped gradually. But in three hours you might want to sit with her. It can take a while. A long while. So you're in for a little wait."

"What about getting her off the ventilator?"

"We'll gradually wean her off. And once we're satisfied she can breathe on her own, the machines will be removed."

Later that night, a few hours after Lauren's dosage of drugs was cut back and her breathing tube was checked by the doctor and nurse, along with her vital signs, Reznick sat down beside her.

The doctor said, "Be patient. Why don't you start talking to her? We'll leave you alone for a little while."

Reznick took a few minutes to get his mind straight. The events since his daughter's accident were catching up with him too. He was overwrought. It was like an adrenaline crash. He often felt like that after intense situations. More so as he got older. But he knew that all that was nothing compared to having his beautiful daughter back with him.

He looked at her one more time. Her hair was fine like her mother's. She had the same pale skin tone.

He waited until the medical staff weren't around. Eventually, Reznick leaned forward and took Lauren's hand. He began to stroke it gently.

"We're back in Maine, darling," he said. "You're in a hospital in Bangor. We're so much closer to home. You can almost smell the sea." Reznick cleared his throat. "I'm looking forward to us walking the Rockland breakwater. They're beginning the process of waking you up. And I'm looking forward to speaking to you again. I've missed you."

Reznick felt his throat tighten.

"We're going to put the incident in New York behind us. We're going to look forward. And we're going to spend some time together, just me and you. I want to know how you're doing at that publishing company—Berman's, right? You need to explain what you do. Editorial intern, I think you said. Reading manuscripts. That's interesting, honey. Tell me all about that.

"I know you like New York, but I for one am glad you're out of that crazy city, at least for now. It'll give us both time. A bit of space. Time to reflect. And who knows? Hopefully we can spend some serious time together." Memories flooded back. "Can't believe my little girl is all grown up. Don't know what's happened to the time. It seems a bit unreal that one minute you were a child, and now you're a young woman making her way in the world in New York. That's where your mom was from. We met there. So it's an important place for me."

Reznick dabbed his eyes.

"It goes by in a flash, honey, let me tell you. That's something people don't tell you. How it's all gone in no time. Blink of an eye. I remember the day you were born, Lauren. I remember like it was yesterday. The doctor handed you to me, wrapped in blankets. I was just a young man myself. Not much older than you. I couldn't believe it. You were mine. I didn't know what to do. What to think. But when I held you close for the first time and kissed your cheek . . . You know what? I realized what love was. I loved your mother. Very much. But having a child is a different type of love. I remember in those early days, Lauren, your milky breath. But I also remember your eyes. You had the most beautiful blue eyes I'd ever seen. I felt calm. For the first time I felt peace."

Reznick felt the tears on his face.

"I don't know if I've been a good father. Could've done a lot better, I guess. I know I wasn't there for big chunks of your childhood. And I hope that one day you can understand why I had to go away. When your mother died, I couldn't go on. I couldn't, in my state of mind, look after you. I thought I was strong. I wasn't. I couldn't cope. Your gran and granddad, your mom's parents, they looked after you for a while. You have them to thank. They're good people.

"A lot of water under the bridge. I'm not the same person now that I was then. I've learned a lot. I've learned about true strength. Guys like your grandfather, my dad. You never met him. But you would've liked him. He would've loved you so much. And I'm hoping that one day you and I get a chance to do more things together. I never seem to find the time. You were either away at boarding school or college, or with your friends. And that's fine. But I hope that when we get you out of here, we get you back to Rockland.

"I'll get your room made up. I know you're not home much. But I'd like you to spend the rest of the summer with me when this is over. I know some great places."

Reznick closed his eyes, bowed his head, and prayed.

Thirty-Seven

The brothel was situated in a depressing high-rise in East Harlem.

Brutka's SUV pulled to the curb, and he walked up to the graffiti-scrawled security door. He pressed the buzzer and then rode the elevator to the twenty-second floor. He knocked on the first door. A few moments later, it was opened by a scrawny young white girl he had taken a fancy to; she was smoking a joint.

"Come in, baby," she said. She spoke excellent English.

Brutka brushed past the girl and headed down the dimly lit hallway until he got to the grimy kitchen. Dirty dishes were piled up in the sink, and old pizza boxes and empty beer cans were strewn on the floor. "You don't like living in a clean house?"

The girl shrugged. "I try, honey. Just seems I have a lot on my mind."

"Clean it up after I leave."

"Of course."

The girl led him to a windowless room filled with candles and shut the door. The space was soundproofed, laced with the sickly sweet smell of marijuana. A leather sofa and a coffee table with pornographic magazines sat in the middle. "You need to relax," she said.

"You need to learn to move your ass. This is America. They work hard here."

The girl's gaze dropped, subservient. "Of course, I'm sorry. You're right."

Brutka grabbed her by the jaw. "I cannot stand lazy bastards. Slovenly, dirty people. The next time I arrive, I want things clean. Do you understand that?"

The girl nodded, tears in her eyes.

Brutka loosened his grip. The girl wiped her eyes and put some Latin music on low. Slowly she began to dance, eyes closed. He went across to the bar and poured himself a large rum and Coke and slumped down on one of the sofas.

The girl sat down on his lap. "You look tired, honey. I'm sorry for upsetting you."

Brutka forced a smile.

"You need to relax more."

Brutka knocked back the drink. "You think I look tired?"

"I've been looking forward to seeing you, honey," she said, trying to change the subject.

"How do I look tired?"

"I don't know . . . Just your eyes. They seem tired. As if you're worried."

Brutka reached out to her and held her hand. "You wouldn't understand. I've got a million things on my plate."

"I want you to forget everything when you're here."

"How are you liking New York?"

"New York is nice. Scary. But nice."

Brutka kissed the back of her hand and ruffled her hair.

"Do you mind if I ask you a question?" she said.

"What do you want to know?"

The girl stroked his cheek. "You promised that I would get my visa. It's just that I've only got another two weeks left before I have to go back home."

"Did I promise you?"

The girl nodded.

"Do I keep my promises?"

"I hope so. I mean . . . I don't want to go home, honey. I want to be here for you, whenever you want to see me."

Brutka grabbed the girl's face in a viselike grip. He pressed his fingers into her jawline, feeling the bones. It would be so easy to crush her face with one hand. He felt in complete control at that moment. He enjoyed the feeling. He allowed it to wash over him. The pleasure it gave him. The sense of omnipotence. The feeling of invincibility. He loved exerting his power how and when he saw fit. His nerve endings were tingling at the very thought of what he could do to her. He saw the fear in her eyes. "Are you insinuating that I will not keep my promise? Is that what you're saying?"

"No, baby. I just wanted to make sure that I can stay here. To be here for you. For your needs."

"I don't know if you mean that."

Tears spilled down the girl's face. "Honey, you know I love you. I would do anything for you. I entertain you whenever you wish."

"And my friends?"

"Of course. I'm here for you. And your friends. But mostly for you. I love you. What do you want?"

"I want people to understand that with freedom comes responsibility. You must get that. Obedience is king. I am your king."

The girl gave a weak smile. "I understand."

Brutka smiled and wiped the tears from her face. "It's all that fucking junk you snort up your nose."

The girl began to giggle. "Yeah?"

"Don't play fucking coy with me."

The girl laughed and kissed him on the cheek. "You're nice. I like when you're nice to me. It makes me feel good."

Brutka began to stroke the nape of her neck. "You know I can make you happy. Make you feel good."

"You always do."

Brutka pulled out a bag of coke from his jacket and held it in front of the girl's face. "Ten thousand dollars' worth of coke should make anyone happy, right?"

The girl hugged him tight before grabbing the bag.

Brutka handed her his black American Express credit card.

The girl burst out laughing.

"Didn't I say I would look after you?"

The girl's eyes lit up and she liberally sprinkled some coke from the bag onto the glass coffee table in front of them. She chopped up the cocaine into four neat lines with the credit card. "Two each, honey?"

Brutka nodded and took out a one-hundred-dollar bill. He rolled it up tight. "That'll get us started." He got up and snorted his two lines. A wave of euphoria engulfed him. He sniffed hard as the coke rocked through his bloodstream. He began to laugh. And smile. He handed the girl the rolled-up bill.

The girl took it and hoovered up her two lines. She leaned over and began to kiss him. "Oh yeah." She got up and started dancing in time to the music, eyes closed, as if in a trance.

"Take some more!" Brutka said.

"Thank you, honey." The girl kneeled down and chopped up four more lines from the bag, immediately inhaling two of them. Then Brutka did his.

The music seemed to get louder. The bass began to throb. The lights were glowing. The girl's skin was glistening. And he felt out of his fucking mind with happiness.

The girl kneeled down beside him and kissed him on the lips. "You OK?"

Brutka nodded. "I need some help soon."

"What kind of help?"

"I have some girls I'd like you to look over. They're coming into town soon. And I'd like you to be there. To take a look at them."

"Who are they?"

"New girls from Ukraine. Most can't speak English. So you'll be able to explain things to them."

The girl's eyes were glassy. "It would be an honor, baby."

Thirty-Eight

Reznick was floating on a black river. The ripples washed against his face. He looked up at the stars. The sound of dark whispers as if in a bad dream. He sensed he was not alone.

"Dad . . ." The voice was soft. "Dad . . ."

Reznick snapped open his eyes. His daughter was awake. He got up and kissed her forehead. "Hey, honey. Dad's here."

Lauren nodded, her eyes getting heavier.

"No breathing tube? No machine? You're breathing by yourself?"

Lauren stared at him blankly. "Where am I?"

"You're in a hospital, in Bangor. Not far from home."

Lauren went quiet for a few moments as if trying to remember what had happened. "I think . . . I thought I was in New York."

"You were."

"What happened?"

Reznick held her hand. It was warm to the touch. "Can't you remember?"

"I remember I was jogging. Then nothing."

Reznick clasped her right hand, lying by the side of the bed, and kissed it. "You've been in a deep sleep, honey. A very deep sleep."

Lauren blinked as she looked around the room.

"Just relax. You're OK now. You're safe."

"I can't remember what happened. I can't remember anything."

Reznick took a few moments to process that information. A knock at the door, and a doctor signaled him. "I'll just be a couple of moments, honey." He left his daughter's side and approached the doctor.

The doctor whispered, "What a fighter. This is very encouraging. She's so strong, fit, and healthy. And young. That all helps."

"She seems very tired. Is she going to recover OK?"

"Well, it's still early, so we'll have to wait and see. But we have every reason to hope."

Reznick turned and saw that Lauren had fallen asleep again. He sighed and turned back to the doctor. "Sleep is good?"

"Sleep is very good. It's about the body repairing itself, about the start of the long road to recovery. She's breathing by herself now."

"But she's not out of the woods yet, right?"

"It's a process," the doctor said. "Waking up takes time. The drugs are still in her system. Some patients suffer hallucinations before they wake up. Your daughter has been very peaceful since she's been here. And the doctors in New York said the same thing when I spoke to them."

"She can't remember anything other than jogging. That's the last thing she remembers."

"That's OK. It happens."

"Is it permanent?"

"We can't rule that out. But it is common to experience some memory loss. Sentence structures may be fragmented. She could have trouble finding the right word. But with speech therapy over the coming months, we believe she can potentially make a full recovery in time."

"Potentially?"

"There are no guarantees. The brain scans, which are crucial, are all clear. No damage. No bleeding. But there might be lingering effects of the concussion. Confusion. But we don't know for sure yet. We need to reorient her when she wakes fully. And we will move her out of the ICU to the high dependency unit."

"You think she's strong?"

The doctor nodded. "I'm confident she can begin her life again. It won't be all smooth sailing. There might be some setbacks along the way. But she's determined. And she's a fighter."

Reznick turned and looked at his sleeping daughter. "Just like her mother."

It was late morning when Lauren woke again.

Reznick was sitting beside her and reached across to hold her hand. "Hi, sleepyhead."

Lauren just stared at him blankly.

"We're going to get you back to normal as soon as we can. You're in a good place."

Lauren didn't respond. She seemed to be in a trance.

Reznick smiled at her and called the doctor in. The doctor began to ask her questions. She didn't speak. Not one word.

A nurse leaned in close and spoke in a loud voice to her. "Lauren, can you hear me, honey?" she said. "Can you tell me your name?"

Lauren stared at the nurse and then looked at the doctor.

Reznick reached out and held her hand. "Lauren, darling, it's Dad here. Can you hear me?"

Lauren turned her face toward him.

"That's good, darling," Reznick said. "You can hear me. Now, tell us what your name is. Can you do that for me, darling?"

But his daughter just stared at him dead eyed, as if unable to find the words. A terrible silence filled the room.

The doctor said, "What's your name?" His tone was sharp.

Lauren blinked once.

The nurse said, "What's your name, dear? Your name? Can you say your name?"

Lauren licked her lips.

Reznick said, "I think she's thirsty. Can we get her something?"

The nurse went away and came back with a cotton swab dipped in water. It looked like a lollypop. She placed it into Lauren's mouth. "That better, honey?"

Reznick smiled. "What's your name, darling? Tell me. Tell Dad."

The nurse gently took the swab out of Lauren's mouth so she could speak.

Lauren's lips began to quiver. Her mouth slowly opened. And then she spoke. "Lauren . . . My name is Lauren Reznick."

Reznick kissed the back of her hand. "That's my girl. Dad's here. Tell me again. What's your name?"

"My name is Lauren Reznick. Didn't you hear me the first time?"

Thirty-Nine

Reznick felt as if he had emerged from a bad dream. But he was still worried about his daughter. He remained wary about Lauren making a full recovery. But the hospital carried out numerous cognitive tests, and she aced them all. Every single one. Then there were brain scans.

The doctors were pleased. "She's doing well," they said.

Reznick helped her to her feet as she began to take her first few tentative steps. She felt dizzy. She walked a few yards from her bed unaided. Then to the end of the high dependency unit. On the fifth day she was strong enough to walk unaided out of the unit down the hospital hallway.

Reznick was by her side the whole way.

Afterward, she said, "I want fresh air, Dad."

Reznick took his daughter by the arm and, along with a nurse, they walked the hospital grounds. The hot summer breeze brushed against Lauren's pale-white skin. She closed her eyes, enjoying the sensation.

The nurse left them together.

Reznick sat down with his daughter on a wooden bench, holding her hand. It was like a new beginning. They sat in beautiful silence as the sun shone and the birds sang.

Every time he thought about it, he realized how lucky she had been. In the blink of an eye, she could have been gone. Taken from him.

Lauren seemed to sense that he was brooding over the issue.

Reznick put his arm around her. "Make sure you don't catch cold."

"I'm fine, Dad. I'm back."

"I know you are, honey. But we need to take it nice and easy for a while."

Lauren nodded and rested her head on his shoulder. "I understand."

"What about any headaches? Vision altered in any way?"

"It's good. No different from before."

"Tell me again . . . What's the last thing you remember before the accident?"

Lauren sighed. "I remember . . . stepping into the crosswalk. I had the walk signal. I started across the intersection. I remember I was wearing my new running shoes. And I had my headphones on."

Reznick pulled her closer. "It's alright."

"I remember . . . I do remember a lady crying, looking down at me. Then . . . I remember hearing your voice."

"In the hospital?"

"Yeah . . . you were talking to me, weren't you?"

"I was praying, mostly. Praying that you would hear me."

"I did hear you."

"I thought I was talking to myself."

Lauren shook her head. "I heard you. I didn't know how far away you were. But I heard you."

"There's a long road ahead. But we're going to get there."

"Sure."

"And you've got a period of rehabilitation and recuperation."

"I'm fine, Dad, honest."

"I'll get your room done up nice."

Lauren groaned. "Dad . . . that's sweet."

"But?"

"But . . . I want to go back to New York. I want to finish my internship."

Reznick hadn't expected that answer. "Honey, you really need to take it easy right now."

"It's important to me, Dad."

"I know it is. But let's get you well again."

"Dad, I understand you're worried."

"Damn right I'm worried. I'm worried you might get run over again. New York drivers are crazy."

"You should take an Uber. Now that is something else."

"That's my point." Reznick shook his head. He couldn't believe his daughter was considering heading straight back to New York. "I really, really think it would be best if you took the next month off. We could spend some time together."

Lauren smiled. "I'd love that. Really, I would."

"Rockland in the summer."

"It is quiet. And beautiful."

"And it's home."

Lauren sighed. "It'll always be my home. But I think it would be best for me to get back to New York. I am feeling much better. Trust me. And my internship. I'm learning so much."

"I think you need space and time to come to terms with this."

"I'm fine, Dad."

Reznick shook his head and smiled.

"What?"

"You remind me of your mom. She was so headstrong it was unbelievable."

"What about you? You're the worst."

Reznick smiled. "Point taken."

"Dad . . . did they find him? The guy who ran me down."

"I think the NYPD has a lead. So that's good."

"A lead? I would have thought it would be pretty straightforward to identify the driver," Lauren said.

"You would think. But these things take time . . . New York is a big, crazy city. You know that, right?"

"I do."

Reznick sighed. "So you want to go back to New York? Do you mean in a week or so?"

Lauren shook her head. "I want to go back now. The doctor said they'll be finished with the last tests tonight. If I'm all clear, I can go back."

Reznick said nothing, already worried about her being back in the hustle, bustle, and nonstop frenzy that was living in New York. "Where are you staying? The same place?"

"I'm still sharing a room in Lenox Hill, on East Sixty-Ninth, with another girl from the publishing house. She's been freaking out while I've been in the hospital. I need to text her to let her know I'm out of danger."

Reznick made a mental note. "Is it OK if I visit? I've gotten familiar with that area in the last week or so."

Lauren shrugged. "I guess. But I work long hours."

"We'll arrange something."

"Weekends are best."

"It's a deal. Look, I know you're an adult and all grown up, but is there nothing I can say or do to persuade you otherwise? Maybe just to hold off and stay here for a few weeks?"

"No, Dad. I want to get back to New York. The sooner I put this behind me, the sooner I can move on."

While Reznick escorted his daughter back to bed in a new ward, where she was going to be monitored for a few more hours, his cell phone rang.

He recognized the number on the caller ID as that of Detective Acosta. "I need to take this, honey."

Lauren's eyes were already heavy. She gave a gentle nod.

Reznick went out into the corridor and took the call. "Yeah, Reznick speaking."

"Hey, Jon," she said. "Is it OK to talk?"

"Go ahead."

"First, I'm sorry your daughter had to be moved from a great hospital like Weill Cornell in her condition. That must've been tough to deal with."

"That was a setback. But she was moved. And now I'm pleased to say she's making a good recovery. Astonishingly so."

"Jon, that's fantastic news. Very good to hear." Acosta sighed. "I've got some news too. I thought I'd share it with you in case you were trying to contact him."

"Contact who?"

A deep sigh. "It's Tom. Tom Callaghan of the *Post*."

Reznick's mind flashed back to his conversation with Callaghan in the bar. He wondered if his story about Brutka's family was about to run. "I'd forgotten all about Tom. He seemed pretty confident that the paper would be running with the story. Has it been published?"

A silence stretched between them. "So you managed to speak to him?" Acosta asked.

"Yeah. We met for a drink. I shared what I knew. And he was pretty forthcoming too. Very disturbing picture he painted of Brutka's family. Far worse than anyone realized."

Acosta sighed long and hard.

"Don't tell me the paper has gone cold on the story."

Acosta remained quiet.

Reznick sensed something was wrong. "What is it? What's the matter?"

"Tom is dead, Jon."

Reznick's blood ran cold. "What happened?"

"He blew his brains out in his apartment a little over an hour ago."

Forty

Acosta was staring at the gruesome photographs that had just down-loaded to her laptop. Callaghan's blood-spattered corpse. Brain matter exposed. The back of his head in pieces. She felt a terrible aching sadness wash over her. He was a good guy. A smart guy. She had known him for years. But she had been the one who had turned his attention, once again, to Brutka after the diplomat had knocked down and nearly killed Lauren Reznick. She had been the one who had mentioned the name of Jon Reznick, putting him in touch with Callaghan.

For a few moments, she castigated herself, thinking *if only*. If only she hadn't called him about Brutka. From that call, Callaghan wanted to know more. He had already unearthed a catalogue of terrifying incidents linked to the diplomat, not to mention Brutka's grandfather's dark past. It was an obsession for Callaghan, according to detectives on the case who had interviewed the journalist's friends and family. An obsession that would lead to his horrible death.

Acosta gazed at the photo, heart breaking. The wound was cata-strophic. But it didn't make sense. The pictures made it look like he had put the gun in his mouth and blown his brains out. But she couldn't believe that this was the same journalist she had fed information to for years. The same guy she had met in the Old Town Bar, a favorite haunt of Callaghan's. He was, like all great journalists, doggedly determined in the pursuit of a story. But suddenly he decides to end it all?

It didn't make sense. Not one bit. The man she knew was funny. Well adjusted. And dogged in his determination. She hadn't known he owned a gun. New Jersey had some of the tightest gun laws in the US. He would have needed to have a justifiable need to carry a gun. Maybe being a journalist working on sensitive stories would have allowed him a handgun permit. That said, maybe he had just bought a gun on the black market. It wasn't difficult.

Acosta logged out, shut the screen, and closed her eyes.

She felt sick. Painfully sick. An emptiness within. Gnawing at her.

Acosta had enjoyed drinks, chats, and coffee with Callaghan over the better part of a decade. He had talked about his wife and their three kids at their home in Jersey City. He never appeared to be down or depressed. But what did that mean? He could've been hiding some acute mental health problems she wasn't aware of.

She had spoken to Captain Arnie Strome in New Jersey and had informed him that Callaghan had been compiling an investigation on Brutka: the corruption, the violence, and the sleaze, set against the background of geopolitics. And she passed on the notes she had from her meetings with Callaghan.

The moment she heard Callaghan was dead, her instincts told her it wasn't suicide. She knew people who would want him dead. And none more so than Brutka. Forensics was still going over the place. But she knew deep down that it was no suicide.

She didn't have proof. She just knew.

Callaghan had needed to be silenced.

Acosta could see that Brutka had the motive. But she knew the diplomat wouldn't have done it himself. It would have been subcontracted. Perhaps the hit had been organized at the foreign government level. Had Brutka used a private security firm from abroad? Maybe a member of the Ukrainian crime underworld in the United States.

The biggest problem was that Brutka was untouchable. He was being protected. And the State Department had, whether they liked it or not, given Brutka carte blanche to get rid of a journalist who threatened to expose the venality of the diplomat. That was the only logical conclusion. Where would the State Department's line in the sand be drawn?

But there was something else that was bothering her.

She had been the one who had pointed Jon Reznick in Callaghan's direction. She had gotten them together. Reznick no doubt would have passed on the details about his daughter being run down by Brutka, and Callaghan would have shared some of what he knew with Reznick.

Had the meeting been compromised? Had Callaghan been under surveillance by those about to do the hit? Had Reznick's presence with Callaghan alerted Brutka or those close to him that the journalist was one step closer to snaring the diplomat?

The bottom line was that Acosta did not know. It was all supposition.

But she couldn't escape the idea that she might've been—indirectly at least—responsible for Callaghan being murdered in cold blood.

Acosta felt pangs of guilt. She leaned back in her seat, staring out the window. She knew she was beating herself up over something that wasn't her fault. Whoever killed Callaghan was going to kill him anyway. Then again, perhaps she had hastened the man's death.

Whatever way she tried to look at it, Acosta felt numb, knowing deep down she had played a part in all this. The reverberations from decisions, the choices people made, echoed down the line. They affected other people.

Her phone rang.

"Yeah, Acosta speaking."

"Isabella, it's Arnie in New Jersey."

"Arnie . . . what's the latest?"

"Slow. Isabella, I wanted you to know something. Thought I'd give you a heads-up."

Acosta felt her insides tighten. "A heads-up?"

Arnie sighed. "We've been checking Callaghan's phone . . . Your number is coming up. Just wanted you to know."

Acosta closed her eyes.

"Forensics has given me a preliminary report, and we're working on a couple of angles."

"Like I said before, Arnie, he called once a week."

"And the last time you spoke?"

"It was about Brutka. I mentioned something about the hit-and-run of the jogger, Lauren Reznick."

Strome sighed. "You and I both know that might be problematic, Isabella."

"It is what it is."

"Unfortunately, it's not that straightforward."

Acosta got a sick feeling deep down in her gut.

"Isabella, I've known you a long, long time, since we used to work together."

"Sure."

"And I've always been straight with you. I like to be up-front."

"So do I."

"Well, we've got another problem."

"What kind of problem?"

"I've been shown footage of you with Jon Reznick, the father of the jogger."

Acosta took a few moments to process the information. She wondered what the hell was going on. "Footage? What kind of footage?"

"Surveillance footage."

Acosta lowered her voice. "I beg your pardon?"

"The Feds were keeping an eye on Reznick intermittently."

"And I was photographed with him?"

"It's video footage of you drinking together."

Acosta felt as if she were slipping into a twilight zone, unable to extricate herself. "I'm sorry, Arnie, am I being implicated in some way?"

"Reznick was also photographed at a bar in the Flatiron District, by an undercover Fed. Old Town Bar. We both know the one."

"So you think I put Reznick and Callaghan in touch, is that it?"

Strome sighed. "Don't be so defensive, Isabella. We're just trying to piece together the sequence of events."

"I might've mentioned in passing that Callaghan was a good guy. A guy I trusted. Reznick was interested and wanted to speak to him. It would've been easy to get his number from the *Post*, but I passed it on."

Strome fell silent.

"I felt sorry for Reznick. I still do. His daughter was the victim. And there was nothing he could do. It's a mess. I know it, you know it, everyone involved goddamn knows it. Brutka is worse than any of us knew. Bad to the fucking bone. The sooner that fucker is out of the city, the better."

Strome cleared his throat. "I know—"

"He's wealthy, he's connected, and he's being protected by people in high places. And he's hiding behind diplomatic immunity."

"I'm sorry to bring this all up . . . but you know how it is. I wanted to let you know."

"You had to ask. Speaking of which, have you got anything about this hit? It is a hit, I'm assuming."

"Too early to say . . . but I believe whoever did this wanted us to think that Callaghan, who didn't have a gun, didn't have access to a gun, somehow acquired a gun illegally on the black market and blew his brains out."

Acosta's instincts were correct. Callaghan didn't own a gun. "What about surveillance footage?"

"Nothing. All we have is a voice captured on audio, part of the surveillance system Callaghan had rigged up. From within the apartment. It's something. But it's got us scratching our heads."

"A voice?"

"Isabella, you've shared intel with me on numerous occasions. And you've been forthright on this. But I can't say too much else."

"Gimme a break, Arnie. What kind of voice? Whose voice?"

Strome sighed. "I think I've said enough. Take care."

Acosta went to the restroom and locked herself in for twenty minutes. She needed some time alone. To think. To get her head straight. She realized that being photographed with Reznick drinking could be construed in the wrong way. She had clearly crossed an ethical line. She had provided Reznick with information. And that had led to Reznick somehow finding out the full identity of the diplomat.

She couldn't have known what would transpire. And she also couldn't have foreseen that Reznick would go after the guy, nor could she have guessed the consequences for Callaghan. To complicate things further, the Feds had been keeping an eye on Reznick. The guy who worked for them as a consultant.

Damn, what a mess.

Now she had become enmeshed, no matter how loosely, in the assassination of a prominent journalist. It didn't look good. In fact it looked like she had broken the code of what was expected of a NYPD officer. She imagined what the NYPD's Internal Affairs Bureau would have to say about that. Her handling of information. Her after-work drinks with Reznick. Tipping him off about Callaghan's work. And a digital trail leading back to the dead journalist's phone.

She wondered why she had gone out on such a limb for Reznick. Was it because she felt sorry for him, for what had happened to his daughter? Did she have feelings for Reznick? Was that it? She did like him. A lot. She liked the way he looked. The way he talked. Even the way he didn't give a shit about rules and authority. That appealed to her. But maybe it wasn't that. Was it that she felt Brutka's victims deserved a better outcome? The fact of the matter was she had gotten too close. Not only to Reznick but also to poor Callaghan. But she wasn't the first cop to speak to journalists. And certainly not the first cop to want to even up the score with the bad guys.

Her cell phone rang as she sat in the stall, snapping her out of her morbid thoughts.

"Acosta," she answered.

A beat. "Ma'am, it's Sergeant Lopez, front desk. I have someone looking for you."

Acosta sighed. "Gimme a break. I'm kinda busy."

"He's not taking no for an answer."

"Fine, who is it?"

"He says his name is Jon Reznick."

Forty-One

Reznick followed a rookie cop up to the second floor of the Nineteenth Precinct. The young patrol officer led him through a maze of dingy corridors until they reached a windowless interview room. Inside was Acosta. She looked tired and drawn. He could see this business with Brutka was taking its toll on her. He knew the feeling.

Acosta stared at him and shook her head. "Jesus, Jon," she said, "what is it with you? I thought we'd seen the last of you."

"Just wanna talk."

The young cop said, "Anything else, ma'am?"

Acosta shook her head and thanked the cop, who shut the door behind him. "How's your daughter?"

"Alive. Talking."

Acosta smiled. "Thank God." She sighed. "Jon, everything has gone to shit. Callaghan is dead. I don't know . . . The whole thing. It's a mess."

Reznick nodded. "That's why I'm here."

"This is not your fight."

"Isn't it?"

"Jon, I don't think we should meet like this. I know you're trying to help. But this is just fucking crazy. I thought I'd just be introducing you to Callaghan. The next thing I know, Callaghan—a lovely guy, a very fine journalist—has blown his brains out."

"You know as well as I do who's behind this."

Acosta sighed. "There are other aspects to this."

"Like what?"

"I've been informed that the Feds had you under surveillance. And they spotted us drinking together."

Reznick took a few moments to process that. "So why are you telling me this?"

"I was the one who put you in touch with Callaghan. And now Callaghan is dead. It doesn't look too good from the FBI's perspective."

"You're in the shit because of this?"

"Damn right I'm in the shit because of this."

"I'm sorry if this has landed you in trouble."

"It's a complete mess. And because the Feds had you under surveillance, my little chat with you at the Bentley bar was no doubt observed as well."

Reznick wondered if the surveillance had been green-lighted by Meyerstein. He wondered if he was reading this right. He knew Meyerstein. Or at least he thought he did. And he couldn't imagine her doing that. It would be a terrible intrusion into his privacy. Especially with his daughter in a coma at the time. But what if this had been green-lighted by the New York FBI? That was certainly possible.

The more he thought about it, the more he began to realize that this had been instigated by the FBI. But the situation had been compounded by the State Department, who also wanted someone to keep a close eye on him after his run-ins with the diplomat.

Nevertheless, Reznick felt more than a little betrayed. It was as if everything he had done for and with the Feds had been for nothing. The trust between them was broken. Their bond gone. But in fairness to Meyerstein and the FBI, it was his reckless disregard of their requests and his actions in going after the diplomat which had sparked the whole chain of events. *His* actions. He would have to take some responsibility for his actions. He needed to face up to that.

Reznick began to pace the room. He didn't want to reveal to Acosta what Callaghan had told him about Brutka's grandfather. At least not now. "Tell me about Callaghan."

"Jon, I've been very forthcoming . . . I think I've said enough."

"You know something, don't you?"

"Jon, gimme a break. I'm glad your daughter is on the mend."

"Callaghan's death is not a coincidence. You know it. I know it. This is linked to him investigating Brutka. Am I right?"

Acosta showed her hands as if declining to get involved. "I've already said too much. Besides, I've got paperwork to do. A mountain of goddamn paperwork."

"I am asking you just this one thing."

"What is it with you? Your daughter is recovering now. Surely that's all that matters."

Reznick shook his head. "That's where you're wrong. It's not all that matters. What about Callaghan? What about his family? What about what Callaghan told me about the young women being terrorized by this low-life scumbag? With his prostitutes, expensive suits, and criminal millionaire lifestyle."

"Try billionaire lifestyle."

"Whatever. Brutka is free to carry on doing this. He's wealthy. He's connected. He's powerful. And he needs to be stopped."

"Are you going to stop him?"

"Well, someone has to. A journalist investigating Brutka has been murdered. The FBI wants Brutka gone. So do you. So does the NYPD. But he's still out there, walking our streets."

"Jon, you can't take matters into your own hands. We don't want a war."

"My daughter isn't out of the woods. The doctors are amazed at her recovery. But they say she may still suffer flashbacks, panic attacks, and all sorts of mental health issues for years to come. They haven't manifested themselves so far. But they might. So, it's not over. Not over for her. And sure as hell not over for me."

Acosta sighed. "The detective in charge of this case is a good guy. If Brutka ordered Callaghan's murder or is linked in some way, trust me, he'll nail him."

"Whatever the cops do, they won't get anywhere near Brutka, you can rest assured of that. You need to get smart. You need to get down and dirty with fuckers like that. I need to know what you know. You know something. Tell me what it is. And I'll be out of your hair."

Acosta shook her head. "Jon, you're driving me crazy."

"One favor. It's all I ask."

Acosta sighed, eyes closed.

"What can you tell me? I'm begging you. Give me something. Where did it happen?"

"Callaghan's apartment was in Jersey City. Nice place on the waterfront."

"Tell me about the weapon."

"Glock, apparently."

"Was it his gun?"

"No. He almost certainly never owned a gun. Very anti-gun, especially semiautomatics. There was no gun registered in his name. If you read any of his articles, you'd know."

"What evidence do you have? Give me something else."

"I think I've said enough, Jon. I wish the best for you and your daughter."

Reznick stared at Acosta. "Isabella, I know you want to help me. I also know you know more than you're letting on. I know how it works."

"Jon, you're killing me."

"This fucker has to be brought down."

"I'm not disputing that. But it needs to happen according to the law."

"Gimme a break. Isabella, are you saying there were no clues at the scene, no evidence whatsoever?"

"I don't know why I'm even speaking to you."

"Because you want that fucker off the streets. Isn't that what your brother, Diego, would have wanted? If he was in Delta, I'll guarantee if he was in my shoes he'd be asking the same questions."

"Jon, I know from my brother what you guys are capable of. I know the lengths you will go to. I understand that pushing boundaries and breaking laws isn't your concern. But it is mine. I work within the law. I'm a police officer."

"Give me one final thing and I'm out of here. Tell me one thing. And I'm gone."

Acosta rolled her eyes. "There is one thing . . ."

"What?"

"There was a voice."

"A voice? What do you mean?"

"A voice was heard in the apartment. It was recorded. Believed to be the killer."

Reznick pondered that. "Callaghan's apartment was under surveillance?"

"I don't know. Home security system picked it up. I do know they're running voice analysis at Forensics."

Reznick smiled. "Isabella, I owe you one."

"Jon . . . one final thing."

"What?"

Acosta stared at Reznick long and hard. "Just be careful."

Reznick left the station and headed out onto the sultry streets. He took out his cell phone and called his hacker friend. He felt the sweat on the back of his neck as he waited for a response. He noticed he was standing opposite the Permanent Mission of Russia to the UN on East Sixty-Seventh Street, diagonally across the street from the Nineteenth Precinct. Cameras watched the street from behind the black iron fence.

The hacker answered five rings later. "Mr. R., how's your daughter?"

"It's early yet, but she's recovering."

"That is good news, man. God bless her."

"Thanks. Appreciate it."

The hacker sighed. "So . . . what's Mr. R. onto now?"

"Things are heating up here in New York, in more ways than one."

"What do you mean?"

"A guy I was introduced to, a journalist, Tom Callaghan, is dead. Apparently blew his brains out in his apartment in Jersey City."

"Whoa! And this is linked to the diplomat?"

Reznick shielded his eyes from the sun. "I don't know for sure."

"Shit."

"What I know is that the New Jersey cops are investigating this death. And I believe that there was a voice recorded at the scene."

"A voice? How?"

"That's the thing. I don't know."

"So is this the voice of the murderer?"

"Possible. I want to know more about this voice."

"And you're sure this is linked to that diplomat?"

"It has to be. First, it's one hell of a coincidence for him to take his life only a few days after meeting me face-to-face to discuss Brutka's latest serious offense. Second, this guy has been working on a major investigation into Brutka and all his criminal activities."

"Motherfucker."

"So, my question is, my friend, can you help?"

"Damn right I can."

Forty-Two

Brutka sniffed the cocaine residue in his nostril as he rode in the back seat of his Bentley on his way to an Upper East Side restaurant. He felt good. His mind was whirring faster and faster. He felt giddy. And then he felt euphoric.

He pulled out his cell and decided to make a call.

"How are you this evening, Grandfather?"

"I feel OK." The old man's voice was slightly strained.

"I haven't got much time," Brutka said, "but I just wanted you to know that the man who was hanging around . . ."

"Callaghan."

"Yes. You won't be seeing Callaghan again. He's been taken care of."

"Forever?"

"Trust me, he won't be back."

A silence stretched between them before the old man began to sob. "Aleksander, to have someone who cares so much for me, an old, old man, is something I cherish. I will not forget you."

"And I won't forget you, Grandfather. Your sacrifices. Your courage."

"We are bonded by blood, Aleksander. Forever."

The private Madison dining room within the Mark hotel had been reserved for Aleksander Brutka and his political attaché, along with two bodyguards, sitting at a table in the corner. He tucked into his veal Milanese with mashed potatoes and sautéed spinach, while his colleague enjoyed North Atlantic black sea bass with hand-cut french fries. The two security guys ordered the Mark cheeseburger with black truffle dressing.

Brutka's mood was leveling out. He felt less crazy as the cocaine high washed over him. He smiled politely as the waiters observed impeccable grace while they served and poured the $3,500 bottle of Domaine de la Romanée-Conti Grand Cru 2012 for him. He tasted the wine, then indicated for the waiter to pour a glass for each of them.

He sat quietly until the waiter was out of view before he took his next sip. He savored the taste. He loved the good things in life. Savile Row suits, fine wines, Bentleys, Rolex watches, prime Manhattan real estate.

Brutka made small talk with his aide about the humidity in New York, but also talked about the views from his penthouse pool over the city. His aide listened attentively, occasionally giving a polite and respectful nod. But Brutka sensed that his aide, a close personal friend and political attaché at the Ukraine mission at the UN, wanted to talk to him about important matters. As if he was just waiting for the right time to broach the subject.

Brutka smiled at his friend. "Do you like my new suit?"

The aide dabbed his mouth with his napkin as he assessed the fine threads Brutka was wearing. "When did you get that, Aleksander?"

"I was measured up about a month ago. I've put on some weight, so I needed to get a new cut."

"It's impeccable."

"Thank you. Got a dozen suits, cashmere and silk, flown in from London."

"Navy suits you, sir."

"Every man must have a good navy suit."

After the main course, Brutka ordered the pecan tart with ice cream, as did his aide. The two security guys passed on dessert.

Brutka ate in quiet contemplation. He sat quietly until the waiters refilled their glasses with more red wine and excused themselves. Then the conversation began in earnest.

The aide took a large gulp of wine, then sighed quietly. "I hope you don't mind me raising a couple of issues this evening."

Brutka shrugged. "Have you ever known me to object to you or anyone raising an issue with me personally?"

"No, I have not. And I appreciate that."

Brutka wasn't really in the mood for deep discussions. He would much rather enjoy his drink and the beautiful food and surroundings. "Is it important?"

"I believe so. There are two things that I would like to draw your attention to. And when I speak, I speak with nothing but the utmost respect, as it is indeed an honor to serve you and our country."

"Thank you."

"As a trusted political adviser, but also as your friend, I believe that it might be worth reconsidering our current position . . ."

Brutka lifted his glass of wine and inhaled the aromas of blackberry and dark fruits and the rich earth it came from. "What current position?"

The aide sighed. "Aleksander, I have daily, sometimes twice-daily, contacts with diplomats from all countries, you understand?"

"Of course."

"But recently, in the last day or two, I have been approached by people I respect, people within the FBI, suggesting that it might be for the best if you excused yourself from diplomatic service for a little while, perhaps eighteen months or so."

Brutka was quiet for a few moments as he contemplated the request. He was irked by the suggestion. It was interesting that the request had come from back channels within the FBI. But he didn't answer to them. Never had. His connections were embedded deep within the so-called shadow government, the coalition of politicians, wealthy industrialists, and the military-industrial complex that operated under the radar, pulling strings to shape foreign policy.

"Why would I do that? I am working on behalf of the President of Ukraine and our people. I work very hard for them. And our interests on the world stage."

"Indeed you do, sir."

"Besides, the State Department has assured me that Reznick and his daughter are out of the way."

"The fact that the FBI spoke to me directly, as a back channel, is important. They clearly believe, and I absolutely agree with them, that this would be a smart move on your part. But not only that, I think the approach from the FBI shows a willingness on their part to understand your role, so there has been a slight change in their position."

"In what way?"

"They suggested that having you return home for a couple of years, maybe eighteen months, could be classified as returning to Ukraine for medical treatment, perhaps."

Brutka picked up his glass and gazed at the blackcurrant-red liquid. "What, don't they have hospitals in New York?"

The aide smiled. "Of course they do, Aleksander. But I believe that this solution would allow you to continue your work back in Kiev, while avoiding a damaging spat with an American intelligence agency. They also said that if heading back to Ukraine is not possible for whatever reason, they would accept—and this is a red line for them—that you could stay in the United States, but outside New York City. They suggested that a sideways move to the Ukrainian embassy in Washington, DC would work for them."

Brutka sighed. "While it is of course prudent to take advice and guidance from intelligence, you must understand my work. My work at the United Nations and my presence in New York are vital to our interests. DC is fine. I liked Georgetown personally. But you know what? It's not New York. I live here. I like it. It has everything I need."

"Aleksander, a move to DC would take the heat off. You have to admit there have been several rather unsettling incidents."

"Listen to me very carefully. The fact that the State Department says one thing and the FBI says another tells me all I need to know about their conflicting agendas. That is their problem. But they do not have the final say about whether or not I stay here. Let's be quite clear on that."

The aide leaned in close. "Indeed, sir. I'm well aware of that. But the mood I'm detecting is that they want to help you defuse any potential fallout from this accident."

"That's very big of them."

"Sir, please, the FBI are not to be trifled with. The Director himself has sided with Assistant Director Meyerstein. What's so bad about DC?"

Brutka took a long gulp of the wine and closed his eyes as he savored the grape while pondering his position. He felt anger begin to rise in him. He had only just dealt with the difficult situation regarding Tom Callaghan, which was now resolved. But he was still having to listen to advice from aides that conflicted with his worldview. He pointed at the man across from him. "Now listen to me. I have heard more than enough. Am I not a pragmatic man who listens?"

"Absolutely, sir. Pragmatism in diplomacy is indeed a virtue. I would say a necessity."

"And I'm open to suggestions, within reason. The problem is, my friend, I don't answer to the FBI. I answer to my father. And to the people of Ukraine. Our country requires representation by me and others who will fight and argue for our country and its people. We need influence at the highest levels of government. And that's what I provide."

"Sir, I don't believe staying in New York is for the best."

"With respect, I do." Brutka sipped some more wine. "This is quite delicious."

"Sir, what should I say to the people who approached me?"

"Just say that I'm giving it serious consideration. And leave it at that."

The aide nodded. "Yes, that should work. It would be good to give them your decision."

"Let's not get ahead of ourselves. Now, what's the second thing? You said there were two points."

"Reznick."

Brutka felt himself tapping his foot instinctively. "What about him?"

"He's back in town."

Brutka stared at his aide and leaned closer. "I'm sorry, I don't follow. I thought his daughter was transferred to a wonderful hospital in lovely Maine. The last I heard he was in fucking Maine looking after his fucking daughter."

"He's back. That's what I heard."

"Mr. Reznick? The father?"

The aide nodded.

"Now why do you think he's back in New York? He doesn't work here, does he?"

"No."

"And he has no business interests here?"

The aide shook his head.

"We need to find out where he is."

"That can be arranged. Anything else?"

"This needs to end."

"What do you want me to do, sir?"

"Figure out how Reznick can be taken out once and for all."

Forty-Three

The Brooklyn Diner on West Fifty-Seventh Street was virtually empty. He settled into a quiet booth and ordered a breakfast of scrambled eggs, toast, and black coffee. Lauren had flown down to New York with him. He had helped her get settled back into the apartment she shared with a fellow publishing intern. He wondered if she wasn't trying to do too much too soon. But he was also relieved that she was taking her first positive steps on the road to recovery.

Lauren was still on medication for anxiety after the hit-and-run, but she was already planning to return to her internship at the publishing house.

Reznick knew he was fortunate. His daughter could have been taken from him. The induced coma that had been meant to relieve the swelling on her brain had taken its toll. She spoke slower, as if the connections in her brain were still not fully mended from the accident. She still suffered migraines. And he knew she was waking up in the night sweating, reliving the accident over and over again.

The scars were real. Mental as well as physical.

But stopping Brutka was about so much more than just his daughter. It was clear that Aleksander Brutka's malign influence extended not only to the highest echelons of the American government but was facilitated by his spectacular wealth—he could buy anyone or anything he wanted. Callaghan's death was no suicide. How convenient. It not only got rid of an investigative journalist who was closing in on Brutka, but it also sent a message to those who got too close to his world. *Stay away or else you'll end up the same way.* Not too subtle. But effective.

Reznick knew how hit jobs like that worked. It would have just been a simple matter of subcontracting to an individual or more likely a security firm that employed mercenaries or assassins. Anyone could be neutralized if the price was right. He knew all about the Right Sector and some of the shadowy groups and people aligned with them. For some in Ukraine, the group only represented a patriotic strand of opinion. But for others—quite a few others—it was a vehicle for extreme nationalism.

It was perhaps not surprising that Callaghan had unearthed links to the fascist elements of Ukraine, none greater than Brutka's grandfather, who'd been instrumental in massacres during the Second World War.

A Nazi collaborator. A murderer.

Reznick's mind flashed back to the grainy black-and-white photo of Ilad Brutka. Ingrained in his mind were the frightened eyes of the naked woman, a rifle pressed to her head, Ilad Brutka parading about shortly before, no doubt, she was butchered.

What was also reprehensible was that the United States had allowed men and women like him to disappear, either through integrating them into America with false names and identities or letting them live out their lives in South America.

Reznick looked at his food and realized he was no longer hungry. Instead, he drank his coffee, then dialed Meyerstein's cell phone number.

"Jon," Meyerstein said, "nice to hear from you again. What's the latest on Lauren? I've been thinking about her."

Reznick gulped the rest of the coffee and signaled for a refill. "She's OK. For now, anyway. So much so that she decided to head back to New York."

"Already? Has she recovered so soon? That's wonderful news."

"She's still a bit fragile, but she's back in her apartment. It's going to take time."

"Give her my regards. So let me take a wild guess . . . I'm assuming you might be back in New York too."

Reznick smiled. "Very astute observation."

"I think we need to move on from this, Jon. Lauren is recovering. Let's be thankful."

"I am, trust me."

"I'm worried, Jon."

"Worried? Why?"

"I'm worried that what has happened has clouded your judgment."

"This is about more than Lauren now."

"Jon, you're letting this get personal."

"Martha, how long have we known each other?"

Meyerstein sighed.

"For years, right?"

"That's correct."

"I just want to say that I'm very surprised and more than a little annoyed that the FBI has had me under surveillance."

Meyerstein was quiet.

"Did you authorize this?"

Meyerstein sighed again. "No, it wasn't me."

"Who was it?"

"Jon, you know I can't divulge that."

"I've busted my ass on investigations for you guys. And that's the thanks I get? Is that where we are, Martha?"

"Jon, you're not thinking straight. You're not seeing the big picture."

A waitress smiled and walked past. Reznick waited until she was out of earshot.

"Are you still there?" Meyerstein asked.

"I'm still here. Listen, I see the big picture all too clearly. And I don't like what I see."

"The State Department has to operate on a grand scale, taking the views and concerns of foreign countries, and our security interests in them, into account."

"Which translates as, if we start throwing out Ukrainian undesirables, our relationship with Kiev, the President, and lucrative arms sales, technology sales, and future oil exploration could be jeopardized, yeah?"

"Jon, you have broken the law several times while in New York."

"Are you kidding me? I've broken the law several times? What about the State Department's pal, Aleksander Brutka? That fucker is out of control. He's dangerous. And he's going to get more people killed."

"That's enough, Jon."

"Martha, you know what sort of person I am. You know how I operate. And yeah, occasionally I cross the line. But it's only in the pursuit of the bad guys. You know that."

"The law is the law."

"Except when you're a billionaire playboy diplomat with serious connections to the State Department."

Meyerstein sighed. "Please back off, Jon. Just be thankful that Lauren is on the mend."

"I am thankful. And I'm going to pray for her. But I can't rest until that fucker is gone."

"Jon, what the hell are you talking about?"

"You know what I'm talking about. You know as well as I do what this guy has done. Leaving Lauren in a coma was just part of a pattern. A long line of stuff. The guy is dangerous."

"You need to move on."

"I will. Eventually."

Meyerstein went quiet as if contemplating what to say next.

"There's one final thing I want to talk to you about. Actually, a couple of things. First, does the name Tom Callaghan mean anything to you?"

"Yes, it does."

"Then you know that he's dead. Shot himself, apparently."

Meyerstein sighed. "I know where you're going with this."

"Do you? Do you know he was compiling a major investigation into not only Brutka but also the father and the grandfather?"

"What?"

"Martha, I don't know if there's not enough sharing between agencies, or if this particular thing is buttoned up tight by Callaghan's paper, but he was not only going to blow Brutka out of the water but had evidence of the grandfather's Nazi atrocities. Brutka's grandfather. He showed me a picture of the grandfather from the war."

"Jon, none of this is making sense."

"He told me that he had been working with the Simon Wiesenthal Center on this."

"These allegations . . . Who else knows about them?"

"I'm guessing only Callaghan, who's now dead, his editor, the Simon Wiesenthal Center, and that's probably it."

Meyerstein was quiet again. "Are you positive this is the story Callaghan planned to publish?"

"I shared with him what had happened to Lauren, and he let me in on what he knew about the grandfather's Nazi past."

"The grandfather—did Callaghan give a name?"

"Ilad Brutka. According to Callaghan, he was smuggled into America by the OSS under the name Bud Smith. Ran a hotel in Vermont, I think he said, a couple of them."

Meyerstein sighed long and hard. "In light of what you've just told me, I need to speak to a friend of mine at Justice. She's in charge of Human Rights and Special Prosecutions."

"Thank you. Finally."

"Leave it to me. This we can't let slide."

"But let's not forget this grandson. We need to stop this guy."

"Jon, I feel like I'm constantly putting out fires since you started going after Brutka. There's only so much I can do to protect you from the fallout."

Reznick heard the veiled warning in Meyerstein's words.

"I want you to be safe," she said. "And I want you to get on with your life. Lauren too. But you need to back off now."

"Martha, there's only so long I can turn a blind eye. My daughter. And now Callaghan."

Reznick ended the call. He wondered if perhaps he was being unfair to Meyerstein. She was only doing her job. A high-level, powerful intelligence job. And he was making her life hell. He pondered that as he ate a leisurely breakfast, washed down with two more black coffees and a couple of Dexedrine. She was a woman he very much admired and liked. Probably more than he would care to admit. He sometimes found himself thinking about her, especially when he was back home alone in Rockland with time on his hands. He imagined what she was doing at that moment in DC. He thought of the handful of times she had met him in his hometown. It was always about work. He didn't mind. But he sensed they were growing closer together. He hadn't wanted to get involved with anyone since his wife had died. Instead he had buried himself in work and booze. His work with the FBI, and with Meyerstein in particular, had given him a sense of purpose. He had begun to think about moving on. Extricating himself from the ghosts of his past. More than anything, Meyerstein was someone who conveyed integrity, honor, and a steely determination to tough out the bad days. She had given his life meaning again. He didn't want to throw that away. Their friendship was strictly business, but it seemed as if she understood his motivations and actions, even if she didn't always entirely agree with how he went about things.

He began to consider why he was taking such a reckless path. His daughter was beginning the process of healing physically and was hopefully going to make a full recovery in time. But here he was, back in New York.

Did he see himself as his daughter's protector? Maybe he did. Was that a bad thing? The fact was, no one could protect their loved ones from getting hurt. Either emotionally or physically. Lauren needed to live her life. Maybe he needed to think about moving on, as Meyerstein had said. She had a point. But something about Brutka, his manner, and his violence against women had left a mark on Reznick. It was something about justice. About being held accountable. Was that what was driving him? Then again, maybe it was just raw revenge. The chance to bring this guy down. Maybe only then, when Brutka was off the streets, would Reznick be able to sleep soundly.

Reznick's senses began to switch on as the Dexedrine kicked in. He felt more alert. Sped up. He looked out of the diner window as the cars, trucks, and people zoomed by. The never-ending buzz and energy of the city. A workman stopped for a drink of water, wiping the sweat from his brow as the sun beat down.

The diner wasn't far from the crosswalk where Lauren had nearly been killed. He imagined a world without his beautiful daughter. His life wouldn't be worth living if she were gone.

He wondered whether he should take her out for the day. Maybe get her mind off things. But what if she was being watched by the Ukrainians? What if they had a security team in place, monitoring his movements? What if they found out where Lauren lived?

He felt his mood darken as he played out the scenarios in his head. He needed to let his daughter live her life, without him hovering over her. Life was hard. It wasn't fair. But the push and pull of life was one thing. It was quite another to let his daughter became embroiled in his shadowy world. Or to leave her to face the danger Brutka posed alone.

Of course, it wasn't the first time his world had encroached on Lauren's. She had been kidnapped as a reprisal years earlier when he had tried to shield a government scientist from an assassination attempt by a foreign government. That operation was how he had gotten to know Meyerstein and begun working for the Feds. It seemed so long ago.

The more he reflected on it, the more he felt like he and Meyerstein were becoming less trusting of one another. The thought bothered him. He sometimes wished she'd cut him some slack. But she never did.

A tapping sounded at the diner window. Reznick turned around and saw his daughter, face flushed from the heat, laughing as she pointed at him. Lauren ambled into the diner, smiling broadly.

Reznick stood up and hugged her. "What's this? I thought you were getting ready to go back to your internship."

"That can wait."

Reznick's mind went into overdrive. "I don't understand . . . Was it a coincidence you seeing me here?"

Lauren grinned as she sat down. She leaned in close. "I was able to track your location. Find My iPhone. Crazy, huh?"

Reznick took a few moments to digest the information. "Honey, I'm thrilled to see you, of course, but shouldn't you be resting up?"

Lauren shrugged. "You said you wanted to spend more time with me. So . . . here I am."

"Well, that's really sweet of you."

"I thought you were going to head back to Maine."

Reznick grimaced, trying to think up a story. "I was . . . and then I thought, Why not just spend a few more days in New York? I knew a guy that used to be in Delta, he lives downtown. Thought I might look him up again."

"Dad, I'm not stupid."

"It's true."

Lauren rolled her eyes as she ordered a skinny latte. "Gimme a break, Dad. I know what you're like. I have an idea what kind of work you do."

Reznick showed his hands. "You got me. Busted."

Lauren smiled. "Dad, don't treat me like a kid."

"Alright. So why am I in New York?"

Lauren whispered, "You know who ran me down and left me in a coma. And I think you want to do something about it. I know about your military background."

"That was a while ago, honey."

"Dad, come on, who are you trying to kid? . . . When I was kidnapped by those Haitians a few years back, you said that it was retaliation for you trying to protect a scientist. And I remember you mentioned that you occasionally work for the FBI."

The waitress returned with the skinny latte. "There you go, honey," she said.

Lauren smiled. "Thank you."

Reznick waited until the waitress was serving another table before he spoke softly. "Let's not talk about that. Let's talk about you. I'm concerned that you're not giving yourself time for recuperation and rest. That's part of the healing process."

"I've gotten the all clear from the doctors. I'm fine, apart from the odd headache. But I'm wondering, are you?"

"Am I what?"

Lauren took a sip of her coffee. "Are you fine? I'm not buying that you're just here in New York to hang around, maybe see an ex-military friend of yours from way back."

Reznick exhaled loudly and sighed. "Lauren, you're killing me. I just wanted to spend a few more days in New York."

"So do you want to go for a drink later?"

"Sure, that'd be nice."

"OK, let's go. Just me and you."

Reznick grimaced. "It's just that . . . I've got a couple of things to deal with, business things."

"Business? Are you meeting up with someone?"

"Yeah, sort of."

Lauren glanced out the window at the passing traffic. "You don't seem too happy to see me."

"Of course I am. It's just that . . . I'm a bit distracted."

Lauren sighed. "Well, I'm glad that we at least had a chance to have coffee, right?"

Reznick smiled. His cell phone began to vibrate in his jacket pocket.

"I think that's yours, Dad."

Reznick nodded. "Yeah, I think so."

"So are you going to answer it?"

Reznick checked the caller ID. The number was jumping around. He knew it was the hacker making sure his location couldn't be pinpointed. The practice was known as caller ID spoofing. Perhaps the hacker had invented his own advanced software to conceal not only his whereabouts but also his name and number. A technique commonly used by collection agencies and private investigators. "Yeah?"

"Mr. R., I got a preliminary assessment for you."

"Already?"

"Man, you make my life more interesting."

"You need to get out more," Reznick said.

The hacker laughed. "It's sad and depressing, my existence. What can I say?"

"What have you got?"

"The voice the cops heard?"

"Yeah?"

"I've been working on this. Distinct French accent."

"Interesting. How was it picked up?"

"A sophisticated home security camera system had been installed. The cops found that the cameras had audio functionality. It could hear what was being filmed."

"Interesting."

"Here's the interesting bit. The cameras had been ripped out and taken. Nothing left."

"Shit. So how do they know about this French guy if they don't have the security system to examine?"

"The voice was saved to a huge server facility. East Coast. New Jersey cops have come up against a wall. But they figure, from what I've trawled of their messages, that the guy was waiting for Callaghan when he arrived home. The guy spoke English when he made a call from a cell phone inside the apartment. His voice was inadvertently picked up by this security camera microphone. The security device itself was taken by this French guy when he left. But the voice recording was saved to a server. And they're analyzing the voice at the Forensic Investigation Division laboratories out in Queens."

"Are they any further along?"

"Not so far."

Reznick looked at his daughter, who had raised her eyebrows as if intrigued by the conversation. "So, we've got the voice of a French guy on a server, and the cops are trying to determine who it is?"

"You got it."

"My next question is simple: Would you be able to identify it with your technology?"

"I'm on it already. I've accessed the voice from the NYPD police software, and I'm running three separate recognition programs, linked to a backdoor into the NSA database via a contractor."

Reznick signaled for another black coffee from the waitress.

"Hang on," the hacker said. "Something's coming through."

"What?"

"Stay on the line."

"Sure thing."

"I got a match."

"You kidding me?"

"Nope."

"Who?"

A beat. "A guy named Henri Bernard."

Reznick took the waitress's pen and scribbled the name on a napkin. "Who is he?"

Lauren turned her head to get a look at the note. Reznick put it in his pocket, away from his daughter's prying eyes.

"French citizen living in New York. Director of a private security company."

Reznick thought that would match the profile of a contractor who could and would do a wet job. Links with a security company, based in New York, a foreign national. Perfect plausible deniability as far as the Ukrainians were concerned. "What else do we know about him?"

"I'm pulling up an FBI file on this guy."

Reznick said, "Go on."

"The thing is, if the FBI isn't sharing the data with the NYPD or Homeland Security, if they're not collaborating and are restricting wider access to the intelligence, this happens, right? You know, everyone working in silos. Protecting their turf."

"Where does he live?"

"Brooklyn."

"Where?"

"Near Prospect Park. What do you plan to do?"

"I'm worried you're starting to live vicariously through me."

"I think you're right, man. I'll text you his address. Be safe."

The hacker ended the call, and Reznick put his cell phone back in his jacket pocket.

Lauren leaned in close. "You know something, don't you?"

Reznick shifted in his seat, feeling very uncomfortable that his daughter was taking such an interest in his work.

"You know a lot, don't you?" she asked. "I'm guessing the name of that French guy is somehow connected to what happened to me. Was the guy that ran me down French?"

"No, he wasn't. I've said enough."

"Dad, don't push me away. I want to help."

"This is totally unrelated to what happened to you."

"I don't believe you."

Reznick looked at his watch and sighed. "I want you to relax, enjoy the rest of your coffee, and get some sleep back at your apartment."

"I'm fine. Look, Dad, I can help you."

"Discussion over." Reznick stood up to leave and left a fifty-dollar bill on the table. "That should cover it. Listen, I've got to see someone. How about we hook up later tonight or tomorrow?"

Lauren looked up at him. "You got it."

Forty-Four

Reznick kissed his daughter goodbye. He felt like a cold bastard just leaving her there. But he had a lead.

A few moments later, the hacker sent Reznick photos of Bernard, his address, and a GPS position obtained via his cell phone.

Reznick hailed a cab and directed it to the nearest hardware store, on East Fifty-Eighth Street. He jumped out, leaving the taxi waiting as he bought some duct tape and nylon rope. He put them in his backpack. Then he got back in the cab.

"Prospect Park, Brooklyn."

The driver nodded and began to speed down FDR Drive as they headed downtown.

Reznick switched off the location on his phone so his daughter, and anyone else who might be looking for him, couldn't track where he was going. A plan was forming in his head. He checked his cell phone. The GPS showed Bernard was at a playground just off Prospect Park West.

The cabdriver dropped him off about a half hour later. He gave the guy a hundred-dollar bill, which seemed to make his day. Then he headed toward the park.

A short while later, Reznick saw a guy doing stretching exercises, headphones on, oblivious to everything around him.

Suddenly the guy took off jogging around the park.

Reznick wasn't dressed for jogging. He was wearing soft-soled Rockports, jeans, and a shirt, with his backpack on. But that wasn't going to stop him. He jogged off after the guy. He got a few awkward looks. But he just ran on after the guy, who headed down a dirt path.

Reznick was closing in fast.

Through a heavily wooded area he ran.

Reznick thought the time was right. He sprinted after Bernard and rushed him from behind. He knocked the guy to the ground and pressed a gun to his head, knocking off his headphones. He grabbed him by the neck. "Name?"

The guy just stared at him as if in shock. "What?" he said, giving a shrug. "I don't know what you mean." The guy was clearly French. But he needed proof.

"Hands on your head!"

Bernard complied.

"Face in the dirt."

Reznick stood over him, foot pressing Bernard's head into the dirt. He bent down and unzipped the guy's fanny pack. Inside was an ID showing it was Bernard, along with house keys and a cell phone. He popped them all inside his backpack.

"I don't have any money," the guy said.

Reznick took out the duct tape and rope from the backpack and tied the guy's hands up tight. Then he wrapped duct tape around the guy's mouth, thighs, and ankles. He wouldn't escape that easily.

Bernard's voice was muffled under the duct tape. "Who are you?"

"One final time. What is your name? I have your ID. But you need to tell me."

Reznick pulled back the duct tape for a moment so the guy could speak.

"My driver's license has those details. I'm French. Bernard is my name."

"Who told you to kill Callaghan?"

Bernard closed his eyes tight and shook his head.

Reznick pressed the gun to his head. "Refuse to answer and you die. Answer and you live."

Bernard said, "I don't know who sent me."

"Did you kill Callaghan?"

"It was a contract. I don't know who sent me."

Reznick had the right guy. He re-covered the guy's mouth with the duct tape. "You lying piece of shit." He kicked the guy in the head, knocking him out cold.

He jogged out of the park. He looked down the street, hoping to find a cab. He wondered if he should catch a train at Seventh Avenue instead. He heard the sound of a motorcycle revving behind him. He turned and saw a biker approach him. He wondered if it was another goon. But the bike stopped right beside him, and the rider signaled him over.

What the hell?

The biker flipped up his visor. Only it wasn't a he. It was his daughter, Lauren, grinning back at him.

Forty-Five

Reznick walked up to Lauren, wondering if she had lost her mind. He looked around to see if anyone was watching.

"What the hell is this?"

"Jump on," she said, handing him a helmet.

"Not until you answer me. What the hell is this? How did you find me?"

"I followed you."

"You followed me? Are you out of your mind, Lauren? I'm working."

"Whatever. Hop on."

Reznick shook his head and pulled on the helmet. He tightened the strap. "We need to lay out some ground rules," he said.

"Fine."

"You ride in back. I'll take this."

Lauren slid back on the leather seat.

Reznick climbed on in front of her. "Hang on," he said as he pulled away into the Brooklyn traffic. He negotiated the streets of Park Slope and then drove through Red Hook as he neared the waterfront. Then through the tunnel into lower Manhattan.

Cars sped past as he tried to figure out what the hell his daughter was doing. Reznick gunned the motorbike north on FDR Drive and all the way up the east side of Manhattan.

Eventually, they were back in the affluent streets of Lenox Hill.

Reznick saw the lights for a parking garage on Third Avenue just off East Sixty-Fourth Street. He headed into the garage and parked. He switched the engine off, took off his helmet as Lauren did the same. He grabbed her by the arm. "You're following me? That's not acceptable. That's definitely not acceptable."

"I want to help, Dad."

"Help? Help me do what? I have some business to take care of here in New York."

"Is that a euphemism, Dad?"

Reznick shook his head as she pulled away from him. He let go of her. "I'm seeing some people."

"In a Brooklyn park? Was that the French guy? Is he connected to what happened to me?"

Reznick pointed at her. "Shut up."

"Don't tell me to shut up."

"I'm your father. Christ, you just got out of the hospital. You were in a coma."

"Don't treat me like a child. I'm not. I'm an adult. And I want to help you!"

Reznick turned away for a few moments before he faced her. "I don't like being angry with you, Lauren. But this is not a game you're playing."

"I never said it was. Listen, I know you just want the best for me. I get that. And I love you, Dad. But don't think I can't look after myself."

Reznick sighed. "You don't have the faintest idea how to look after yourself."

"That's where you're wrong. You taught me to look after myself. To learn to fend for myself. And I do."

"Lauren, honey, I love that you're such a bright, smart young woman. I don't want you to be someone you're not."

"Over the past year, you know what I've been doing apart from studying?"

Reznick shrugged. "I don't know."

"I've learned Krav Maga. Self-defense. I'm doing martial arts. I'm learning. Fast."

"Why haven't you told me this until now?"

"You haven't asked. One of my professors, she's a member at a shooting club. And she's mentored me. She used to be in the Israeli army. She teaches Krav Maga. And she taught me how to shoot."

Reznick shook his head. "Are you kidding me?"

"I've got a nine millimeter. And I'm ready. I know what I'm doing. I don't know what you know, obviously. But I can look after myself. That's what you wanted, wasn't it?"

Reznick sighed. "You've got a gun?"

"Yup. And I can use it."

Reznick took a few moments to figure out what to do. "I don't know what to say."

"How about, *That's cool, honey, let's go for a beer.*"

Reznick smiled. "You're too young."

Lauren shrugged as if unfazed.

"You're crazy, you know that?"

"Yeah, and guess who I take after?"

Reznick cocked his head. "Let's get out of here. Then we can talk."

Forty-Six

The Bedford Falls bar was a low-key establishment on East Sixty-Seventh Street.

Reznick ordered a couple of Heinekens and headed with his daughter to the beer garden at the back. He sat down in a quiet corner and took a sip of the cold beer. He looked around at the other drinkers sitting in little groups before he turned to look at Lauren. "So . . . what are we going to do? I can't have you following me around. Nothing personal. Just work."

"That's not a problem. And I'm glad we're sitting down talking like two adults."

"I'm your father. And there are rules in my world."

"I know that."

"Rule number one: I protect you at all costs. That's my main concern. And if I have you hanging around, I can't guarantee anything."

"I understand. But you have to know one thing: I love you, and I want to help you do what you're doing. I want you to open up about what you know. And why this is important to you."

Reznick said nothing as he enjoyed his beer, still trying to wrap his head around what was happening. He felt sweat trickling down his back.

"Don't shut me out. And don't think you can. I don't want to be thought of as a victim."

"That's good."

"But I also just want to be with you right now. And let's see where it takes us. If you think that I might be in danger, Dad, I was in danger on the crosswalk that day. Life is messy. You should know that better than anyone."

Reznick sighed. "It's just that I don't want any further harm to come to you."

"I get it. You're protective. And thank God you are. But just let me help. At least for now."

"To do what?"

"Be with you. I won't get in your way. I promise."

"Things are complicated, Lauren."

Lauren took a sip of her beer.

Reznick looked at his beautiful, defiant daughter and smiled.

"What? Is a woman not allowed to have a beer in your world?"

"Not at all. You want a beer, you have a beer. But remember one thing: nothing annoys me more than people who moan or whine. I can't abide that."

Lauren nodded slowly.

Reznick leaned closer and whispered, "I've got things to do."

"Let me come with you."

Reznick sighed. "Tell me . . . You say you can shoot."

"Yes, I can."

"What gun you got?"

"Glock nineteen."

Reznick nodded, impressed. "Why the nineteen?"

"Slightly smaller than the Glock seventeen. It's a compact."

"Not allowed in New York City, unless you're a cop, Fed, or other authorized individual. Very strict laws. But there are exceptions, I grant you."

"I'm a part-time resident of New York City, and a few months ago I joined a pistol club. Flatiron District, if you must know. And before you ask if that's lawful, in 2013 the New York Court of Appeals affirmed this stance."

"You kidding me?"

"Dad, I'm legit. I have an NYC handgun license for the city. And in Vermont it is lawful to carry a firearm openly or concealed."

Reznick smiled and began to shake his head. "I had no idea. And Krav Maga?"

"Don't fuck with me, Dad. That's all I'm saying."

Reznick burst out laughing before giving Lauren a big hug.

"So am I in?"

"You need to be discreet. You need to listen more than you talk. And you need to be aware all the time. Can you do that?"

Lauren nodded and sipped her beer. "Oh yeah."

Reznick began to outline the information he had about the diplomat, the hacker who was helping him, the attacks on other girls, how he had been warned to leave town by the State Department but then had returned after hearing about the murder of Callaghan. "So, my question to you is one final time: Do you still want in?"

"Damn straight I want in."

Reznick hugged her tight. "This is a fast-moving situation. But I'm going to let you come with me. At least for today. Maybe I'm crazy, I don't know. But I know you're smart. And you say you can shoot and fight. Hopefully we won't need that. But . . . that's where we are."

"Great."

"Listen, the hacker I told you about?"

Lauren nodded.

"I need to give him a call."

"Go right ahead."

Reznick looked at his daughter and smiled. "You are as stubborn as your mother, let me tell you."

"That's a compliment, right?"

"Damn right it is." Reznick took out his cell phone and called the hacker. "Hey, man, superquick favor, just back from a little trip to Brooklyn."

"How did it go?"

"I've got the guy's cell phone in my backpack. I want to access it and get that information."

"I can do that." The sound of tapping of keys in the background. "I'm in. I'm downloading the information from his cell phone as we speak."

Reznick clenched his fist. "Find any links between the Ukrainians and this guy. Is he connected? And in what way?"

"Might take some time."

"Better get on it, then."

Ten minutes later, Reznick got a call.

"Bernard . . . ," the hacker said.

"Yeah, what about him?"

"I've got a message on his cell phone from a political aide to Brutka."

"Bullshit."

"You want me to send it to you, the conversation?"

"Sure. Can you tell me the gist of it?"

"Here's the verbatim quote: 'Mr. C needs a long sleep.' Sent to Bernard the day before Callaghan was killed. The following day, Bernard replies, 'Mr. C is having a long sleep. Night night. Sweet dreams.'"

"Motherfucker. It's him."

"GPS tracking of his movements also confirms he was right outside Callaghan's home too."

Forty-Seven

It was nearly midnight in Meyerstein's hotel room. She was looking down onto Sixth Avenue when her cell phone rang. She recognized Reznick's number, and her heart sank. She knew that he was not going to forget about Brutka. This wasn't going to end well for anyone.

"Are you kidding, Jon, at this time of night?"

"I want to talk."

"So talk."

"Martha, I'd like to do it face-to-face. And have an assurance that it won't be recorded."

Meyerstein sighed. "Why all these precautions?"

"Doesn't matter. Where are you?"

"I'm at my hotel."

"Where's that?"

"The Quin, near Central Park."

"I'm not far from there. How about I meet you there in fifteen minutes?"

Meyerstein wondered if this was wise. She knew he was angling to try to bring down Brutka, no matter the consequences. "Jon, it's really, really late."

"Please. It's important."

"Very well."

Meyerstein ended the call and reapplied her makeup. She put on a pastel-pink blouse and a navy suit. She picked up her handbag and headed down to the bar. The place was buzzing despite the late hour. She sat down at a leather banquette.

A few minutes later, Reznick strolled in with a young, quite beautiful woman.

He grinned as he walked up to where she was sitting.

"Martha," he said, "I want you to meet someone."

Meyerstein stared at the girl, who smiled beatifically.

"I'd like to introduce you to my daughter, Lauren."

Meyerstein felt her cheeks flush. She got up and hugged Lauren tightly. "So nice to meet you. And I'm delighted you're making such a good recovery."

Lauren smiled and sat down in between Meyerstein and her father.

Reznick said, "A nice bottle of red?"

Meyerstein and Lauren both nodded.

Reznick ordered a bottle of Pinot Noir, and the waiter returned with three glasses, pouring a modest amount into each.

Meyerstein looked at Reznick. "And to what do I owe the pleasure of your company at this time of night?" she asked.

Reznick took a sip of his wine. "First, my daughter knows what I know. I hope you're fine with Lauren being here."

Meyerstein looked at his daughter before saying in a low voice, "I'm delighted to meet you at last. But you have to understand that your father and I discuss matters that occasionally have security implications. I'm talking classified. And you don't have any clearance."

Lauren nodded. "I understand."

Meyerstein took a large gulp of wine. "This better be good, Jon."

Reznick leaned forward, glass in hand. "Thanks for meeting me on such short notice."

Meyerstein gave him the once-over. "You been fighting? You've got dirt under your fingernails. Scrapes on your knuckles."

"What I'm about to say didn't come from me."

Meyerstein shook her head. "Oh God, Jon, what are you up to?"

"This is no ordinary investigation."

"I'm well aware of that. Look, I'm surprised you're back in New York. The only reason I'm still here and not in DC is because you came back. But I can't get back home as long as you're here dragging this out."

Reznick whispered, "I want to talk about the assassination of Tom Callaghan."

Meyerstein closed her eyes for a moment. "Jon, that's a matter for the police."

"It most certainly is. But I'm not convinced the cops have the clout to deal with this."

"What do you know? And how do you know it?"

Reznick looked around and sipped his wine. He leaned in close. "What if I said the person linked to Callaghan's death has been in touch with one of Brutka's political aides?"

The color drained from Meyerstein's face. "I'll tell you this now, Jon: if this information has been accessed illegally, we won't be able to use it."

"That's your choice. I have it on good authority that the assassin was a French national, Henri Bernard."

Meyerstein stared at him long and hard. "What?"

"His was the voice captured on Callaghan's security system audio and saved to the cloud."

Meyerstein sighed and turned to Lauren. "Is your dad always so obsessive?"

Lauren rolled her eyes. "You have no idea."

Meyerstein looked at Reznick. "And you know that for sure? And he's French?"

"I'd bet my house on it."

"OK, let me deal with it. I'm not going to ask how you got that information. But I'll deal with it. You want some advice?"

"Why not?"

"Let the NYPD know. I'll let my people know. We all want the same thing."

Reznick nodded. "I know you do. And I appreciate that. This guy needs to be stopped. Before someone else gets killed."

Forty-Eight

Just after seven the following morning, after four hours sleep Reznick was standing across the street from the Nineteenth Precinct, drinking a cup of coffee, next to a police cruiser that was parked up on the sidewalk. He wore a Yankees cap pulled low to shield him from the sun. He stifled a yawn. He had gotten back to his hotel just after two in the morning after walking his daughter back to her apartment. He was still struggling to get his head around Lauren tracking him down to the diner and then shadowing him to Brooklyn. But part of him was immensely proud that she was learning Krav Maga and shooting.

Out of the corner of his eye, Reznick saw Detective Acosta headed toward the precinct.

Reznick threw his coffee cup in a trash can and walked across the road to greet her. "Morning," he said.

"What the hell is this, Jon?"

"I've got something to help you get back in the game."

Acosta shook her head and stopped. "Jon, you're killing me. I'm trying to move on."

"A few minutes of your time is all I'm asking."

"What is it with you? You really are crazy."

Reznick shrugged. "What can I say? Five minutes."

Acosta shook her head. "I've got a life to lead, Jon. I'm trying not to lose my job."

"You helped me . . . Now I want to pass on new information."

Acosta cocked her head, and Reznick followed her into the precinct. Up to the second floor and into an interview room.

Reznick shut the door behind them.

"So what's going on?"

"I know the identity of the man in Callaghan's apartment."

Acosta stared at him and shook her head. "Unbelievable. This is way out of left field."

"Henri Bernard. French. Security consultant, lives in Brooklyn."

"How the hell do you know that?"

"I've got a hacker friend."

"What the hell?"

"He is phenomenal."

"This all sounds very illegal, Jon."

"Maybe it is. But I'm telling you, the information is sound. The voice was Bernard's. It was detected by the microphone contained within a security camera."

"OK. So why wasn't the device recovered from the apartment?"

"It was stolen. But the voice was recorded to a cloud server. And my guy, my hacker friend, retrieved this information." Reznick handed her a cell phone.

"What's this?"

"This belongs to Bernard."

"And how did you get your hands on this?"

"I don't want to go there . . . However, my hacker analyzed it, and he said there's at least one message from a political aide of Brutka's on that cell phone."

Acosta stared at the phone and shook her head. "We've got people working around the clock trying to figure this out," she said. "How did your guy come up with that result?"

"You guys take too long. I'm willing to cross lines. I'm not interested in boundaries. And neither is the hacker."

"It's called the law."

"Whatever. I do what has to be done. But that's immaterial. I want to help. That's why I'm passing that on."

Acosta shook her head as she wrote down what he told her. "You're a nightmare, do you know that, Jon? But I appreciate the heads-up. Unfortunately it doesn't help put Brutka away, does it?"

"Get it to your forensics guys. I'm tired of all this bullshit. Figure it out."

Acosta's cell phone rang, interrupting the conversation. She rifled in her pocket. "I need to take this."

Reznick shrugged. "Sure."

Acosta went over to the corner of the room. "Calm down, Zuki. Have you been to the hospital? . . . You were warned? By who? You need to give me a name!" She scribbled down *Brutka* on a pad in front of her. "Are you sure?" Acosta shook her head. "Listen to me, I'm on my way. Don't move." She ended the call.

Reznick said, "Who was that?"

"That was another one of the hookers Brutka uses."

"Another? Beaten up?"

"Middle of the night he turns up. Drinks some beer. He's high. Cocaine. Beats her senseless. And he chokes her until she passes out. But she was lucky. She didn't die, unlike another girl I found, Daniela."

Reznick shook his head. "Callaghan said there were more. He was right."

"Fuck."

"When is this going to end? How can this be allowed to continue? It needs to stop."

Acosta sighed and looked at her watch. "We need to speak another time, Jon."

"Are you headed to see the hooker?"

Acosta nodded.

"I want to tag along."

"Jon, that's not going to happen."

"I want to help. I'm bringing you information. Information you didn't have. I'm not here to hinder your efforts."

Acosta was quiet for a few moments. "It goes against all our protocols. You're a civilian."

"I've got high-level intelligence security clearance. I've worked for the Feds. You can trust me."

"What is it with you?"

"Let me go with you. What do you say?"

When Reznick and Acosta arrived at the girl's one-room apartment in East Harlem, a block from Daniela's, the girl was sitting on the bare floorboards, shaking, her face swollen. Specks of dried blood dotted the wooden floorboards. The girl broke down when she saw the look on Acosta's face.

Acosta wrapped the girl in a hug and wiped away her tears. "Zuki, this can't go on," she said. "It has to stop."

"I want to help, but I'm scared. I don't want to speak to you."

Acosta held the girl's swollen and bruised face. "Listen to me: he will kill you. You said so yourself. It's just a matter of time."

"You can't protect me. No one can."

"We can protect you. This needs to stop."

The girl closed her eyes. "He says he will have me returned to Ukraine in a box. A coffin. I can't go back."

"As it stands, you have no rights. He holds all the cards. But you need to help me help you."

The girl shook her head. She picked up a packet of Marlboros and shook out a cigarette. She lit up and dragged hard on her cigarette, watching the blue smoke.

"I will protect you."

The girl closed her eyes. "He is free to do what he likes with me. And all the girls."

Reznick said, "We can bring him down. But the police need your help."

The girl pulled up her T-shirt to show cigarette burns all over her stomach. "He did that. Do you think someone like that will allow me to escape?"

"Listen to me," Reznick said. "Detective Acosta will make sure you and your friends are protected. You're in America. We will protect you."

"I can't go back to Ukraine! You don't know what it's like there."

"I don't know much about your country," Reznick said, "that's true. But I know that my daughter was nearly killed by that same bastard."

The girl blinked away the tears for a few seconds as if struggling to comprehend how to escape her predicament. "How did he nearly kill her?"

"His car ran her down in a crosswalk. He didn't stop. She just came out of a coma."

The girl nodded sympathetically.

Reznick pulled up a picture on his phone of his daughter and showed it to her. "Aleksander Brutka left her to die on a New York street."

"She's very beautiful."

"Trust me, she didn't look beautiful when she was in a coma."

The girl looked at him.

"You need to be brave now," Reznick said. "Braver than you've ever been."

The girl pointed at her face. "Look at me. He beats me. I've nowhere to turn. And I know he'll find me. He killed my friend."

Acosta took out her notebook. "Name?"

"Bondar. She used the name Carmel. She's disappeared completely. I think he killed her. She was from a small village outside Kiev. Now I have no one."

Acosta said, "Do you know Daniela?"

"I've heard of her."

"She's dead."

The girl closed her eyes tight as if trying to block out the pain.

"What if he turns up tomorrow?" Reznick said. "Or the day after. Do you think this is just going to end because you want it to? It won't. And it's only a matter of time before he ends your life too."

The girl began to cry. "I'm scared of him. I'm scared every day. I don't want to live like this. He rapes me. He hurts me. He feeds me drugs and laughs at me. I want to die. I want to die!"

Acosta held her hand. "You never told me you'd been raped."

"Well, I just did! He raped me. Several times. He's a beast. I pretend to like him. But only because I'm scared."

"Tell me about Brutka's friends. You told me previously he lets his friends visit you and abuse you."

"They're filthy pigs too. I hate them. I hate him and all his disgusting friends."

"Who are his friends?"

The girl dragged hard on her cigarette, crushing it in an overflowing ashtray on the floor. "Diplomat friends. Bodyguards. A Frenchman. He has friends in high places."

Reznick and Acosta exchanged knowing glances when she mentioned a Frenchman. He sat down on the floor beside the girl. "I've got friends in high places too."

"Do you?"

"Yes, I do. People who will protect you and your family. The NYPD could help get you to safety and a better life. But you need to help us too."

The girl looked at Acosta. "What if he finds me?"

Acosta shook her head. "I want you to help us help you and stop this once and for all. But it means you will have to entrap him."

"What do you mean?" the girl asked.

"What if I said we could bring down Brutka? We need your help. Think about it. The next time he turns up, he might not stop at raping and beating you. He might very well kill you. You've told us he choked you, right?"

The girl went quiet.

"When do you think you'll see him next?"

"Tonight."

"Tonight? What's happening tonight?"

The girl's head hung low as if it was all too much to bear. "He wants me to meet the latest batch. Consignment."

"Consignment of what? Girls?"

The girl nodded. "Fresh. Young. Innocent."

"Where are they from?"

"Ukraine, mostly. Some girls from Belarus. Straight from a container ship. From Odessa."

"Odessa?" Reznick said. "What, and this is happening tonight?"

Acosta fixed her gaze on the girl. "You seem to know a lot about this. He told you all this?"

"That's why he came in the early hours. To let me know I was needed to accompany him. I said I didn't want to be part of it. But . . ."

Reznick said, "Take your time."

"I just wanted the beating to stop. So I agreed."

Acosta said, "We can help you. But you need to help yourself."

The girl closed her eyes and hugged herself tight as if for comfort. "He scares me. He is a terrible man. I hate him."

Reznick said, "Let's nail him. Once and for all. But like Detective Acosta said, we need your help. Can you do that?"

The girl didn't react.

Acosta said, "You said he's coming back tonight. What time?"

"He just said he would collect me. And I was to be with him. He wants me to check the girls."

"Why?" Reznick asked.

The girl sighed. "Me being there is to reassure the girls. I remember when I was brought in last year it was the same scenario. A girl was with him, holding his hand, smiling at the new girls. We were all frightened."

"So he wants you to do the same thing? Why?"

"Because I speak English fluently. They will relate to me more, I guess. Most of the girls only speak Ukrainian or Russian."

"Why haven't you told me this before?" Acosta said.

"You didn't ask," the girl said.

Acosta sighed. "Give me some details about tonight."

The girl said, "He says he will pick me up. And we will drive to check on the girls."

"Where?"

"Long Island."

"Why Long Island?"

"They're arriving by boat."

"Where?"

"I have no idea. Three or four miles offshore, they are transferred from a container ship to a boat. A yacht. And they are taken below. Then they are put on a dinghy about a mile out and taken to an isolated beach. Then they are put in the back of a truck and driven somewhere. Unless it's all changed since I was smuggled in last year."

Acosta said, "There is one way for you to end this for good."

"How?" the girl said.

"You wear a wire."

The girl shook her head. "I can't do that. He's a very smart man."

Reznick said, "What about another way? What about if we track your cell phone?"

The girl went quiet for a few moments. "You need this to trap him, right?"

Reznick said, "This way we can monitor where you are. Record what is said. And then end this for you and all the girls."

The girl nodded. "It will end?"

Reznick said, "It will end tonight. If you agree to this, it will end tonight."

Forty-Nine

Reznick and Acosta accompanied Zuki out of her East Harlem apartment. She was taken for a full medical examination by an NYPD doctor. Her injuries were treated and catalogued, and she gave a full statement. She was then sent home in a cab, having agreed to help nail Brutka. Reznick was in awe of the girl's resolve after all she had been through. But he couldn't help wondering how this was all going to play out.

Reznick and Acosta headed back to an interview room at the Nineteenth Precinct to discuss if the operation would work. "My concern, Isabella, is, can she pull this off? Will she get cold feet?"

Acosta said, "She seems determined enough."

"I don't know. I'm wondering if she's putting on a brave face for our benefit."

Acosta nodded and scribbled some notes.

"I appreciate you letting me in on this."

"I've OK'd it with my boss. Although it would be best if the Feds are on board."

Reznick sighed. "Tell me about the resources you're going to call on."

"So, the NYPD is pulling together the best team we can for this. Surveillance experts. Vice Enforcement. And the whole operation will be run in tandem with our Intelligence unit."

Reznick said, "This is high risk. Zuki does know that."

Acosta said, "She knows this is high risk. But she's got guts, that girl."

"Let me speak to the Feds. If you guys can work alongside the FBI, draw on each other's expertise, it will be better for everyone."

Acosta smiled. "Let's do it."

Reznick called Meyerstein, and they spoke for a quarter of an hour. He explained the situation in detail. And in particular what was going to go down that night.

Meyerstein said, "Are we going to be doing this without the State Department's knowledge?"

"Got to. Otherwise, the whole thing could be compromised."

Meyerstein remained quiet for a few moments. "Do you want to stick with Acosta on this?"

"Why?"

"You're not officially FBI. But if she's happy for you to ride along, then I'm fine with that."

Reznick covered the mouthpiece and asked Acosta if that was possible.

Acosta said, "No chance."

Reznick relayed the information to Meyerstein.

"Jon," she said, "if this goes down and we have covert audio and video showing Brutka in the act trafficking, then we have proof."

Reznick looked across at Acosta. "How about if I get a motorcycle?"

"That can be arranged. Harley, unmarked, I would imagine."

"Perfect. I could be connected to the operation. But still separate. Plausible deniability and all that."

Acosta shrugged. "That would work. I have no problem with that. But you would be at greater risk."

"Don't worry about that," Reznick said. "Martha, did you hear what I said? What do you say?"

"And this girl is convinced it's happening tonight?"

"Correct."

"Very well. But, Jon, if this goes south, you're on your own."

Fifty

Reznick picked up a black leather biker jacket from a nearby store and headed back to his hotel room. He freshened up and put on a fresh T-shirt, jeans, and battered Nike sneakers. He popped a couple of Dexedrine, washed down by a bottle of Coke from the minibar. He stood beside the window and stared out at the skyscrapers all around. A world away from his day-to-day life in recent years. But in a city he loved, all the same.

The city his late wife had called home. The city where they had married. The city that had endured despite 9/11. The city that never stood still. He was glad. It was a sign that America would endure. It wouldn't stop the energy of this city. Nothing could.

In his darkest hours, after 9/11, when Reznick had retreated to Rockland to bury himself in a haze of booze, unable and unwilling to move on, he could never imagine returning to the city again. Not after what had happened to Elisabeth. The way she had died. But over time, over years, Reznick had finally made it back. Alone. He had wandered the streets of lower Manhattan. He had seen that the city was determined to build again. On the sacred spot where the towers had stood, there would emerge two enormous waterfalls and reflecting pools.

Hundreds of trees had been planted around the site.

Sometimes he just stood and stared at the water. It was a place to contemplate. Invariably he contemplated his wife's life. Their beautiful daughter. And her love. Unconditional love. Lauren talked about art, philosophy, and all sorts of stuff. Reznick just listened, content to hear her explain it to him.

Reznick wondered if he was trapped by the past. Beholden to the tragedy that had occurred that day. In many ways it was inevitable. But he was thinking about moving forward. He hadn't dated since Elisabeth had died. It hadn't felt right. But years had gone by, and Reznick was only now beginning to wonder if he needed someone else in his life. He had his daughter. Thank God she had pulled through the accident. But he needed someone to be there for him. To talk to. To have a drink with. He missed that. In its place he had retreated into a world of the familiar. A bar. A drink. Friends of his late father. They talked about politics. The bullshit going on in America. But he needed more than that.

He knew he was closed off. He wasn't by nature the most gregarious person in the world. Quite the opposite.

Reznick's cell phone vibrated on the desk beside the TV. The caller ID showed it was his daughter.

"Hey, Dad," she said.

"Hey, Lauren. How are you? How are you feeling?"

"I'm feeling good. I had a nap this morning, and I'm feeling refreshed."

"Good stuff."

"Dad, you were talking about getting to know each other better. At the diner, remember?"

"Sure, honey."

"And I was wondering if you'd like to come to my apartment tonight. Tracy won't be back until eleven tonight, and I'll cook you dinner. How does that sound?"

Reznick grimaced. He hated letting his daughter down. "Tonight?"

"Yeah, I thought it would be great. I'm feeling so much better and stronger, and how cool would that be? I'll get the food—I know you like steak—and you can bring the wine."

Reznick groaned. "I can't. Not tonight, honey. I'm sorry."

"Oh. I'm sorry . . . I thought it would be a nice surprise."

Reznick wanted the earth to swallow him whole. "It's a beautiful thought. It's just . . ."

"You got some business to attend to?" Lauren's voice faltered for a moment.

"That's right. It's unavoidable."

"Are you going after the guy who did this to me?"

Reznick sighed. "I don't want to talk about that, honey. I just want you to know that if it's alright with you, we can do dinner tomorrow. How does that sound?"

"That's fine, Dad."

"I'm really looking forward to that, if your friend's OK with that."

"She's fine, trust me. She's always out at night."

"Know what we can talk about tomorrow?"

"What?"

"I want to hear more about your marksmanship. Your Krav Maga skills. And all that."

"I can shoot, Dad. I'd be useful to you tonight."

"I know you would. But this isn't your fight, Lauren."

"But it is, can't you see?"

"Sometimes things get messy. This has the scope to be messy, trust me."

"I just want to help. I don't want to sit around twiddling my thumbs while you're out there battling in my corner."

Reznick sighed. "Sadly, it's about more than just you, Lauren. There are quite a lot of young women affected by this guy."

"I'd like you to change your mind."

"Not this time, honey. How about I take you to a shooting range, see what you've got? And then, perhaps, we can talk some more."

"Promise?"

"I swear." Reznick checked his watch. It was nearly five o'clock. He had to move. "I love you, Lauren."

"Love you too, Dad. Be careful."

Fifty-One

Three blocks away from the Ukrainian girl's apartment, Acosta was getting antsy in an unmarked Ford Crown Victoria. She checked her watch. Where was Brutka?

NYPD surveillance vans and cars were set up within a one-hundred-yard radius of the apartment. In addition, three unmarked FBI cars were spread out across the neighborhood. It was going to go down tonight. But still there was radio silence.

The minutes dragged as Acosta contemplated the operation. She watched a Latino street hustler wearing a baseball cap and low-slung pants skulk down the street, peering in vehicle windows. He was smoking a joint. But that would have to wait for another day.

She felt the adrenaline rushing through her body. The intel from Reznick had jarred everyone. It was possible that if they had some luck Brutka could be snared once and for all. But they were going to need a good slice of luck for that to happen, and to avoid Reznick or any police officers getting injured in the process.

She knew from years of experience at the NYPD that good intelligence gathering was crucial. She couldn't help but wonder if the information supplied by the damaged Ukrainian girl about the shipment of young women being brought into Long Island was correct. Only Zuki knew what she had been told by Brutka. Maybe she had picked it up wrong. It was possible that it was misinformation. Was that a realistic scenario? Could Brutka have deliberately supplied false information to determine if the girl could be trusted?

Acosta sighed as the doubts plagued her mind.

The radio buzzed into life, snapping her back to the present. "Stand by. Vehicle has arrived," a male voice said. "Verified ownership of target. Black Bentley SUV. Got a visual on someone."

Acosta said, "Copy that. Is the visual the target?"

"Negative. Bodyguard has entered the building."

Acosta said, "Shit! Where's the target?"

"Can't tell. His cell phone GPS is showing he's in Midtown."

Acosta shook her head. "Copy that." She realized that Brutka, if he was in the car, was using a new cell phone again. Probably as a precaution. But with the amount of surveillance on his tail, Acosta was confident they wouldn't lose him.

The radio again crackled into life. "The girl is leaving the apartment."

"Copy."

"She is wearing dark glasses. Bodyguard is holding her wrist tight. She is now in the rear left seat. Repeat, rear left seat. Bodyguard upfront. And they're pulling away. I think we're on. Repeat, they're pulling away from the address."

Acosta said, "Copy that. Let's do this."

"The girl's cell phone has been activated. We've got a fix on her location."

"Copy that." Acosta spotted the car in the distance. "Not too close. Headed north on FDR."

The driver said, "Where they headed?"

"We expect they will take a turn onto the Triborough Bridge."

And sure enough a Fed surveillance vehicle confirmed that the Bentley was headed over the bridge.

But instead of heading down through Brooklyn, out through Queens, and toward Long Island on the expressway, the Bentley drove north into Port Morris and then the Bronx. She knew the area better than anyone. It never seemed to change.

Acosta sighed. "Shit. What's going on? What is this?"

The driver shook his head as they headed north on the Bruckner.

Acosta realized the original plan given to Zuki had either been scrapped or revised somewhat. It wasn't a great start. "OK, this could be pointing to a rendezvous in the Bronx. But let's just focus on the target and his vehicle. Let's see where it leads us."

Fifty-Two

Brutka shielded his eyes from the shards of sunlight reflected off the industrial buildings as they drove through the bleak Bronx landscape. He was sitting in the back seat of the Bentley; the girl, smelling nice, sitting beside him was quiet. The way he liked it. He turned and looked at her. "I like your shades," he said.

"Thank you."

"Where did you get them?"

"Drugstore."

Brutka smiled. "Very cool. I'm glad you can help me out tonight."

The girl nodded, hands clasped.

"I'm sorry about last night. I think I got a bit carried away. Are you OK now?"

"I'm good, thanks."

Brutka reached over and took off her sunglasses. The girl flinched. The swelling and purple bruising around her eyes was pronounced. "I need to work harder on my anger management, I know that," he said.

The girl gave a forced smile. "I forgive you."

Brutka stroked her hair again and kissed her on the lips. "It'll get better. I promise." He reached into his pocket and handed her a small box. "This is a small token of my love for you."

The girl looked at it. "What's this, honey?"

"Open it. It's for you."

The girl carefully opened the paper. Inside was a Tiffany's box wrapped in a crisp white ribbon.

"Open it."

The girl untied the ribbon and opened the box. A smile crossed her face as she lifted up the diamond-encrusted bracelet. "This is beautiful. For me?"

Brutka smiled and stroked her head. "A special gift for a special girl. I try so hard to be a good person. But I find it difficult."

The girl looked unsure whether to touch it. "I can't believe this . . . It's too much, honey."

"Nonsense. We all deserve special treats. Especially my special girl."

"This is . . . so unexpected. This must've cost you a fortune."

"Better part of twenty big ones."

The girl whistled, then burst out laughing. "For me? Are you sure?"

"Put it on."

"Now?"

Brutka nodded as he stroked the girl's swollen cheek. "You're so beautiful. And understanding. I like that combination."

The girl wrapped the bracelet around her slender wrist and clipped it into place. Tears filled her eyes. "I'm sorry I upset you last night."

"It was my fault. But anyway, the bracelet . . . You like it?"

"Yes, honey. I love it. It's sparkling, like your eyes."

Brutka kissed her and wiped away her tears. "You say the nicest things. I love you. You're a very special girl."

The girl's gaze dropped.

"Put your sunglasses on," he snapped.

The girl did as she was told. "Where are we going? I don't know this area."

"It doesn't matter. What does matter is that you stand beside me, smile, converse with any girls who are nervous. To reassure them. That a new life awaits. And if they are very good in the first few months, I can secure them a ten-year visa. And an apartment. But only after they have proven themselves to me. Do you know what I mean?"

The girl gave a tired smile. "Yes, honey."

Fifty-Three

Reznick was discreetly tailing the Bentley on a Harley chopper, headed north through the Bronx, a hundred yards or so behind the diplomat's car. His 9mm Beretta was holstered inside his leather jacket. The NYPD had attached a metallic stars-and-stripes badge with a pinhole camera to his lapel. But Reznick also had a gun taped to his left calf and a knife taped to the other leg. He always liked to be prepared.

As he sped through the postindustrial wastelands of the Bronx, Reznick's earpiece buzzed to life.

"Jon, you got a visual?" The voice of Meyerstein.

"Affirmative, I see him. I'm three cars back."

"Copy that. We're tracking from the phone. So we have the GPS and the real-time conversation being recorded. But do not, repeat, do not get too close."

"So we're 100 percent sure this is the target vehicle?"

"Copy that. We got a visual. She's in the rear left seat. The target is sitting beside her. And we can be sure he's absolutely not conducting official diplomatic business."

"Copy that. What about the consignment of girls?"

"Latest electronic surveillance we have is that the boat dropped the girls off at Hunts Point, close to the fish market. That's all we have."

"And that's where the target is headed?"

"We don't know for sure. The signal dropped in the last few minutes."

Reznick saw the Bentley head off the expressway. "OK, he's taken a right. A right onto . . ."

"Hunts Point Avenue."

"Copy that. He's speeding up."

"Hunts Point, for your information, Jon—low-income, high-crime area."

Reznick rode past graffitied buildings and farther and farther into the heart of Hunts Point. Past industrial warehouses and repair shops. Then down sketchy side streets. "Where the hell am I?"

"Whittier Street."

"Thought we were headed to a scrapyard."

Meyerstein said, "It's all very fluid . . . Hold on. Jon, I've just been informed by Detective Acosta that this particular area is used by prostitutes. And their johns."

"What a fucking dump."

"Jon, just be eyes and ears in the vicinity."

"Negative. We can't just wait. I need to be closer in case this goes south."

A beat. "Jon, that's an order. You need to hang back. Only for emergencies."

"I don't work for the Feds anymore, remember."

"Jon, let's not have this discussion now. You know as well as I do that going in by yourself is suicide."

"Wouldn't be the first time. Let Acosta and the NYPD know."

"Brutka and his men will kill you."

"Not if I kill them first."

Fifty-Four

The Bentley SUV disappeared from sight through an iron gate into what looked like an industrial warehouse. Reznick continued down the street, surveying the scene. Barbed wire on the slate roofs and broken glass embedded in brick. He turned a corner and rode down the parallel street, Drake Street. It was filled with the same collection of industrial units and run-down auto shops and bottling plants.

Reznick dumped the motorcycle behind a truck, knowing it would almost certainly be stolen if he left it unattended. But that wasn't his concern. At least not now. His concern was Zuki. And the other girls.

Reznick walked down Drake.

A trucker wound down his window. "Be careful around here, man. They'll fucking kill you soon as look at you."

"Appreciate the advice."

"Take care, bro."

Reznick walked around the corner and down Whittier Street. Cameras surveilling the area around the warehouse. He crossed the street.

Out of the shadows a black woman wearing a tight dress appeared, smoking a joint. "Hey, honey, you want some fun?"

Reznick shook his head. "Just walking around."

"Like hell you are. Walking around . . . shit. You want some action? You want to do some business? Don't be afraid. I don't bite. Much." She gave a guttural laugh. "You need some weed? Crack? Speed? I know some really cool guys around here, trust me."

The voice crackled in his earpiece. "NYPD cars in position. We're waiting until they come out, and then we're going to head them off."

Reznick kept walking away from the sad, debauched woman in front of him.

The woman followed him. "I ain't cheap. But I'm good. You know what I'm saying? You look like you got the cash, man."

"Do you mind . . . Might be safer for you to make yourself scarce."

"You a cop?"

"Do I look like a cop?"

"Yeah. Actually, you do look like a cop."

The woman made a hand signal.

"What was that you just did?"

The woman dragged on her joint and shrugged. "I ain't do nothing, honey."

Reznick saw a black guy farther down the street walking toward him and the woman, a switchblade in hand.

"Yo, white boy, what the fuck are you doing wasting my girl's time?" he said. "You bothering her?" The guy walked up to Reznick, knife aloft. "I don't like people wasting her time. Time is money."

Reznick stood his ground.

"Are you deaf, motherfucker?"

Reznick stared at him, wanting the guy to get in his face.

The guy was waving the knife around, agitated. "You crazy, white boy? They let you out of Bellevue, that it?"

Reznick stood and stared.

The guy lunged forward and Reznick feinted. Grabbed the guy's arm. Knocked the knife to the ground. Then he head-butted the guy. The pimp crumpled in a heap. Reznick kicked him once, hard in the head. Blood spilled out of the guy's nose onto the street. A few moans. Then the guy passed out.

Reznick pointed at the woman. "You! Out of here! Now!"

The woman just nodded and ran back down the street, high heels clacking on the asphalt.

Reznick kneeled down and checked the pimp's pockets. He took out the cell phone and a penknife and a Glock from his waistband. He called in support. "Need a vehicle to quickly get this fucker out of the way!"

The earpiece crackled into life. "Copy that, Jon."

Thirty seconds later, a Ford Suburban pulled up and two burly plainclothes cops got out.

"You OK, bro?" one said.

"I'm fine. Get him out of here. And pick up the hooker too. Get them both out of the way."

The pimp was thrown in the back of the Suburban, and the cops were gone in a matter of seconds.

The voice of Meyerstein echoed in his earpiece. "Jon, you need to stand down on this. We don't know who's in there."

"Zuki for starters. Brutka. And other girls. We can't let this go. I need to get in. We need proof. We need to prove he's there and get a second audio feed too if we can."

There was silence for a few moments before she spoke. "Jon, be careful. This guy's crazy. We don't want to lose you in there."

Fifty-Five

Brutka gazed at the line of young women standing in front of him, their hands tied, eyes downcast. He walked down the line as he began his inspection of the girls. He looked at their cheekbones. Checked their teeth. Then he began to smell them. Their scent: a mixture of stale sweat and soap. He glanced around. His bodyguards were grinning, as if enjoying the show. Eyes crawling all over the young flesh in front of them.

Brutka winked at them and turned to face the girls. "You need to know one thing about your new life," he said. "You must listen very carefully."

The girls nodded. Zuki, his most beautiful girlfriend, wearing sunglasses, smiled reassuringly at the girls and translated his words into Ukrainian.

"Very good. I like good listeners. You now work for me and my associates. You step out of line, and you will be taken back to Ukraine. To your families. What is left of your families. And your country. Don't think Russia won't be contemplating another land grab like Crimea. You will be slaves to Moscow. And you will likely starve like dogs. Am I making myself clear?"

The girls nodded, a handful giving respectful bows of subservience.

"You are all very beautiful. That is why you have been picked. You are very lucky that you have been blessed in this way, and that has opened up opportunities for you."

Zuki translated.

"But with opportunity comes responsibility. You will be able to make money. A lot of money. And that of course can go back to your families. But do not take my charity as weakness. Quite the contrary. I can be harsh. And I can be cruel. But if you obey my each and every word, then we will get along just fine. You see, I want to help you.

"Your families want you to be here. And that is why they are now in my debt. That can only be paid back by hard work. I have spoken personally to each of your fathers, and they are very grateful for this opportunity. When I stressed the importance of hard work, duty as you entertain clients and friends of mine, they understood exactly what my intentions were. I'm a good Ukrainian. I love Ukraine. And we must not let this opportunity pass us by, yes?"

Zuki translated. The girls nodded.

"When the Russians came to take the eastern part of our beautiful country, we resisted. But it came at a price. An economic price. I can't imagine the horrors your parents went through. I know many lost businesses, families became homeless, and people got desperate. Your fathers, every one of them, have decided that the cash sums—substantial sums—I have sent to them will allow them to try and rebuild their lives."

Zuki cleared her throat and translated, hands on hips. The girls again nodded.

"And in return you will work for me. Be at my beck and call. Do as I say. And as my associates say. Why? That is the legal agreement which is your duty as the fine daughters of Ukraine to uphold."

The translation prompted a few tight smiles.

"I will provide all food, accommodation, and a good salary for each of you each and every month."

The translation followed. The girls smiled, looking happier at the prospect of making money.

Brutka's gaze lingered on the girls. He estimated their average age was eighteen. "So here's what's going to happen. We're going to get you all photographed, prints and DNA taken in the adjacent room. You will each have a medical exam. And this will make sure you are not carrying any diseases."

Zuki translated and the girls nodded.

"Do not worry. The doctor is a lady doctor, a Ukrainian working in New York City, so don't be afraid. It's just so that we have up-to-date information on your physical health. Then we can let you see what the city is all about."

Fifty-Six

When he was satisfied the area fringed by industrial units was quiet—no hookers, pimps, or clients lurking in the shadows—Reznick headed back onto Drake Street. He climbed up a wall and pulled himself up and onto the roof of a nearby building.

He stayed low as he crawled across the tiles of the one-story building. He saw the black Bentley SUV parked in a dingy courtyard. Sulfurous yellow lights bathed the area. He peered down.

Reznick whispered into the pinhole microphone on his jacket, relaying the information.

The earpiece crackled back into life. "Jon, copy that." It was Meyerstein. "We have all units in place. We'll have them covered when they leave."

"The warehouse extends over three separate units, as far as I can see. It's far larger than we thought. So it's not just the front. I'm concerned that there are other ways to get out of there without being observed."

Meyerstein went quiet for a few moments.

"Whittier Street, behind the buildings," Reznick said. "Have we got a unit there?"

There was a pause as Meyerstein checked with the team, but Reznick couldn't wait any longer. "I'm just going to go check out Whittier Street to scope out the scene."

"Copy that, John."

"Radio silence, people."

The radio went quiet.

Reznick held his breath. He looked down on the courtyard. He was spread-eagle on the roof about twenty yards to the rear of the Bentley, out of sight of the rearview mirror. He waited for a few moments. Suddenly, the shaven-headed driver wound down his window, elbow out, smoking a cigarette. He saw his chance.

He crawled a yard to the edge of the building and peered over. The guy was looking away from him.

Reznick got on his side and slid a few inches to the edge, gripped the tiled roof, and lowered himself down softly. He crouched down and then crawled underneath the car.

His heart was beating. The smell of cigarette smoke mixed with gasoline fumes.

Reznick rolled out and emerged, gun pointing at the driver's head. "Nice and easy, step out," he said, one finger to his lips. "Hands up."

The driver reached down inside and cracked open the door.

Reznick grabbed him by the throat and hauled him through the window, kicking away his legs.

The guy whined in pain as he collapsed to his knees.

Reznick pressed the gun hard into the man's neck. "Where's your boss?"

The guy just shrugged.

"Dumb move, asshole."

Reznick bent down and punched the man hard in the side of the neck, knocking him out. He reached into the guy's jacket pocket. Took the guy's cell phone, car keys, and wallet, put them in his own jacket pocket.

Out of the corner of his eye, Reznick saw a rifle butt. Suddenly it smashed down hard against his face. Then he was swallowed up in darkness.

Fifty-Seven

Meyerstein felt a sense of dread as she watched the real-time footage from Reznick's pinhole camera. Glimpses of two stocky men of Slavic appearance briefly appeared in the shot, kneeling down to check on him. Then speaking in what sounded like Ukrainian.

There was no movement from Reznick. Had he been knocked unconscious?

She picked up the radio and spoke to Acosta.

"Detective Acosta, you watching what we're watching?" Meyerstein asked.

"Tracking the whole thing. I'm tempted to go in now. This whole thing is messed up."

Meyerstein sighed. "I think we should wait."

"Why?"

"What we have won't nail Brutka."

"I don't know if I agree with that."

"Ideally, we want footage of him. We have audio. But footage showing him in there would be a clincher."

Acosta went quiet for a few moments.

"It's a tough call, I know, Acosta. But I say we hang tight for the moment."

Acosta sighed. "Ma'am, Reznick's life is in jeopardy. And I'm worried Brutka and his goons might kill one or all of the girls."

"It's a possibility. But here's the problem: we don't have Brutka beyond a reasonable doubt so far. Audio is good, but that could be disputed as dubbed or fake. Trust me, I've come up against bastards with great lawyers before."

Acosta cleared her throat. "So you're saying we watch and wait?"

"That would be my call. Wouldn't it be best to have video footage of Brutka with the girls in the room?"

"That's what we want."

"Agreed. Something so incriminating but also, crucially, not something that can be passed off as official diplomatic business."

Acosta went quiet for a few moments. "The last thing I want is for this fucker to get off on a technicality. 'Yeah, that was me talking, but I was just fooling around with friends.' I see what you're saying."

"You need to call it."

"I feel uncomfortable letting this go on. My concern is Reznick's life is on the line now."

"I know Jon. And I know what he can do," Meyerstein said. "He wants to nail this bastard."

"Even if he's injured doing it?"

"Jon is brave. A warrior. And I know he will take it to the wire, do whatever is needed. He's that kind of guy. But this is your call, Acosta. We go in now, we've got them all. But for the best evidence, we need to wait."

"Damn. Damn . . . Fuck. Does Reznick always take the hardest route to get to a destination?"

"Almost always."

A beat. "I say we watch and wait," Acosta said.

Fifty-Eight

Reznick was drifting in darkness. He tasted blood. Heard voices. Eastern European. Shouting. He tried to open his eyes, but his vision was blurred. He felt his hair being grabbed and a gun to his forehead. Then a hard slap to the jaw.

He felt himself coming to.

"Who are you? Are you police?"

Reznick managed to finally open his left eye; his right seemed to be heavily swollen. A Mohawk buzz-cut thug wearing a dark suit pressed a gun to his head.

The guy again slapped him hard on the jaw. "Answer me."

Reznick played submissive, as he had been trained to do. "No, sir. No, I'm not."

The guy hauled Reznick up. Frog-marched him through a dimly lit repair shop. He was pushed and prodded into a windowless room. The Ukrainian girls were lined up as if for a slave auction. Standing in front of them was Brutka, Zuki standing beside him. Two heavies leered at Reznick.

The shaven-headed guy pushed Reznick forward and kicked away his feet.

Reznick slumped to his knees.

"Hands on head!" the thug shouted.

Reznick complied, tasting blood again. He squinted in the harsh light as Brutka walked slowly toward him.

Mohawk said, "Look what I found outside."

Brutka was wearing a navy suit, pale-blue shirt and maroon tie, black loafers. He screwed up his eyes as he stared down at Reznick. "I thought we'd seen the last of you, Mr. Reznick."

"You guessed wrong, Brutka, you fucking scumbag. What's this you've got going on? Do these girls know they're going to be working as prostitutes? As drug mules?"

The Mohawk guy smashed a monkey wrench down onto Reznick's forehead. Pain erupted as blood gushed down the front of his face.

A piercing scream came from one of the girls.

Reznick wiped the blood away with the sleeve of his leather jacket as he stared at the girls. "Meet your new boss, girls."

Brutka stared down at Reznick. "You're becoming tiresome, Mr. Reznick." He turned to face the girls, a couple of whom were now sobbing. "This gentleman has been suffering from delusions and is trying to stop opportunities for girls from Ukraine. And he has tried to harm me. Make no mistake, he is not a good man."

Reznick spat blood onto the floor. "He's going to be your pimp."

Brutka laughed and looked down at Reznick. "They don't understand a word you're saying." He looked at Zuki, who still wore her dark glasses. He cocked his head at his bodyguard. "Check my friend."

A bodyguard grabbed Zuki and patted her down. He took out the cell phone from her pocket.

"Is this how they found us?" Brutka asked.

She began to cry. "Honey, you gave me that to call you."

Brutka approached her and whispered in her ear. "Did you speak to the police?"

"No, sweetie." She looked at Reznick. "I don't know that man."

Brutka smiled and turned to face the other girls. "Rule number one," he said as Zuki began to translate into Ukrainian. "You learn the meaning of respect. And the meaning of fear. Otherwise . . ." He turned and nodded at the bodyguard.

The heavy pressed the gun to Zuki's head and shot her stone dead. Blood sprayed onto the walls. Her body dropped to the floor. The screaming from the other girls echoed around the old stone walls. Blood pooled around Zuki's head on the floor. Some of the girls began to shake as shock set in.

Reznick felt as if his brain was going to explode. He seethed. He needed a plan. He needed to find a way out for all of them. He realized he was going to be killed. And quite possibly the girls too.

Brutka looked at the girls. "We all need rules," he said as the bodyguard who killed Zuki began to translate. "You need to learn to obey. This is America." He turned and looked at Zuki's blood-spattered body. "She learned the hard way what we need to avoid." He began to speak in Ukrainian, perhaps repeating his words to the girls.

Mohawk looked down on Reznick and grinned. "You next?"

Reznick just stared at him, and Mohawk turned away.

Reznick surreptitiously reached up his right trouser leg to the back of his calf, pulled out the second Beretta, and trained it on Mohawk. He shot him twice in the back. The guy slumped to the floor as the girls screamed again. But before the other two goons could act, Reznick did a double tap to their foreheads. The two thugs fell to their knees, then collapsed facedown, red splatter congealing on the floor.

Brutka put his arms up in the air and walked backward. He lunged at one of the girls and grabbed her, spun her around, and stood behind her, cowering, as he took a gun from his jacket and pressed it to her head. "What do you think, Mr. Reznick? You think this is going to end well for this fragrant beauty?"

Reznick slowly got to his feet, gun trained on Brutka. He wanted the pinhole camera to capture the rogue Ukrainian diplomat in all his terrible glory. The eyes of the girl he had his arm around were filling with tears. "It doesn't have to go down like this, Brutka. This stops today. It's over."

"Who are you working for, Reznick? Whatever they're paying you, I will quadruple it. Forget that. I will transfer ten million dollars to an account of your choice. Just as long as you get me out of here."

Reznick said nothing, just focused on Brutka's hand with the gun pointed at the girl's head. "You must have me mixed up with some other guy. I don't do deals."

"Reznick, I know powerful people. My father can get an audience with anyone in the world. You need to look at the big picture."

Reznick focused on Brutka's trembling hand that was holding the gun.

Brutka smiled. "You're crazy, Mr. Reznick. I didn't mean to run over your daughter."

"Why didn't you stop? Why didn't you take responsibility?"

"Let's do this deal. You'll never have to work again."

"Let the girl go."

"I do deals each and every day. I'll ensure your daughter has a significant trust fund so she can pursue her studies. I will make sure you are richly rewarded, and we can all move on. What do you say, Mr. Reznick?"

Reznick fired two shots at Brutka's wrist. He fell to the floor, screaming, as the gun dropped to the concrete. Blood seeped out of the diplomat's wrist as he writhed and wailed in agony.

Reznick stepped forward and kicked the gun away as the girls fled from the space.

"What the hell?" Brutka shouted. "Have you lost your mind?"

Reznick pressed his shoe down hard onto the bleeding wound, gun trained on Brutka.

Brutka screwed up his face in pain and began to scream.

"How do you like that? That feel good?" Reznick pointed the gun at Brutka's head. "You're not above the law."

"Please, let's work this out man-to-man."

"What do you think I'm doing?"

Out of the corner of his eye, Reznick caught sight of two SWAT guys.

One shouted, "Reznick, you can put it down! NYPD SWAT."

Reznick shook his head. "I'm not standing down."

"That is an order."

Reznick kept his gun trained on Brutka as he seethed. "You wanna make a deal now?"

Brutka was shaking uncontrollably. "Please! Help me!"

A split second later, Meyerstein and Acosta burst in through a side door, guns locked and loaded, aimed at Brutka.

Meyerstein said, "Jon, we've got this."

Reznick didn't move.

"He's not worth it, Jon," Meyerstein said. "Don't do anything you'll regret."

Acosta said, "Think about this, Jon. The rest of the girls are fine."

Reznick pressed the gun to Brutka's head. "Why did your bodyguard kill the girl?"

"It's how we operate! We lay down the law!"

Reznick sneered. "The law! What do you know about the law?"

Acosta went over to where Zuki lay. "Oh my God, no."

Reznick said, "Why did you kill her!" He pressed his gun to Brutka's head. "Why did you kill her, you fuck?"

Brutka closed his eyes, as if expecting a bullet in the head.

"Tell me!" Reznick ordered.

"I wanted to teach her a lesson. She needed to learn obedience."

"Obedience? Is that what it's all about?"

"Please . . . I'm begging you."

Reznick stared down at Brutka. "You killed an innocent girl in cold blood. I have a good mind to blast you to hell myself."

Meyerstein said, "We've got him, Jon. We've got it all. It's recorded. We have the footage. And the audio."

Brutka had tears in his eyes. "I can explain."

Reznick said, "You weren't on official business, were you, Brutka? This is not official business."

"Of course it's not." Brutka was breathing hard.

Meyerstein looked at Brutka. "Your diplomatic immunity is gone now. What do you have to say for yourself?"

Brutka shook his head. "I want my lawyer. I want to see Lionel Morton."

Meyerstein looked at Reznick. "Nothing can save him. Not even his father. We got him, Jon. You need to stand down."

Reznick pressed the gun tight to Brutka's sweating forehead. "Welcome to America, you fuck."

Fifty-Nine

The minutes that followed went by in a surreal blur for Meyerstein. The diplomat was screaming in pain as he was handcuffed, still bleeding heavily from his wrist. Meyerstein watched impassively. The SWAT team hustled him into a waiting ambulance. Then the traumatized Ukrainian girls were taken outside to waiting ambulances, wrapped in blankets, given warm tea from a thermos, and taken to a hospital for a checkup, before being interviewed by the NYPD. Reznick was being treated by a paramedic for his head wound.

Meyerstein stared at the body of the dead Ukrainian girl, Zuki, blood still congealing around her head on the warehouse floor. She walked over to Detective Acosta, who was standing in the corner by herself. "I believe you knew this girl quite well."

"Not well enough, unfortunately."

Meyerstein handed Acosta her business card. "Don't hesitate to contact me in the future."

Acosta stared at the dead girl. "Poor little thing. I tried to get her out of that apartment. But she was too scared to move."

"She was brave enough to help us nail that bastard."

Acosta said, "True." She smiled sadly as Reznick approached her. "You OK?"

"I'm fine."

"I appreciate what you did on this, Jon. It was crazy how you went about it. You crossed the line. But you got him."

"I'm just glad he won't be terrorizing any more girls in New York. Or anywhere else."

Acosta sighed. "There's always lowlifes like him out there, Jon. But we'll keep going after them. Trust me on that."

"I would expect nothing less, Isabella. Been a pleasure."

Acosta blushed. "It was nice to meet you, Jon. I wish you had known my brother. You would've liked him."

"I know I would."

"Next time you're in New York, look me up. I'll buy you a beer."

"You got it."

Meyerstein felt an unusual pang of jealousy. It was not that she envied Acosta, though she was clearly beautiful. But the detective's flirtatious response to Reznick's presence didn't sit right with her. Especially in the immediate aftermath of the cold-blooded murder of Zuki. Her cell phone rang, and she sighed. "Sorry, I have to take this."

"Sure," Acosta said.

Meyerstein went outside to the courtyard to take the call. "Assistant Director Meyerstein," she said, eyes closed.

"Martha, quick heads-up." The voice belonged to Alisa Fonseca, head of Human Rights and Special Prosecutions at the Justice Department. "We've got the paperwork in place."

"For what?"

"Ilad Brutka, Aleksander Brutka's grandfather, also known as Bud Smith. We've had three experts confirm through medical records and photo identification this is our guy."

"So when are you getting him?"

"That's why I'm calling. I know you're in New York. So am I. I had to stop off to pick up a Justice Department lawyer who we want to be there."

"Where are you?"

"LaGuardia. We're leaving in thirty minutes. We're just getting refueled."

"I want to be there. We're thirty minutes away."

"Not a problem."

Meyerstein ended the call and walked over to Reznick. "We're going to LaGuardia."

Sixty

It was just after midnight, and Reznick was wired on Dexedrine and adrenaline as the Cessna touched down at Lebanon Municipal Airport in New Hampshire. The night air was steamy and sultry. The events in the Bronx were still running through his head like an out-of-control freight train. He accompanied Meyerstein in one of two SUVs, which drove them across the state line to Norwich, Vermont.

Meyerstein turned to Reznick. "How's your head?"

"Tylenol taking the edge off."

Meyerstein gave him a rueful smile. "You really need to think about cutting back on those other pills."

"Gimme a break."

Meyerstein looked ahead as they drove down a quiet road outside Norwich until they came to a dimly lit colonial, a US flag flying near the front door. She got out and walked across to the first car as Reznick followed close behind.

Fonseca, from the Justice Department, spoke into her cell phone for a few moments. "This is it. We've got the green light to arrest this guy."

The lawyer checked over the paperwork in the back of the SUV as two Justice Department special agents introduced themselves to Meyerstein and Reznick.

Reznick thought it all looked very unscripted. Not thinking about any potential dangers, hidden or otherwise. As if a ninetysomething frail old man posed no problems. "So how are you gonna work this?" he asked Fonseca. "Just stroll right up?"

"We've got this covered, thanks for asking."

"How?"

"How what?"

"How have you got this covered? I'm talking preparations."

Fonseca shrugged. "One of my guys will take the rear door just in case. I will arrest Brutka with my other colleague from the Justice Department."

"And that's the plan?" Reznick said.

Meyerstein intervened. "What intel do we have on this guy and his house?"

"Nothing. We're assuming he will be in bed. And we will wake him up."

Reznick said, "You're assuming?"

"There is no indication he's a threat," Fonseca said.

Reznick shook his head. "Apart from the crimes committed during the Second World War, you mean."

Fonseca looked around the area for a few moments before fixing her gaze on Reznick. "I don't appreciate your tone, Mr. Reznick. We're all on the same side, after all."

Reznick didn't think there had been even a minimum level of planning. And it worried him. "So you got the arrest warrant? All the legal stuff."

Fonseca showed it to him. "Here it is. You ask a lot of questions, Mr. Reznick."

"You can never ask enough questions," he said. "Never."

Meyerstein held up her hand to silence Reznick. "Jon and I will accompany you into the house if that's OK, just in case there are any problems."

Fonseca seemed stung but acquiesced. "Fine. Let's do it."

Reznick was surprised they were going in without a basic SWAT team. He didn't care if the guy was in his nineties. It was better to do it right. It would have been better to arrest him on the street when he left the house the next morning. He pulled out his 9mm Beretta from his waistband and flicked off the safety. If nothing else, he was ready.

He pushed the negative thoughts about the lack of planning aside and followed Meyerstein to the front door. One of the Justice agents indicated he was going to go around the rear of the building, gun in hand.

Fonseca knocked hard on the front door. She waited for a few moments. The only sound was the whirring of cicadas carried on the warm New England breeze. But no answer at the door. She tried again. And again.

Meyerstein said, "Try the handle."

Fonseca turned the handle and slowly pushed open the door as the moonlight bathed the dark corridor. She flicked on a light switch. But nothing. "Damn. Mr. Brutka?" she called. "Justice Department special agents." She turned to Meyerstein. "I'll take the first floor. You guys want to take the second and third?"

Meyerstein nodded. "Got it."

Reznick brushed past Meyerstein. "I think I hear something."

Meyerstein stopped and listened. "Is that music?"

Reznick nodded and headed up the creaking stairs. He scoured the rooms on the second floor. He tried a light switch. Nothing. The sound of music grew louder. Military music. Marching music. He beckoned Meyerstein. "Someone's up there."

Meyerstein nodded.

Reznick bounded up the stairs two at a time. He was on the third-floor landing. He pushed open a door straight ahead, gun pointed. Nothing. Then a second room, adjacent to the first. It was a neatly made-up bedroom.

Was the music coming from the third room, at the end of the hallway?

Reznick indicated for Meyerstein to keep out of the line of sight. He had his back pressed to the wall as he approached the door. The music was rousing. Patriotic songs.

He turned the handle and pushed open the door.

The room was in darkness, pale moonlight coming through the net curtains.

Reznick realized the hall forked off down another narrower corridor for a few yards. Heart beating fast, he peered around the corner. Stairs to an attic. He signaled Meyerstein toward him. She crouched down, gun drawn. The music played on. Drawing up the rear were Fonseca and the Justice Department crew. He whispered, "Let me have a look."

Meyerstein nodded, as did Fonseca.

Reznick approached the wooden stairs, floorboards creaking with every step. He hoped the music would mask the noise. He wondered if the guy was waiting for them. He grimaced and climbed the stairs. He peeked his head up and looked into the attic. Cloaked in darkness was a skeletal figure sitting in a chair, gun pressed to his head.

The man said, "I've been waiting for you."

Reznick edged into the attic, gun trained on the figure, as the music played. "FBI! Put down the gun!"

The man didn't move.

Meyerstein entered the attic, gun pointed at the silhouetted figure. "Put down the gun!"

Reznick took a step closer.

The man said, "Stop right there."

Reznick froze, gun still trained on the guy. His eyes were getting accustomed to the darkness. The man was wearing a military uniform.

"I've been waiting for this moment for a long time," the man said.

Meyerstein said, "Are you Ilad Brutka?"

The man said, "That's very perceptive. Who are you?"

"FBI Assistant Director Martha Meyerstein. Put down the goddamn gun! We have a warrant for your arrest."

"Meyerstein . . . What an interesting name."

Reznick took a step closer. "Put the gun down!"

"Meyerstein," Brutka rasped. "Is that a Jewish name?"

Meyerstein didn't flinch. "Sir, you need to put the gun down!"

The music was playing, and Brutka smiled. "You are Jewish, aren't you? I take a keen interest in these things."

Reznick focused on Brutka's hand holding the gun. He knew the Justice Department wanted to take him alive. But his gut instincts were screaming at him that the guy was a danger to them all as well as to himself.

"Sir . . . put down the gun!" Meyerstein said.

"I knew the Jews. They were all Bolsheviks. No one understands what we were facing. You would never understand. How could you? And you dare to come for me? An old man. I wear the uniform of the Fourteenth Waffen Grenadier Division of the SS with pride. The First Galician we were known as. What do you know about me? You know nothing."

"Final warning, Brutka!" Meyerstein said as the marching music blared.

"I am not afraid of you. I am afraid of no one."

Meyerstein kept her gun trained on him.

"I thought I could live out my days. But somehow you've come for me. And for it to be a Jew, well . . . How ironic. Do you think you will be able to take me alive? I am not afraid of death."

Suddenly, Brutka edged the gun away from his temple.

"Drop the gun!" Reznick shouted.

Brutka directed the gun toward Meyerstein, his finger on the trigger.

Reznick fired off a double tap to Brutka's head. Muzzle flash lit up the room as gunshots rang out. Blood and brains exploded from the old man's forehead. A deafening silence followed. The smell of cordite. But all he could think of in that split second was the grainy black-and-white photograph of that poor naked Jewish woman being paraded through the streets by Brutka and his fellow Nazis.

Today was a belated payback, nearly eighty years later, for that woman. Cold vengeance.

Reznick stared at the old man. The music continued playing. Then the gun dropped from Brutka's bony hand.

The old bastard was dead.

Sixty-One

The first tinges of pale morning light began to bathe the interior of the attic through a skylight. Forensics and local cops mingled with Fonseca, her team, and Meyerstein. Reznick had given statements to Fonseca and the cops. The flash and the clicking sound of a camera cut through the investigative chatter.

Meyerstein said, "I think we're done."

Reznick headed out into the street, where there were cop cars, FBI guys, some folks wearing Justice Department jackets. He and Meyerstein headed past them all, his mind still flashing up images of Ilad Brutka's head exploding. Blood-smeared walls. The smell of decay. An hour later, they caught the Cessna back down to New York with Fonseca and her team.

Not a word was spoken.

A Lincoln picked up Reznick and Meyerstein at LaGuardia before the short journey to the Upper East Side. He was dropped off at his hotel, where he showered and shaved, pleased to get the film of dirt and decay off his body. Waves of tiredness washed over him. But he needed to speak to his daughter first. He called her number.

"Dad," she said, "I've been trying to contact you."

"I'm back in town. Are you OK, honey?"

"I'm good, Dad. I'm working through some manuscripts. Like I've never been away."

"That's my girl. Lauren, I just wanted to tell you that I love you."

"I love you too, Dad."

"But also . . . I got him."

"The guy that ran me down?"

"Yeah. You won't be seeing him again, trust me."

"Did you kill him?"

Reznick closed his eyes. "No. But we got him. That's all you need to know."

"I love you, Dad."

"I'll talk to you tomorrow, honey."

Reznick laid down and slept until dark. He was woken by a text message from Meyerstein. He joined her for a meal at the Quin.

"How's your head, Jon?" she said.

"I'll survive."

"You need to rest up."

"I intend to, trust me."

Meyerstein was flicking through some papers in front of her. "I can't believe what's happened in such a short time span. Nothing's easy with you, Jon. Why is that?"

"Stubborn, I guess."

"And it all started not far from here, with your daughter getting hit early on a summer morning."

"Seems like a lifetime ago."

"First, and most importantly, I want to say how happy I am that Lauren has recovered. And I'm glad she's back in the city. It's important not to let what happened affect how she lives her life."

"She loves New York. But yeah, sure, glad that she has no lasting physical problems. I spoke to her earlier. She seems to have made a helluva recovery."

J. B. Turner

"What about psychologically? That might be more of a problem, I'd imagine."

"Maybe. She's tough. She'll have flashbacks for a while. But it's a small price to pay to be alive. In one piece."

Meyerstein sighed. "What you have unearthed, through this whole thing . . . It's crazy. With your doggedness and sheer pigheadedness."

"It was just something I couldn't let go of. I couldn't walk away from it all."

"You're being very modest. Your help almost single-handedly brought down Brutka and his grandfather."

Reznick said nothing. He felt empty inside.

"But in the future, Jon, you need to see the bigger picture. Do we have a deal?"

Reznick nodded as he knocked back his second glass of red. "I'm not a fan of the State Department, truth be told."

"Well, I'm not going to get involved in a discussion about that."

"What about Aleksander Brutka? What do you think's going to happen to him?"

"He's in the hospital, recovering from the bullet wound, blood loss, trauma—bone splintered, by all accounts."

"He got off lightly."

"But . . . we have undeniable proof that he was engaged in violent criminal activities."

Reznick sensed where this was going. "Is he actually going to face charges?"

"The White House has gotten involved."

Reznick's heart sank. "What a surprise."

Meyerstein sighed. "I'm hearing Brutka's going to have a choice. Either a full jury trial or another avenue. But . . ."

Reznick groaned. "But? There's a but?"

"I'm not so sure how it's going to play out in the real world."

"What makes you say that?"

"You might not like this."

"Try me."

"I've heard already there's some behind-the-scenes stuff. High-level State Department and Justice Department."

"Don't tell me: he'll be allowed to return to Ukraine."

Meyerstein nodded. "That's what I've heard."

"After everything that's happened? Unbelievable."

"The way I look at it, Jon, he'll be off our streets, out of our country for good. So that's something."

"What about the Ukrainian President? How's that playing out? His father was a Nazi, and his son is being accused of murder, human trafficking, you name it."

"This has all yet to come out to the public. I'm hearing the *Post* is publishing Callaghan's investigation in full in the next twenty-four hours. The fallout from that should be interesting."

"What about the poor girl Brutka killed in cold blood? Zuki. And you said there was another, Daniela. He should be standing trial."

"Yes, he should be. But he's not."

"We could've insisted he stand trial."

"But it won't work out like that. Both of us know that."

"And what about Tom Callaghan? What about his widow and kids?"

"That's not my call, Jon. It is what it is."

"That's bullshit. That's what it is."

"Tell me about it. Look, I'm sorry for giving you a hard time on this. We were trying to get Brutka to leave the country. But . . . but he was . . ."

"Protected?"

"You were putting yourself at severe risk going it alone. You know that, right?"

Reznick cleared his throat. "I was well aware of that."

"The lone wolf."

"With stitches in his goddamn head, thanks very much."

Meyerstein took a small sip of her Pinot Grigio. She leaned closer. "You saved me in that attic."

"You would've killed him if I wasn't there."

"Maybe."

"Trust me, you would've had him."

"I owe you."

"You owe me nothing."

Meyerstein sighed and looked around the restaurant before focusing her gaze on Reznick. "I'd like to meet Lauren again. Would that be possible?"

Reznick smiled. "I need to warn you, she's very stubborn and opinionated."

"That's not a bad thing."

"Yeah, well, I don't know about that." Reznick was quiet for a few minutes.

"What are you thinking about, Jon?"

"Thinking about Lauren. About what she says."

"What does she say?"

"It's not easy, her growing up without a mom. But that being said, increasingly she's not shy about sharing her thoughts."

"Sharing her thoughts . . . What kind of thoughts?"

"Lauren doesn't think I've moved on since 9/11." Reznick's mind flashed to an image of his late wife on their wedding day. "She thinks I'm stuck."

Meyerstein shifted in her seat. "What do you mean?"

"She's concerned that since her mother died . . ."

"You mean your late wife?"

Reznick nodded. "That's right: Elisabeth. Lauren thinks I'm sort of trapped in limbo, so to speak. All these years."

"And are you?"

"Maybe. I don't know."

"It can't be easy."

Reznick said nothing.

"I'd imagine when you're here in the city, there must be some very powerful memories for you."

"It's hard not to think about the past . . . what happened on that day . . . when I'm in Manhattan. The memories are always there."

"The FBI has some terrific psychologists. Talking it over might help."

"I don't know."

"Sometime, when you're ready, it might be time to move on . . . A new chapter, so to speak."

Reznick's mind flashed to the footage of the plane hitting the first tower.

Meyerstein sighed. "It's been a little while since I visited the memorial. Usually do when I'm in New York. Might do that tomorrow."

Reznick stared into his drink.

"Do you still visit the memorial?"

Reznick smiled. "I used to . . . Not so much now."

"We'll always remember them, Jon. We'll always remember that day. I know I will. Everyone who was alive will remember that terrible day. But we can't live in the past forever. Sometimes we need to move on."

Reznick felt emotions rising to the surface. His head was swimming with pictures of Elisabeth.

"It's been a long time," Meyerstein said. "Maybe it's time to lay some ghosts to rest."

Reznick felt his throat tighten. "Amen to that."

Acknowledgments

I would like to thank my editor, Jack Butler, and everyone at Amazon Publishing for their enthusiasm, hard work, and belief in the Jon Reznick thriller series. I would also like to thank my loyal readers. Thanks also to Faith Black Ross for her terrific work on this book, and Caitlin Alexander in New York, who looked over an early draft. Special thanks and gratitude to Detective Arlene Gonzalez, NYPD Nineteenth Precinct, on the Upper East Side. And thanks also to Detective Roman Ilustre and Captain Kathleen Walsh.

Last but by no means least, my family and friends for their encouragement and support. None more so than my wife, Susan.

About the Author

J. B. Turner is a former journalist and the author of the Jon Reznick series of conspiracy action thrillers (*Hard Road*, *Hard Kill*, *Hard Wired*, *Hard Way*, and *Hard Fall*), as well as the Deborah Jones political thrillers (*Miami Requiem* and *Dark Waters*). He loves music, from Beethoven to the Beatles, and watching good films, from *Manhattan* to *The Deer Hunter*. He has a keen interest in geopolitics. He lives in Scotland with his wife and two children.